I0561300

# SECRET PUCKING UNICORN

## PARANORMAL HOCKEY LEAGUE

JENNY FENSHAW

Copyright © 2024 by Jenny Fenshaw

All rights reserved.

No part of this publication may be reproduced, distributed, or transmitted in any form or by any means, including photocopying, recording, training of artificial intelligence, or other electronic or mechanical methods, without the prior written permission of the publisher, except as permitted by U.S. copyright law.

Contact information: www.JennyFenshaw.com

This is a work of fiction. Names, characters, places, and incidents are either products of the author's imagination or used fictitiously, and resemblances to actual persons (living or deceased), business establishments, events, or locales is entirely coincidental. All text in this book was generated by Jenny Fenshaw without use of artificial intelligence.

Book Cover Designed by Dark Water Covers Premades and Formatting

Editing by Empowered Writing Author Services, HEA Author Services, and Patricia Raine Lam

 Created with Vellum

# 1

## DECLAN

I'M IN POSITION TO SHOOT THE PUCK INTO THE GOAL WHEN A TINGLE RUNS down my spine. *She's here,* my wolf tells me.

*Who?* my unicorn asks.

I don't answer either of them. I have to stay focused on the play. But I can't resist taking a quick glance around the arena where my team, the Atlantic City Devil Birds, is holding their first practice after the Christmas holidays. I don't see who I'm looking for. I don't see *her.*

"I don't have time for this," I mumble to myself. Well, to the two shifters inside of me who are insisting on having a conversation while I'm trying to freaking play hockey here. But since they are part of me, it still counts as myself.

Coach blows his whistle to stop the play.

"What was that, Mackenzie?" Coach Liam Morgan asks. "Are we keeping you from something important?"

"No, Coach," I reply. "I was telling myself I don't have time to second-guess. No thinking about it. I need to shoot when I get the puck."

"Good save, Mackenzie."

He doesn't look like he's buying it, but he lets it go. My wolf gets restless when I look around again. She is here. I know it. How? Why?

We reset the play and the puck has been fired at me when I see her at the glass. My mate. Miranda. My heart skips a beat, and I can picture my unicorn tossing his mane and giving an equine smirk. *Told ya so*, my wolf says.

The puck sails past me and ricochets off the boards. Reflexively, I slap the puck toward the goal when it hits my stick, but our goalie, Brick, catches it. Coach blows his whistle and skates toward me.

"Mackenzie, what the hell was that?" He's waving his clipboard in agitation. "The puck practically had an engraved invitation to hit your tape and you let it get past you."

"Randi," my teammate Carter calls out as he skates toward the glass where Miranda is standing. *My* Miranda.

Coach looks over his shoulder and follows Carter to the glass. I head that way but veer off to the bench and climb over the boards. At six feet and nine inches tall, it's more of a step than a climb. Miranda is next to the bench and I'm not letting the glass keep us apart. Her long, black hair falls like an onyx river down her back and I long to run my fingers through it. There is a pink tinge to her ivory complexion—I don't know if it's from the cold or excitement. The faint purple shadows under her lovely gray eyes have me worried. Isn't she sleeping? Is she worried about something? Is she sick? She's smiling and waving at Carter and Coach as I remove my helmet and drop it on the bench. She seems happy. When she notices me, her eyes widen with shock.

"Declan?" She moves to the half wall separating the stands from the bench. This is the practice arena, and the glass isn't as all-encompassing as it is in the main rink we use for games.

Wrapping Miranda up in a hug, I lift her off her feet and swing her over the half wall to my side. Laughing, she hugs me tightly and then leans back.

"What are you doing here?" she asks.

A happy grin spreads across my face as I answer, "I play here. I'm a Devil Bird."

"You are?" Her brow furrows in confusion before a beautiful smile spreads across the lips I'd give anything to be able to kiss—to claim. "We are finally in the same place at the same time."

"I'm not even going to ask how you two know each other. Are you going to carry her around all day?" Carter, the jackass, asks with a smirk.

I realize I'm still holding Miranda a foot off the ground. She's five foot six. I have to lift her to be eye-to-eye with her at my normal height of six foot nine. I'm even taller when I'm in my skates.

"I haven't hugged her in almost two years. I'm making up for lost time," I say, still holding her in my arms.

"Well, she's our new roommate and you'll be sharing a bathroom with her. How about you put her down so the rest of us can hug her?"

I reluctantly lower her to stand on her own. "You're Randi?"

"Yeah, that's what everyone calls me. But you can keep calling me Miranda."

"That's okay?

"Yeah."

"Please let us know when you're done, Mackenzie. We'll wait," Coach says, his arms crossed over his chest. The way his jaw is ticking has me seeing extra skating drills in my future.

My cheeks heat even though we're in an ice rink.

"Go," she says. "I can't get fired on my first day." She gently pushes against my chest, a silent request to let her go. I back up a step, but my wolf is howling in my head in protest. My unicorn is more genteel in his reaction, but he's disappointed too.

"Fired?" I ask.

"Meet my new assistant, Randi Quinn," Coach calls out. "She is here to work. You—"He narrows his eyes at me."—are to let her do her job. No flirting."

Miranda's face turns pink, the color rising from her neck and into her cheeks, and she lowers her eyes. I respect Coach, but I want to punch him for embarrassing her.

"I take it you two know each other?" Coach asks.

Miranda nods. "We grew up together."

"You're Irish, and he's from Scotland. What's up?" Carter glares, his gaze snapping from me to Miranda and back again.

"Long story. I'll tell you later," Miranda says.

I grab my helmet and turn to go back on the ice.

"Your number is eighty?" Miranda asks with a laugh.

Buckling my chin strap before snagging my stick from where I left it leaning against the boards, I nod. "Aye, I told you I'd pick it if I ever played. It's been my number on every team I've been on."

I feel her eyes on me as I skate back to my spot to run the drill again. It's taking every ounce of my willpower not to turn my head and look at her. I can't help it, I'm weak. A quick glance shows me Miranda is back behind the protection of the glass. Good. Nothing can happen to my Miranda now that she's back in my life.

Carter skates up to me and taps my shin with the blade of his stick.

"Dude. I had no idea you and Randi knew each other. She's my best friend from college and arrived from New Zealand today. She is going to be in the spare room. She has nowhere else to go. Are you good with that?"

I can't stop the grin splitting my face. "Better than good. You can be my best man at our wedding."

Coach blows his whistle twice, never a good sign.

"You want to make the PHL All-Star Game, Mac, you're gonna have to stay focused. You too, Carter."

Coach's words light a fire under me. Now with Miranda here, I can see everything I want for my future, and the All-Star Game, along with the prize money offers, will help me get it.

# 2

## MIRANDA

Liam jerks his head toward the tunnel. I assume it's a signal to get the hell out of his practice and stop being a distraction to his players. Daphne, the team's social media manager and my friend, must interpret it the same way because she stands.

"Let me give you the tour of the rest of the place and get you settled in your office. Liam will want to talk to you after practice."

As I follow Daphne to the tunnel taking us out of the practice rink, I look back to the ice. Declan is bent over with his stick on the ice, ready to start the next play. Even his helmet and cage can't hide his strong jawline or the tendrils of black hair escaping the edge of his helmet. Wearing his pads, he's gigantic, but I know under them he is muscular with broad shoulders and strong arms that give the best hugs. The few times we've cuddled together when visiting I got to enjoy being near all his muscles. He wasn't playing hockey then. I bet there are more, larger muscles now. I shouldn't think about my best friend's older brother like that, but I do. Like always, our connection is strong because he lifts his beautiful blue eyes to mine, and a jolt of electricity shoots through me.

We leave the practice rink and Daphne gives me a tour of the locker and training rooms before ending up in my office. It's off the locker room and next to Liam's office. The space is nice with a chair and desk, a couple of armchairs, and a couch I'm longing to take a nap on. I don't sleep when I travel. I can't let myself relax enough to be vulnerable and sleep on a plane. I cheated and did my trip in two segments. First, I flew from Auckland to Los Angeles yesterday. I got a room at an airport hotel for Christmas Day and tried to nap for a few hours before going back to the airport to catch an overnight flight from L.A. I arrived in Philadelphia early this morning and took a hired car to the rink here in Atlantic City. I can't wait to get to my room at Trevor's and crash. If I can get a solid twelve hours of sleep, I'll be okay.

I take the chair behind my desk and before Daphne's ass can hit the couch, two heads pop through the door, grinning. Kendall is my best friend and roommate from college, and Mallory Carter is Coach Liam Morgan's fiancée and Trevor Carter's older sister. I don't know her very well but it's nice to see another friendly face. They bounce inside and sit on either side of Daphne.

"So," Kendall says. "You and Mac?"

"Mac?" I ask.

She rolls her eyes in exasperation. "Declan Mackenzie. You know damn good and well who I'm talking about. I saw everything on the ice this morning. Spill the tea."

"Ooh, yeah, tea sounds good. Daph, where can I get a cuppa?" I rise from my chair. I don't want to discuss me and Declan. Not that there *is* a me and Declan.

Daphne gets up and walks through a second door in my office, leading to a dining area. We can choose from juice, water, coffee, and some mass-produced tea bags. Hot water is from the water cooler. I sigh. I should be used to this, but I miss making a proper cup of tea. I'll need to see if I can find a tea shop and get some good loose-leaf tea. I can pick up an electric kettle.

The girls grab drinks too, and we wander back into my office. *My office.* I like the sound of that. In Auckland, I had a cubicle in the offices of the professional rugby team I worked for. It wasn't my own private space. I could get used to this.

"Keep these doors closed and maybe locked if you don't want the players walking in randomly or using your office as a pass through from the locker room to the dining room," Daphne advises.

Mallory winks. "Or get an eyeful of naked shifters walking back from the showers."

Heat rushes to my cheeks. "Thanks for the tip."

"That's what she said," Daphne cries, holding her hand up for a high five.

Mallory and Kendall laugh as I slap Daphne's hand. I don't get it.

"Just the tip of his penis," Kendall explains. She's used to me not getting jokes.

My cheeks are blazing hot now, and I curse my fair Irish complexion.

"Back to Mac..." Kendall doesn't give up when she gets a thought in her head.

I nod. "He's my best friend's older brother. We grew up together. Our parents were best friends. I stayed with them while my parents were traveling with clients."

My parents are equine veterinarians, and when I was a child, they worked at different estates and race tracks throughout the UK, Ireland, and Europe. It was easiest to leave me with the Mackenzies when I was younger. They had a houseful of kids, and adding me to the mix was no problem.

"Hey," Kendall exclaims., "I thought I was your best friend!"

I shrug. "She's my best friend from childhood. You're my best friend from college, besides being the best roommate ever. Honestly, you and Sophie would get along great."

"What's up with his number? Does eighty have some special significance?" Mallory asks.

"His initials are AD—Alexander Declan. It sounds like the number eighty, and he always said it would be his number if he was ever on a team." I take a deep breath. "I didn't know he was playing here. Playing at all, actually. We haven't spoken lately."

When I contacted Trevor to see if he knew of any job openings with the Devil Birds, it didn't occur to me to ask about the players. Everything came together quickly. I was rushing to tie up the loose ends in New Zealand and preparing to come here, and I didn't bother researching the team roster. I assumed Trevor—I guess I should get used to calling him Carter like his teammates do—was the only person on the team I knew.

My degree is in sports management, and eventually I want to work in the front office of a professional sports team. Advancement wasn't going to happen with the rugby team I worked for in New Zealand and I didn't want to settle there permanently anyway. I want to be close to my friends. And my parents are here now. We aren't close—I haven't spoken to them since before I left for New Zealand—but I keep hoping to have a closer relationship with them and we need to be near each other for it to happen. I wanted to be back in New Jersey anyway, and discovering they were at a racetrack near where I went to high school and college sealed the deal. They couldn't be here for the six years I went to school in New Jersey, but within a year of me moving across the globe, they find a spot.

I'm thrilled to see Declan, of course, but my goal is to work hard, prove my value to the team, and make this a long-term situation. I'm tired of moving all over the world at the drop of a hat. From the ages of ten to sixteen, I went to eleven different schools in five different countries. Some schools I didn't even stay for the entire term. It wasn't until my junior year of high school that I landed at the boarding school I graduated from. Then I spent four years at Wickham University with Kendall and Carter. It was the most stability I'd had since I left Ireland and the Mackenzies when I was ten.

I want to settle here. Find a house with a little bit of land where I can plant flowers and watch them grow. Maybe get a cat or a dog. Live somewhere no one can make me leave. It would be mine and no one could take it away from me. I can't let my silly crush on Declan distract me from my goal. He's here while he's playing hockey. Once he's done, he'll move back to Ireland to start the horse farm he's always dreamed of.

Love of horses is what we have in common. We'd spend time sitting on fences, watching them run around the practice track or grazing peacefully in the fields. Discussing bloodlines. Dreaming of the day Declan would have his own farm and could breed the horses he wanted, train them, and coach riders. His father's stable was full of thoroughbreds for racing. Declan wanted magnificent black Friesians for dressage and warmbloods for eventing. He wanted to raise horses to do more than run around a track. I was his first coaching project. I didn't need him to coach me. I took to riding like a duck takes to water. But it was a way I could spend time with him, and it made him happy. Even as a little girl, I had a crush on him, despite not realizing that's what it was.

I realize staring off into space, lost in my memories, is not going to go unnoticed by my friends. Hopefully, they'll chalk it up to jet lag. I focus on them and try to get conversation rolling again with topics other than me and Declan. Daphne is wearing a baggie team hoodie, but I can see the start of her baby bump. She's expecting her first child with her husband, and I couldn't be happier for them.

"When are you due?" I ask Daphne.

"End of May. We tried to time it for the offseason, but it turns out I was already pregnant when we started trying on purpose." She shrugs with a blissful grin.

"Oops," I say with a giggle.

I turn to Kendall. "You're dating the captain? How did that happen?" I'm impersonating a talk show host interviewing my friends, but if I keep them talking about themselves, they won't ask awkward questions about my life.

"We pretended to fake-date, but with real benefits." Kendall wiggles her eyebrows. I can't miss what she's implying. "So people would stop trying to fix us up with each other or with other people.

There were some hiccups along the way, but fake became real. You and Declan..."

For a cougar shifter, she has the memory of an elephant.

Shrugging, I say, "There is no me and Declan. We were friends as kids."

"So you haven't seen him since you were a little girl?" Mallory asks.

My comfy office chair is more like a hot seat. "I saw him a couple of years ago."

Kendall cocks her head. "When? You didn't go to Scotland or Ireland while we were in college. Did you go before you went to New Zealand?"

"No." I shake my head. "He came to the Wickham graduation."

"Oh." Kendall at least has the grace to look embarrassed. None of them were at the graduation ceremony because Kendall had run off a couple of weeks earlier to elope with her asshole ex. When she skipped walking at graduation, none of her family went. During college, I had spent holidays at her home when I didn't go see my parents. I felt included and even loved there. But it was all fake. They were there for me when Kendall was there. They were always kind, of course. They are nice people. But I wasn't one of them.

I walked across the stage, knowing no one in the crowd was there for me. I thought I had been lonely as a ten-year-old when I got dropped off at my first boarding school in England and watched my parents drive away. That was nothing compared to walking across the stage to accept my diploma from the Dean in silence. My classmates received applause and whoops. They announced my name, and I started my trek in silence. There weren't even crickets. Then I heard it, a lone "Yay, Miranda," in a distinctive Irish/Scottish brogue along with a heavy-handed clap. I looked out and there was Declan, standing tall and proud, with a huge smile on his face. Others started clapping too, but his was the applause I heard most clearly. For once, I wasn't alone.

It's not a big deal. I'm used to it. Luckily, I like my own company and am self-sufficient. I don't need anybody. I'm a pro at being friendly and forming relationships, but I know they aren't genuine. It's proximity and convenience. I don't let anyone truly get close. I learned that letting people in means letting them hurt you. No more of that. Fool me once, shame on you. Fool me four or five times...well, I finally get a clue. Sure, it took a while, but it was a lesson I learned by the time I was twelve years old. Having busy parents teaches you a lot of things young.

But I'm ready to change that. Kendall, Daphne, and Trevor weren't at graduation for assorted reasons, but they have been there for me many other times through the years. Daphne is like the older sister I always wished I had, and I think I fill the little sister role for her. Neither of us have siblings. Her parents passed away when she was a teenager and my parents...yeah. The moment I mentioned thinking about coming back to New Jersey, Trev opened his home to me. Daphne and Kendall helped me get this job. I owe them a ton and I'm not going to let these friendships fade. I have to trust more and be more open. I have to try, even if it's scary and may open old wounds.

And I'm going to try to establish a new relationship with my parents. Maybe now that I'm an adult and independent, we can connect on a different level. I don't need them. I want to be close with them. Like a normal family. Someday I want to have a family of my own and even if they weren't present in my life the way I wish they were, I'd love for them to be grandparents to my children.

I realize everyone is waiting for me to answer. What were we talking about? Oh, the last time I saw Declan.

"He was in New York working at a vineyard owned by one of his classmates from Cornell. He was close," I say. "I went to his graduation, and he was returning the favor."

"Wait, wait, wait." Mallory is bouncing in her seat. "Mac went to Cornell?" She looks at Daphne and Kendall. "Did we know that?"

"No, Burke and I haven't been spending our time talking."

Kendall wiggles her eyebrows like we wouldn't know. I can be dense sometimes with flirty innuendoes, but I'm not completely stupid.

"What did he major in there?" Daphne asks.

"Are you asking out of personal curiosity, or for stuff to use for content?" I ask. "I don't want to tell tales out of school or share stuff he doesn't want known."

"I'm being nosy. I get approval from the athletes before I post stuff."

"Hospitality management and a viticulture minor," I say.

Kendall scrunches her face. "Really? He doesn't seem like the hotel type, and I don't think I've ever seen him drink wine."

"He isn't." I sigh, feeling disloyal talking about Declan's personal business.

"Oh, his family is in the hotel business, right? Somehow connected with the Clardmore hotels?" Daphne exclaims.

"Yeah," I say.

"That's nice he was close. Did you guys visit a lot through the years?" Daphne asks. Man, she's all kinds of nosy today.

"Some—more video calls than in person. We were both busy, and I moved a lot before college. At Wickham, I was busy with cheer, and courses limited me to seeing him a couple of times a year. I went to his graduation mostly because his family was attending, and I hadn't seen them in years. It was easier for me to go up there. They would have come down to Wickham if I couldn't have made it, but it wasn't necessary. I talk with his sister Sophie more."

I hear a bunch of male voices approaching, and Liam pokes his head in from the locker room.

"There you all are. Randi, did you want to join me while I talk to the team or wait until after they stop stinking?"

Grabbing the legal pad and pen on my desk, I rise. "I'll go with you. That's what I'm here for."

"Do you need a ride to the barn?" Mallory asks. The house she shares with Liam is on the same property as the converted barn I'll be living in.

With an eye roll and a sigh, Liam says, "We'll make sure she gets home, Mallory. Half of the team is going to the same place she is. We won't leave her stranded."

"I'm good, Mallory," I say. "Catch up more later."

Looking over my shoulder and giving a quick grin, I follow Liam into the locker room. I hope no one is naked. I think.

# 3
## DECLAN

SITTING IN FRONT OF MY STALL, UNLACING MY SKATES, I WONDER IF IT'S possible to put my wolf on ADHD meds. He won't shut up about Miranda being here and being our roommate and how pretty she is and how good she smells, and on and on. It was impossible to pay attention to the drills we were running. I was always a step behind. Eventually, Coach stopped screaming at me because he knew I was a lost cause. I have to focus. I can't risk my position on the team by being distracted by Miranda. I'm counting on the money I'm making from hockey to enable me to buy a horse farm. That's my dream. Even though hockey isn't my lifelong dream, it is something I've committed to. When I make a promise, I keep it, and I've promised my team I will do everything in my power to help us be winners. I can't let my feelings for Miranda interfere with that.

I never planned on being a professional hockey player. Until the Paranormal Hockey League formed and I got picked up to play in this inaugural season, I was trying to decide whether I was going to work for my family's hotel chain or whisky distillery. I didn't want to do either of them but if I was ever going to have enough money to do what I truly want, I had to earn it. My parents are very loving and supportive, but even though our family is incredibly wealthy, my siblings and I are expected to make our own way. There's always a place for us in the family businesses and I'm grateful for the security, but I want more.

Carter and Burke Bedard, our team captain, flank me.

"What the hell was that today, Mac?" Bedard asks. He's not quite as big as me, but sometimes he seems bigger. He's built like a bear and lumbers like one too.

I shrug. I can't bloody well say, *my wolf was a wee bit distracted since our fated mate is in the building, and we've known she was ours for at least twenty years.* They'll think I'm daft. Maybe I *am* daft. She doesn't feel the same for me as I do for her. I'm her best friend's big brother. That's it. She didn't come here for me. This is coincidence, not fate. She wasn't looking for me. She's here because her friends are here.

"Stay here," Coach says to someone behind him before entering the room.

Sweeping us with his gaze, he jerks his head and Miranda walks in. She looks exhausted. I mean, she looks beautiful. She always has and always will in my eyes. I want to bundle her up, take her home, and put her to bed. She needs to sleep. In my bed. And never leave.

She smiles uncertainly as she looks around the room and takes in all my teammates. What is she thinking? Other than Bridget Waller, our number one goalie we all call Brick, she's the sole female in a room full of large male shifters. I don't know if she's ever been in a situation like this before. I'm not sensing fear, but I can sense her uncertainty and fatigue.

Coach steps forward. "For those who didn't hear already, this is Randi Quinn, my new assistant. She will handle the travel logistics, communication about practices, PT, appointments, and whatever else we drop in her lap. She is here to work, as are all of you. I know today was a clusterfuck with it being the first practice after the holidays and a new pretty girl around, but get your heads screwed back on and use them. We are here to win hockey games, not play *Bigfoot Finds a Bride* or *The Bachelor*." He rubs the back of his neck, looking sheepish. "I watch a lot of wedding and dating shows with my fiancée. Beautiful cakes on *The Baking Beaver*."

Miranda's pale cheeks turn a pretty pink, but I hate it's from embarrassment.

Coach turns to her. "Randi, anything you want to say?"

She steps forward, clutching her notepad to her chest. Clearing her throat, she looks around at all of us; her gaze lingering on me long enough to get my heart racing, before moving on to Carter and giving him a genuine smile.

"Hello, everyone. I'm excited to be here and to be part of the Devil Birds' organization. My previous job was working in a similar role for a professional rugby team in New Zealand. I went to university in New Jersey. It is nice to be back here. I look forward to working with all of you and will do everything I can to make things run as smoothly as possible. All you need to worry about is winning games. I promise when I'm not suffering from jet lag, I will stand a chance at remembering your names."

That gets a chuckle. Sven Lindholm—Lindy—our young Swedish forward with pale blonde hair, raises his hand.

With a nod and a friendly smile, Miranda looks at him and says, "Yes?"

"Are you a shifter? You don't smell like a shifter. You smell like Mac."

Damn right she smells like me, and no one better forget it. I will scent mark her every day to keep these arseholes away from her. I don't care if they are my friends and teammates.

Her eyes widen.

Brick reaches out to slap Lindy with her blocker. "Lindy, you can't ask people that. It's impolite."

Lindy rubs the back of his head. "What? Mama said to not bring home any non-shifter girls. I need to know these things."

"You're not bringing her home to your mother," I say, barely keeping my wolf from adding a snarl for good measure.

"Um, I'm human," Miranda rushes to say, whether to get rid of Lindy's interest, break up the tension, or simply answer the question. "I hope that won't be a problem."

She casts an uncertain glance at Coach, and he gives her arm a reassuring squeeze. The tiny touch causes my hackles to rise.

Bedard nudges me with his foot. "Dude, you're growling."

A couple of glances and knowing smirks are being thrown my way. Damn it. I don't need this kind of attention. My teammates are good people, but they are competitive shifters. The more apparent my interest in Miranda is, the more they will be sniffing around her. I don't want to have to beat them up for getting too close to my mate, but I will.

"Not a problem at all, Randi," Coach says.

Turning to us and pinning me with a glare, he says, "Get showered and get out of here. Practice is at the same time tomorrow. We'll watch video and then get on the plane for our game against the Spokane Sasquatch the day after tomorrow."

"Randi," Carter calls out. "I'll give you a ride home."

She looks at Coach, who nods. "You're done for the day. You look like you're ready to drop. Get settled at the barn, sleep, and get ready for tomorrow. Daphne has the travel details. She's going with us and will give you the info on what you need to pack. You're shadowing her for a bit to get the lay of the land."

"Okay, thanks," Miranda says before turning to Carter. "I'll be in my office. My bags are with the security guard upstairs."

"We'll get them on the way out. I'll be twenty minutes, tops." Apparently, Carter doesn't remember I drove us here today. I rush through my shower and am dressed first.

"Oh, shit. You'll drive us, Mac, right?" he asks after his shower as he comes back to his stall with a towel around his waist.

"Aye," I say. "Wondering when you'd remember you don't have your wind-up car."

Carter drives a BMW sports car instead of the SUVs and trucks the rest of us prefer. It's like riding in a clown car. I did it once, with my knees around my ears, and will never do it again. If I want to do yoga, I'll go to the class Brick runs in the gym at home. I don't need to ride in a tin can to get twisted into a pretzel.

I rap my knuckles against Miranda's door.

"Come in," she calls.

I open the door and walk in, Carter on my heels.

"Mac is driving us home. I forgot he drove today," he says.

Looking around her office, I furrow my brow.

"Let me know if you want your furniture rearranged," I say.

"Why would she do that? It looks nice in here," Carter says.

"Her view is the shower and there's a door at her back. If she flips her desk, then the wall is at her back and if she looks out that door" —I point out the door to the dining room—"she can see out the window."

Miranda's smile tells me she likes my idea.

"Declan is right, Trev, that's a great setup."

"Okay. Randi, do you want us to do it now?" Trevor asks.

She laughs. "No. It's not a priority. I want to get settled, eat, and collapse. I'm flexible on the order, but I need to at least eat and collapse."

"You slept on your flight, right?" Carter asks.

"No. I don't sleep on planes. I haven't slept in almost forty-eight hours and I'm not sure what day it is."

Carter reaches out his hand and Miranda takes it and rises from her seat behind her desk. I swallow the growl my wolf tries to make.

"Then let's get you home, sweetheart."

*Sweetheart?* Oh, hell no. He helps her put on her coat and it is a massive feat of willpower not to punch him when he lifts her hair where it's trapped in her coat collar to allow it to fall around her shoulders in a waterfall of black silk. The intimacy in the gesture twists my stomach. Are they in a relationship? Have they been?

There's so much about Miranda's life once she left for boarding school and then university that I know nothing about.

I may have been waiting for her but that doesn't mean she's been waiting for me. My poor wolf wants to howl in despair. Me too, wolf, me too.

# 4
## MIRANDA

A HALF HOUR LATER I'M ABOUT TO COLLAPSE. I'M IN MY NEW ROOM AND there's a bed, but Trevor keeps asking a question I can barely register as I stare at the naked bed.

"Sheets?" I shake my head, feeling like it's moving through molasses. "I have a computer. And some clothes. That's all I own."

Then Declan's big body is behind me, and his reassuring voice is saying, "No worries, Miranda. I have extra sheets and blankets. We'll get your bed made, get you fed, and let you collapse. Almost done."

He gives my shoulder a gentle squeeze before turning and going through a door.

"That's the closet. You guys share it too," Trevor says.

If Declan doesn't hurry back with sheets, I'm sharing his bed too.

"Here are sheets from my bed. We have the same size mattress." Declan puts a pile of bedding on an armchair I didn't even notice in the corner. He grabs the fitted sheet and snaps it to lay it over the mattress.

I go to the opposite side to help. "Ooh, Scottie dogs."

Trevor grabs the pillowcases and starts stuffing them with

pillows. "Dude, you get paid millions of dollars, and you sleep on flannel sheets from Target with dogs on them?"

Declan shrugs. "They're comfortable and the print reminds me of a dog we had."

"Fergus!" I loved the feisty Scottish terrier the Mackenzies had. He liked to bark and growl at everyone, but he was always sweet with me. He'd follow me around and sleep at the foot of my bed. I run my finger over a Scottie with a plaid bow tie. I hadn't thought about Fergus in years. He was a wonderful dog. I'm sure he's passed.

"Ma has his grandson," Declan says. "The next time he is at stud, maybe we can get you a puppy from the litter."

I smile. It's a kind offer, but I can't have a dog. I'll be traveling too much with the team. But soon. A shiver of anticipation rushes through me. It's hard to kick the impulse to leave, to not make a home, but that's what I came here for. I've got to start thinking differently. Maybe getting a dog would help with that. Someday, when I have my forever home, I'll get a dog. But that's not possible now.

"How the hell are you getting laid with Scottie dog sheets?" Trevor asks.

"I guess if you're doing it right, no one is paying attention to the sheets," Declan retorts.

Heat rises from my throat and into my cheeks. I don't want to hear about this. Of course he brings women home. No one as gorgeous and sexy as him lives like a monk. I try not to let the thought of him with someone upset me.

"Anyway..." Declan looks at me as he tucks in the second corner on his side. "These are brand new sheets. I've washed them but haven't used them yet. And I'm not bringing anyone home."

Trevor nods and shoots him with finger guns. "Good plan. Stick to hotels or their place. Less complicated that way and they won't know where you live."

Declan shoots a look my way as he flicks the top sheet to unfurl it. "No, I'm not dating."

Trevor scoffs. "No one said anything about dating. Whatever, you do your thing and I'll do mine." He tosses the pillows he put in cases at the head of the bed and leaves the room.

Declan turns and grabs a plaid blanket. I grin when he turns back toward me with it in his hands. It's the Mackenzie tartan.

"This, I have used, but I swear only for sleeping."

"Thank you." I smooth out the cover with the rich green and blue pattern I have always loved. I wish I was sharing this blanket with him. And the sheets. And the bed. And so much more.

I give my head a shake—I need to stop these thoughts. Declan is my best friend's brother. *My* friend. My gorgeous, talented, and kind friend, who is also a sexy wolf shifter. He can have anyone he wants. He isn't going to want me. Hell, sometimes my own parents don't seem to want me. Why would anyone else?

"I know you're exhausted," Declan says. "Why don't you take a shower and get ready for bed, and I'll make you a cheese toastie?"

My eyes widen and fill with tears. No one has made me a cheese toastie since I was ten. I've had grilled cheese sandwiches, of course, in the cafeterias of the schools I attended. But not a real toastie made especially for me. What I'd get was something mass produced and plopped on a tray as I shoved it along the rails.

"Really? You'd do that for me?" I whisper.

Declan rounds the foot of the bed and takes my hand. Sparks shoot up my arm at his touch. If anyone asked, I'd chalk it up to exhaustion, but I know it's the stupid, unrequited crush I've harbored for years on a man I can't have.

"Miranda, don't you know I'd do anything for you? A cheese toastie is simple. Go do whatever to get ready and I'll make your sandwich. Do you want chips or soup with it?"

I shake my head. "The sandwich is all I need. If I eat too much, I'll have weird dreams." I grab my backpack holding what I need for tonight in it. I made sure I had the basics in my carry-on because I knew I wouldn't want to deal with unpacking.

When he leaves the bedroom, I walk into our shared bathroom. It's clean, but I can smell the faint scent of the soap he uses. It's a fresh, clean scent, not too heavy. It's like a meadow after a rain shower. I remember sitting in a gazebo during a rain shower and smelling that scent. It wasn't soap—it was the rain and the land. I've missed it.

I undress and climb into the huge shower. The spray washing over me is incredible. Whoever designed this bathroom was a genius. The dual vanity area is in the hallway connecting the two bedrooms and the shower and massive soaking tub are behind one door and what I presume is the toilet is behind another. Two people could use the bathroom for their personal needs in privacy. Declan can shave at the sink while I'm in the shower. It will make getting ready much easier.

I'm entering my bedroom in my moose-print flannel pj pants and baggie Wickham U t-shirt when Declan pokes his head in.

"Toastie is almost done. Do you want to eat at the counter, or should I bring it in here? I've made tea as well."

"I'll come out there."

He turns to walk down the hall to the kitchen and I follow, trying to not stare at the firm, denim-clad ass the hockey gods blessed him with. On the counter are two plates with a toastie on each and two steaming mugs of tea. Trevor is in a recliner with a bag of chips, flipping through channels on the massive TV. I sit on one stool and Declan takes the one beside me.

"Thank you," I say, giving him a smile.

Declan returns my smile with a soft one of his own. "You're welcome. Eat, while it's still hot." Declan picks up his sandwich and I follow suit. The mixture of shredded cheeses oozing out of the sliced middle reminds me of the happy times from my childhood. He made a real cheese toastie with fresh shredded cheese, not some fake cheese from a plastic wrapper.

I take my first bite and close my eyes as I groan in delight. This sandwich is an experience. It's flavorful, it's comforting, and someone who wanted to take care of me made it for me it. I will remember this sandwich and this moment forever.

"Oh my gosh, this is delicious. Declan, I could kiss you." The words slip from my mouth without thinking.

"I'd be okay with that," is his quiet reply.

Oh, if he truly meant it.

# 5
## DECLAN

I'M AN IDIOT. WHY DID I SAY THAT? THEN MIRANDA LEANS OVER TO PRESS A kiss to my cheek and I know why I said it. Best idea ever.

"Hey. None of that," Carter calls from his recliner. "If you're going to be kissing a roommate, Randi, I'm it."

Miranda rolls her eyes. "Yes, Trevor."

Before I can ask if there is a relationship between them, Miranda hops down from her stool and takes her plate to the sink.

Grabbing her mug of tea, she rests her hand on my forearm and gives me a squeeze that ripples throughout my body.

"Thank you, Declan. Best thing I've eaten in years. Thank you for everything. I'm thrilled you're here."

Turning away, she says, "I hate to be the boring roommate, but I'm going to bed before I collapse. What time are you going to the rink tomorrow?"

"Ten in the morning," I say.

"Cool, I should be human by then."

She walks over to Carter's recliner, leans over the back, and places a kiss on Carter's cheek while pushing back the lock of dark reddish brown hair that always falls over one of his eyes like a floppy dog ear.

"Thank you for everything, Trev. You're a lifesaver."

"Aw, Randa Panda, you don't need to thank me. I'd do anything for you."

She straightens, says good night, and goes to her room. I pick up my mug and take a seat on the sofa, my stockinged feet plopped on the ottoman.

"What do you want to watch?" Carter asks.

"I don't care. Whatever you want."

He turns on one of the home makeover shows he's obsessed with. This one is *From Dud to Den*. It's a shifter-focused show. In this episode, a bear shifter's family is getting an upgrade to their cookie-cutter, builder standard home. The makeover leaves them with beautiful wood touches everywhere. Almost everywhere. The rock walls some of the bedrooms feature call to mind cozy caves for hibernating.

"Would you ever do a reality show, Mac?" he asks.

I whip my head around to look at him. By the way he's casually munching on his chips, I assume it was a random question.

Taking a sip of my tea is a good delaying tactic. It's a lovely herbal, full of flavor. It's decaffeinated, and hopefully it's helping Miranda get the sleep she desperately needs.

"Depends on the show. Something like that"—I gesture to the TV—"would be okay. I wouldn't do a dating show."

"I was going to try out for one. With Miranda. We were going to try out for a dance show."

"As a couple?"

"We were auditioning together, but we would have been competing separately."

Our other three roommates come in the main door, their animated conversation about the upcoming game interrupting whatever else Carter was going to say. Sean Waller, we call him Stone, is carrying a grocery bag and his sister, Brick, has a loaf of bread. Our team captain, Burke—we don't have a nickname for him yet—is the last in and he's carrying a bakery box from the Half-Cocked Bake Shop, the local bakery we all love. Its name is because the owner and head baker is a rooster shifter.

Stone looks around. "Where's our new roomie?"

"In bed," Carter says. "She hadn't slept in about forty-eight hours. Mac made her grilled cheese—"

"A cheese toastie," I interject.

Carter rolls his eyes. "He made her a *sandwich*, and she went to bed."

Stone starts unpacking his grocery bag and Brick and Bedard add their parcels to the counter.

"I'm making spaghetti," Stone says. "Should we wake her when it's ready?"

"No, let her sleep," Carter says. "She sleeps like the dead and is grumpy if you wake her up before she's ready to be conscious."

He turns to me with a furrowed brow. "Dude, what's up with all the growling?"

"Knock, knock. Hello." The door opens and more people wander in. Coach and Mallory, Daphne and Logan, who is her husband and our team photographer, and Kendall. Mallory has a few bottles of wine and Coach has a couple of six packs of a local IPA.

"Where's Randi?" Kendall asks, looking around before kissing her boyfriend, Burke. "Ooh, you got the cookies from Half-Cocked. Thank you, honey."

"She's asleep," Carter says, rising from his recliner and putting the clip on the bag of chips.

Coach is putting the beer in the fridge. "Who's growling? Mac? I thought he was going to shift and rip my arm off in the locker room when I touched Randi's arm."

A hot flush rushes to my cheeks. Crap.

Rising from the sofa, I rub the back of my neck and turn to face everyone. "I'm sorry. My wolf has opinions and isn't subtle in expressing them lately."

With a heavy slap to my shoulder, Coach laughs. "Been there, done that. But man, you gotta get it under control." Even through the laughter I see the message in his eyes. I have to control myself and not let Miranda's presence distract me. He's serious. I don't know what he'd do first—fire Miranda or trade me, but I don't want to make him have to choose. I'd quit the team before I put Miranda's job in jeopardy.

"I will. It was the surprise of seeing her. I didn't know she knew any of you and that she was coming to work for the team. Or living here."

Carter cocks his head. "I talk about Randi all the time. Do you ignore me?"

"She's always been Miranda to me. I thought Randy was male."

A collective "Ohhh..." flows throughout the room.

"Does she know?" Daphne asks.

"Know what?"

"That you're in love with her."

My cheeks burn hotter. "No. She doesn't think of me that way."

I hope that's enough to satisfy them. Everyone keeps looking at me. Damn.

"Ever since we were kids, we've had this connection. She gets me in ways no one else does. We both love horses, and we'd spend hours sitting together looking at my father's horses, going over auction catalogs and daydreaming about being able to buy the horses, what she'd name the foals. She wanted to ride in the Olympics, and I was going to be her coach. She'd ride one of the horses I bred and trained. We'd be a team."

Everyone is looking at me intently, like they know there is more to the story.

"She was sent to boarding school when she was ten and I had turned thirteen a few weeks prior. I suspect it's because our connection was becoming obvious. We were kids, nothing was going to happen, but it was inevitable. And it did happen, I fell in love with her. By then she was here in the U.S., and I was finishing high school in Scotland. My plan was to declare my feelings on her eighteenth birthday and see how she felt. Our parents were not on board with that and made me promise to wait until she finished university to try to date her. I did and was there at Wickham on her graduation day ready to tell her my feelings and instead she told me she was accepting a job in New Zealand. I didn't have a chance."

"That's heartbreaking." Daphne sniffles into a napkin she snagged from the holder on the counter. "Stupid hormones make me cry at everything. But I love you, Birdie." She pats her belly. Logan is a golden eagle shifter and, since they don't know the sex of the baby yet, they have taken to calling it Birdie.

"Everyone good with spaghetti?" Bless Stone Waller for changing the subject.

"Sounds great," I say.

"Sure," Kennie says distractedly. "Randi went to boarding school? I mean, I know where she went to high school, but I didn't realize she was there as a boarder."

She turns to Carter. "Did you know that?"

He shakes his head.

"She went to a bunch of them," I say. "Her parents traveled all over the world for work, and they put her in boarding schools."

They look surprised. They are her closest friends. They've known her for six years. How do they not know these basic things about her?

Coach claps me on the shoulder again. "Let's save the interrogation for another time. We have all season and lots of time on planes and buses to poke around in their business. Who wants to play pool?"

"I will," Stone says. "Let me get the water started for the pasta and go check the sauce I have in the slow cooker. Be right back."

Taking a swig of my beer, I accept the pool stick Brick hands me.

She winks. "I can't wait to watch this unfold. So many items for the betting pool. This is going to be great. And hopefully profitable."

I can't wait for something else to distract everyone. Maybe we can get Carter a girlfriend. He's always good for some drama.

# 6

## MIRANDA

IT IS EITHER THE SMELL OF BACON COOKING OR THE INSISTENCE OF MY bladder waking me. Whichever one it is, I roll out of bed and stumble to the bathroom.

"Oh," I cry. Declan is shirtless at the second sink, brushing his teeth. His surprised blue eyes swing to me, and his toothbrush hangs out of his mouth.

"Morning," he mumbles around his toothbrush as he goes back to his business. Needing to take care of mine, I go into the toilet room and close the door, locking it to be safe. I'm not sure if he can hear me pee, so I wait until he runs the faucet before letting loose. I didn't consider this when I thought it wouldn't be a big deal sharing a bathroom. I've shared bathrooms with other females, but never a man. A man I'm attracted to. Well, this will probably kill any crush I have on him.

Of course, walking in to find him shirtless was a wonderful surprise. He's huge. I looked up his bio on the team website before I fell asleep last night and saw from the official stats he's a few inches shy of seven feet tall and two hundred eighty pounds. But that's all muscle. I'm seeing miles of smooth skin and not an ounce of fat.

Stupid bladder. If it hadn't been insistent about its need to be emptied, I would have had more time to enjoy the view. Instead, I mumbled good morning and rushed in here like a crazy woman.

I flush and come out, going to the other sink to wash my hands. He's still at his sink, shaving now. I'm surprised he doesn't use canned shaving cream. He has a tin with soap in it and a brush he wets and rubs over the soap, then he rubs on his face to get a lather. I watch, fascinated, as he takes the razor and scrapes it over his square jaw. His gaze flicks to mine as he rinses the foam and whiskers off in the sink.

"Did you sleep well?" His accent is the softer tone of his Irish side than the stronger Scottish brogue he had yesterday. Like mine, his accent absorbs what he is around. My Irish lilt is practically non-existent when I'm in America. When traces slip through, the assumption is I'm either from the southern US or sometimes Canada.

Nodding, I try to keep my gaze above his neck and not follow the drop of water trailing down his neck and between his pecs.

Swallowing my drool before it drips out of my mouth, I say, "I did. The sheets were perfect. Thank you for sharing."

"I'll share my sheets with you anytime. All you have to do is ask."

It's fascinating to see when he realizes how suggestive that sounds and watch the red flush stream up from his chest, up his neck, to the one shaved cheek visible and to both ears. It's like a cartoon thermometer with the red rushing up the tube and exploding out the top.

My giggle sets off his laughter, and the sounds of our merriment echo off the tiles of the bathroom.

He's the first to regain his composure. "Stop making me laugh or I'll slit my throat and that would be a terrible start to the day."

I can't resist. I need to touch him. Before he resumes shaving his other cheek, I pat his biceps. His warm, hard, huge biceps I want to squeeze. But don't. Because that would be creepy, and Declan is my friend.

"We can't have that. I'm going to get dressed. Can I hitch a ride with you to the rink?"

"Aye. Whichever one of us gets to the table first, we'll save bacon for the other, yeah?"

"Deal," I say as I let myself out of the bathroom, closing the door behind me. Leaning against it, I let out a long breath. Being around Declan, working together, living together, sharing a freaking bathroom is going to be both wonderful and difficult. It would be easy to let him in and get used to him being there, but I know it won't last. It never does. He'll get traded or find a girlfriend. Crap. Does he have a girlfriend? Does it matter?

Pushing away from the door, I go through my bags to dig out my clothes for the day. Pausing, I look at the small parcel carefully wrapped and protected in my bag. It's some random trinkets I've collected through the years. A black plastic unicorn cupcake topper, a little blue flower shaped eraser reminding me of forget-me-not blooms, the keychain with a tiny plush bear wearing a red Cornell sweater Dec gave me one of the weekends I visited him. It's silly I've kept them—I'm not usually sentimental and with how often I move, it's not practical. I should take them out and put them on a windowsill or something to make room in my bag. But what if I don't come back here? What if they realize I'm not a good fit for the job after all and I can't come back to get them? I'll bring them with me. They aren't taking up much room. I dress quickly in trousers and a black argyle sweater. Add warm socks and comfy lace up booties and I'm dressed.

"What am I doing with you?" I ask my hair as I look in the mirror on the dresser. I braid it since that's the simplest and will keep my hair out of my face. Once I'm done with that, I go to the bathroom door and knock on it. Not hearing anything in response, I cautiously open the door and peek at the mirror. Declan is gone and the door to his room is closed.

Pushing the door open all the way, I enter. The spicy scent of his shaving soap lingers in the air. Brushing my teeth and washing my face, I wonder what the day has in store for me. I know we will travel to Washington State for tomorrow night's game. I don't know if I should pack now and take it with me or if we will come back here for our bags. Opening my bedroom door, I see the apartment door open. We must be eating in the common room.

I haven't met the other three roommates yet. Guess there's no time like the present. After being the new girl in school almost every term, I should be used to it and stop being nervous, but like all of my first days of school, the butterflies are present and my hands are clammy. I wipe them on my trousers and prepare my mask of serenity. One thing I've learned through the years is if I can hide my fear of not being accepted, then people don't know they can use it to hurt me. They'll still reject me like everyone else has and it will still hurt but if I want to have the life I want, I need to take the risk. For years, I refused to care, but that's a lonely way to live. I don't want to be lonely anymore. Taking a deep breath for courage, I walk out of the apartment.

# 7
## DECLAN

I DON'T SLIT MY THROAT, BUT I NICK MY CHIN. SHARING A SPACE WITH Miranda is going to be a heavenly kind of hell. As I dress in my practice gear, I mentally run through the checklist of what I need for the road trip. My garment bag with my suits is hanging on the back of the door. My travel toiletry bag is always packed and ready to go. My equipment is at the rink, and I took care of my suitcase last night. My iPad and charger are in the small carry-on I take on the plane. I'm all set. It's back-to-back games in Washington state and Colorado, four days. Did Miranda pack already? Does she know what she needs?

Following the scent of bacon, I walk to the counter in the common kitchen where Miranda is on a stool watching Brick cook. Looks like bacon, scrambled eggs, and toast.

"Good morning," I say to Brick, taking the stool next to Miranda's and pouring myself a glass of orange juice.

"Do you want tea?" I ask her.

Stone comes in and goes to the coffeepot. "Oh, no, tell me you're not a tea snob too, Randi."

"No tea snob here," she says with a bright smile.

"Good, because Earl Grey over there," Stone jerks his thumb in my direction, "is enough."

I get up and fill the electric kettle with water. "It's not Earl Grey, it's Irish breakfast tea."

Miranda's wistful sigh drifts to me, but before I can ask again if she wants some, Stone puts a cup of coffee in front of her.

"Thanks," she says.

This will be interesting. I rest my back against the counter, cross my arms, and watch as she adds four spoonfuls of sugar and as much milk as the mug will allow. Watching her take a cautious sip, her shudder has me shaking my head. She hates coffee. Why is she forcing herself to drink it? Whatever. The kettle shuts off and I turn to fill the thermos I take with me to the rink and the travel mug I use in the morning. When I have time, I make a pot and use the quilted tea cozy my mother sent me, allowing me to drink my tea like a civilized man. Today it's the insulated mug and a thermos. I drop my tea bags in and turn back around. Miranda is staring at me with wide eyes and mouth agape.

"You're using *tea bags*?"

"What else would you use?" Stone asks.

"Loose leaf tea and an infuser," Miranda says.

She's scandalized, and I love it. I still don't understand the coffee charade, but at least I know she's true to her tea loving roots.

"Ma made me the tea bags. It's her loose leaf blend. It's easier to travel with the bags than the tea tin and equipment. Thanks," I say as Brick puts everything she cooked on the counter. I hand Miranda a plate from the pile at my elbow.

She takes the plate and looks around uncertainly. Carter and Bedard have joined us.

"You need to take what you want first because the boys will fall on it like starving hyenas and there will be nothing left," Brick explains.

"Oh, okay." She takes a couple strips of bacon, a slice of toast and a scoop of eggs. She's going to be starving in two hours, but whatever.

Brick fills her plate next because the rule is whoever cooks gets first dibs. Then, true to form, the rest of us attack it and fill our plates.

Carter takes the stool on the other side of Miranda. "Since when do you drink coffee?"

"Since this morning," she mumbles. Adding more milk to refill her mug after her last sip, she takes another taste. Then she adds more sugar. She's going to end up with a mug full of milk and sugar.

I realize she is having breakfast with people she hasn't formally met yet, so I make introductions.

"Nice to meet you," Miranda says. "Thanks for letting me stay here."

"Don't thank them, I get all the thanks," Carter says. "Without me, you'd be homeless."

I know he's teasing, but by the way Miranda's already fair face goes chalk white, she doesn't realize it.

"Of course, sorry. Thank you, Trevor." Her Irish lilt is coming through. That's something I've noticed happens when she's tired or upset and can't fully disguise it.

I wait for him to tell her he's teasing, but he doesn't. He stuffs another forkful of eggs in his mouth. I like Carter, I really do, but right now I want to punch him.

Nudging Miranda with my elbow to get her attention, I ask, "Did Daphne give you information about what you need to pack for the trip?"

"Um, I don't know. Will we be coming back here for our bags, or do we take them with us this morning?" She's biting her bottom lip, and my wolf licks his. "Let me go check my phone. Thanks for break-fast, Brick, it was delicious."

"You're welcome," Brick says. "Can you cook? We take turns. Not every day, but a few times a week we eat together and rotate playing chef."

Beautiful gray eyes widen in panic. "I've cooked for myself. Never for a group of people and certainly not shifters. I don't think I can make enough food for all of you." She gives a shaky laugh.

"We'll team up until you get the hang of it," I offer.

Her hand rests on my forearm and gives a gentle squeeze that shoots right to my dick.

"You're a lifesaver, Declan. Let me go check my phone to see if Daphne sent anything and put stuff in my carry-on. We fly out this afternoon, spend tonight and tomorrow night in Spokane, the next in Colorado Springs, and fly home after the Colorado game? Do I have it right?"

"Yep," Stone says. "Then we have three days off and a home stand. It's a shame you didn't arrange to join us in Washington. All this flying must screw up your body clock."

"Whatever," she says. "I'm used to adapting. Nothing I haven't dealt with before."

She heads back to her bedroom, and we continue eating. I know she's used to traveling and adapting to wherever she ends up, but I want her to stay somewhere long-term. Okay, what I truly want is for her to stay with me. Would she want to settle down? Miranda seems ready to always go on a new adventure and move somewhere new. I dream of having a home and a family. I want to raise horses and babies. With Miranda. If she'd stay. Can I convince her I'm enough and worth settling down for? Or can I sacrifice my dreams to follow hers?

# 8

## MIRANDA

DAPHNE'S TEXT GIVES ME THE SCOOP ON WHAT I'LL NEED FOR THE TRIP. SHE has a stash of team branded gear I can wear to the games. I open my carry-on bag and repack it. We fly on chartered flights, which is wonderful. The rugby team I worked for often flew commercial when we weren't taking a bus. The players would always get first class and business class seats, and I'd be back in economy with the other travel staff.

I can pack with my eyes closed. After confirming the temperature for where we are going, I add more sweaters and cozy socks. I left the southern hemisphere in the middle of summer. It will take time to acclimate to winter in the northern hemisphere. The next week is going to suck between jet lag and not being warm. At least we will have a few days off and then home games. I'll have to ask if the team does anything for New Year's Eve. I'd be happy with a quiet night home but knowing Trevor's love of being in the center of the action, he'll probably throw a party.

I grab my coat and wheel my carry-on out to the common room. Burke is there. No. I should call him Bedard, start using everyone's nicknames and last names. Everyone else comes out with their bags. Declan takes mine to carry downstairs before I grab it.

"Dec, give me my bag. I can carry it. Brick is carrying her own."

"He tried to carry mine, Randi," Brick says as she follows me down the stairs. "His default setting is to be a gentleman. It's refreshing."

"How did you get him to stop?" I ask over my shoulder.

Stone chuckles, tossing his head to get his shaggy brown hair out of his big brown eyes framed with beautiful long eyelashes. His grin is mischievous. "She threatened to put Bengay in his cup."

My nose wrinkles, and Declan glances back at me.

"You have access to my shampoo," he says. "Are you going to put hair remover in it?"

I reach out to ruffle his thick, black hair. It's cool and crisp in my fingers. It has a bit of curl to it. I love it when it grows out and the curls appear. Reminds me of the boy who meant everything to me as a child. He normally keeps it cut short, but through the years when we had our video chats or we'd have infrequent visits, there were times it was longer and the curls were there.

"No, I love your hair. I'd double check your toothpaste, though."

Everyone laughs as we make our way downstairs. We pile into Declan's Suburban, and I sit between Declan and Bedard in the front row. Stone, Brick, and Trevor—I guess I should call him Carter now —are in the row behind us.

It's nice being in relative silence. The past few days have been almost constant noise with the airports, flights, rink, and all the new people. I give off an air of being social and extroverted because it makes it easier to be accepted when I'm someplace new, but I love being able to have some solitude. I've always been like that. When I was a girl living with the Mackenzies at their home in Ireland, they could usually find me in a gazebo on the grounds of their home. It was on the edge of the woods and surrounded by a field full of daisies and forget-me-nots. It was my favorite place in the entire world. I could get away from the other kids. Declan has four younger brothers and his sister, Sophie.

Declan would usually find me there making daisy chains or cloud watching. He'd sit next to me quietly. Occasionally pointing out an interesting-looking cloud. I think he wanted to be away from his siblings too. I wonder if the gazebo is still there.

Stone speaks up from the back seat. "So, if Randi is Irish and you're Scottish, Mac, how did you grow up together?"

Dec glances down at me, and I motion for him to explain it.

"Our parents are best friends. My mother is Irish, Da is Scottish. We lived mostly in Ireland but would go to Scotland for the holidays and school breaks. I went to senior school in the north of Scotland. Miranda's parents traveled a lot for work. There was a passel of us kids—I have five younger siblings—so Miranda stayed with us and was part of the tribe."

"They're equine veterinarians," I chime in.

"We've been best friends for six years, Randi, and this is the first time you mentioned what your parents do," Carter says from the back seat.

I shrug. "It never came up."

"Do you have siblings, Randi?" Bedard asks from next to me.

I shake my head. "No, just me."

"Lucky," Brick mutters, and we all laugh.

"It was lonely a lot of the time, especially when I went away to school when I was ten." Dec's hand leaves the steering wheel to give my knee a gentle squeeze. My tummy flips. "But I'm great at adapting to new people and places. It's a benefit."

We park and head from the parking garage to the rink. I'm not prepared for the icy wind sweeping down the Boardwalk and off the Atlantic Ocean when we leave the parking garage. It steals my breath and I stumble into Dec. He immediately wraps his arm around me and hustles me across the boards into the doors of the pier.

When I catch my breath and reluctantly step out from under Declan's arm, I laugh.

"Whoa, I was not expecting that. Next time, I'm buttoning up my coat and wearing a hat and gloves. That's brutal."

"Bet you're wishing you stayed in New Zealand," Carter says. "You could be on the beach now."

Hopefully, they chalk the red in my cheeks up to the frigid wind when I say, "No, this is where I want to be." Maybe I'm imagining the uptick of Dec's lips at my statement, but I hope not.

We part ways and I go to Daphne's office, rapping my knuckles on the door frame to alert her to my presence.

"Hey Randi, did you get some sleep last night? I feel horrible we're dragging you back and forth across the country."

I return her warm smile as I drape my coat over the arm of the sofa in her office.

"I slept well," I say, settling in the chair in front of her desk. "Honestly, it's better I came here first. My rhythm is screwy anyway and when you factor in time zones and the hemisphere flip, I don't know what day it is or what season I'm in. Working gives me something to focus on at least. I'll adjust soon enough. This isn't my first rodeo."

"When Logan and I travel, I usually spend the first day in bed."

My eyebrows inch toward my hairline. I'm not stupid.

"Daph, that has nothing to do with travel and everything to do with Logan."

Her hand drops to rub her belly while a pretty pink flush stains her cheeks.

We both laugh. Daphne was a major factor why I wanted to come back to New Jersey and work for the Devil Birds. I don't truly connect with very many people. Daphne is one of the few. She would have been at my graduation from Wickham, but she and Logan had the flu and were staying home. She was heartbroken to miss it and was relieved when I told her a friend from home attended. I didn't tell her the friend was Declan because I didn't want to explain our relationship. I *can't* explain our relationship. I'm trying to figure out where we stand.

Daphne gestures to a black duffle bag on the sofa behind me. "Oh, there's your Birds gear. Let me know if you want something in a different size or more of something."

Pulling the bag onto my lap, I unzip and go through it. T-shirts, hoodies, joggers, hats, jerseys—there is a bit of everything. I look to see whose jerseys I have. They are for the mascot, Shifty the Seagull, who wears double zero as his number.

"I figured Shifty was the most diplomatic choice. If you want a player jersey, we can do that."

I shake my head. "No, Shifty is a good choice. I don't want to appear to play favorites."

"But if you were to pick, you'd go with Mac, right?" Daphne's brown eyes are bright with mischief. And maybe a gleam of match-making too.

My bark of laughter slips out. "You and I both know Carter would pout if I wore anyone else's number but his. I don't want to end up homeless."

"Carter?"

Shrugging, I scrunch up my face. "It's weird, but I'm trying to get used to calling everyone by their last name or their nickname. I want to fit in."

"So, Mac?"

I roll my eyes. "I don't know if I can do that one. He's been Declan since I could talk. His name was my first word."

"Aw. That's adorable." Daphne holds her clasped hands to her heart. "Were your parents upset it wasn't Mama or Dada?"

"Doubtful they even knew. They were off in Italy or Austria. Maybe Dubai."

"Have you been in touch with them lately?" she asks.

I repack the duffle bag, happy to have something to focus on. "Nope. But I hope to be now that we're all in New Jersey. I'm tired of being alone."

Sniffling, Daphne grabs a tissue and wipes her eyes. Getting out of her chair, she comes around the desk and bends down to hug me.

Her baby bump is pressing into my arm that's trapped between us. "Randi, you're not on your own. You have me. You have us. You're not alone."

I know she sincerely believes what she's saying, and I love her for that. But once Birdie arrives, she's going to be busy building her family with Logan, and I will be an afterthought. The focus will be on the baby, as it should be. Every baby deserves to be the center of their parents' world. I know that's how it will be, if I'm ever fortunate enough to have a family of my own. If I can create some stability here, then maybe I can take the steps to make that part of my dream come true.

After Daphne composes herself, she sits behind her desk again, and we chat some more about the travel plans. We go through the routine for game day when we are away. Of course, some aspects are unique because this is ice hockey and not rugby, but enough is similar despite being in the US and not New Zealand. Professional sports is a universal language to a certain extent. I'm not fluent yet, but I'm certainly conversant. Kinda like I am with German. Why my parents enrolled me in a German school in Portugal still doesn't make sense to me. But I was eleven then and realizing very little my parents did when it came to me was based on logic. I assume it was the only school willing to accept me as a boarder on short notice. For the term I was there, I picked up enough of both German and Portuguese to get by. Of course, most of it was slang words not appropriate for an eleven-year-old girl, but you do what's necessary to fit in.

Grabbing my coat and duffle bag, I go to my office. Entering through the doorway from the dining room door, I gasp when I see the furniture rearranged how Declan suggested it yesterday. It's perfect. There is a thermos on my desk with a note propped on it. Sitting down, I take a moment to appreciate the view of the beach and the ocean. When I grab the note, I recognize Dec's handwriting.

"Let me know if you don't like the furniture. I'll move it back. I was going to ask, but you weren't around. Tea in the thermos. Why did you drink the coffee?????"

He signed it with a "D," like there was any doubt who had done this for me. He even put a mug from the dining room next to the thermos. Talk about service. Taking the hint, I unscrew the lid and close my eyes to enjoy the soothing fragrance of the tea carried on the rising steam. Pouring my mug, I cup it in both hands and lean back in my desk chair with a sigh. My first sip is what it must have been like for any lucky mortal to get their first taste of ambrosia. It is a heavenly experience. First a cheese toastie and now a thermos full of tea. I will end up completely spoiled if this keeps up. He'd do this for anyone, I'm sure. He's a kind man. He's doing it to be nice and because we're old friends. I'm not special. I need to remember that.

But I can break the pattern. I'm in charge of my life now. I'm an adult who gets to choose where I live and it's up to me when I leave. If I leave at all. I can make connections and if they don't grow, I can make new connections. It is going to be okay. I am going to make friends. I will figure out how to make sure they like me. My life is going to look like the old sitcom where everyone would sit around the coffee shop and talk and be best friends. Sure, it was a made-up TV show, but it doesn't mean I can't have it too.

# 9
## DECLAN

I do everything I can to focus on practice and not let my mind wander to Miranda. Does she like that I moved her furniture, or did I overstep? Is leaving her tea creepy? I can't help it. Every instinct I have is to take care of her. To protect her. To make her happy. It has been since I was a boy and hated to see her lonely or unhappy, and it's gotten stronger through the years. Shifters throw around the term fated mate to explain how they feel about their partner, but true fated-in-the-stars meant-to-be mates are extremely rare.

That's not to take away from the deep feelings of love people have for each other. It's a wonderful thing. But having a fated mate goes beyond love. You are destined to be together and if you ignore the dictates of fate, there are consequences. It is wonderful when you are together and torturous when you are apart. That's how it has been for me in the years we've been thousands of miles away from each other. I knew she was more than the girl I had a crush on when I was eighteen and she was sixteen when we saw each other in person again. She was my fated mate. That was it. My heart started pounding. I couldn't form coherent sentences. My wolf was all, *She's cute, we like her!* I agreed wholeheartedly. Then my unicorn cleared his throat, tapped me on the shoulder, and informed me, *She's your mate. She's the one you are fated to be with. There is no one else. There will be no one else for you. If you are not with her, you will be alone. Forever.*

Not everyone has a fated mate. People throw the term around like they do saying someone is a friend when all they are is an acquaintance. But it's a real thing that means something. I will never have what I feel for Miranda for someone else. Now that we are finally in the same place, I need to get Miranda to have the same feelings for me as I do for her. Without freaking her out and scaring her away.

Non-shifters don't feel the same sense of fate shifters do. At least, I don't think they do. I've never discussed it with Miranda. I've been afraid of pushing her too hard, too fast, and losing her altogether. I dream of her, and it feels like we're together. I'm always in my unicorn form, never as a man or as my wolf. We're in the field near the gazebo where we spent much of our time together as children. The daisies and forget-me-nots are blooming. The sun is warm on our skin. As time has passed, we've gotten older in my dreams and it's like being together in real time. We never get to touch or speak but just being together brings me peace. That's our fate bond at work. I don't know if she has the dreams. But the glimpse of what our future could be is what keeps me going.

Since it is a travel day and we aren't playing, we dress in our team-branded gear for our bus ride to the local airport. It's nice not to be flying in a suit. We had a light practice and now we are all showered and dressed, and we are getting on the bus parked across from the pier. I can easily see over the crowd and am looking for Miranda. I'm hoping we can sit together on the bus and on the plane.

Did something happen, and she's not traveling with us after all? My wolf stirs. If I were shifted, he'd be pacing. But I'm me and I need to keep my cool. This is her second day here. I don't want to make her the center of attention because I can't control myself. Yes, I'm a shifter and I have that side to me, but above all, I am a man and in control of myself at all times. No longer am I the boy in the throes of puberty learning how to deal with changes, not only to my human body, but also to the two other creatures who are part of and growing with me. Sometimes arguing with each other and making me be the swing vote like a chaotic tribal council on Survivor. I'm past that.

I don't see Daphne either. Maybe that's a good thing? They are together and we wouldn't leave Daphne behind.

"They're already on the bus," a voice says from over my shoulder. Glancing back, I see Logan.

My cheeks heat. I didn't realize I had been so obvious.

"Dude, I'm an eagle shifter. I'm observant," he murmurs.

I follow my teammates onto the bus, ducking my head out of habit. My eyes automatically find Miranda sitting with Daphne in the third row behind the driver. The seat across the row from her is open. It's next to Colby Alvarez, a capybara shifter from Texas and our fourth-string left wing. I like Colby. He's quiet, but he always has cookies or cupcakes from the Half-Cocked Bake Shop. It's hard not to like a guy with a bakery box. It's Carter and Brick between me and my goal. They'd understand getting mowed down. If there was enough room, I'd climb from seat to seat and avoid the aisle completely, but the seats are full and I'm too tall to maneuver like that.

Miranda looks up and the smile breaking across her face when she sees me has my hand uncontrollably reaching up to rub my chest over the heart that has kicked up in rhythm. When he sees Miranda's smile, Carter looks back at me with a smirk and prepares to sit down next to Alvarez. He never sits with Alvarez. Carter is always in the back of the bus, never up front. In a flash, Miranda tosses her purse in the seat, startling Alvarez into choking on cookie crumbs.

"Sorry Trev, Alvarez is saving that seat for Declan," she says with the sweetest, fakest smile I've ever seen on her lips. Still sputtering, Alvarez nods. He's my favorite teammate.

"You can't save seats. That's not fair," Carter protests.

"You know that's bullshit. You save a seat for Stone whenever he has a new game downloaded you want to play," Brick says from right in front of me. Shoving Carter past the empty seat, she turns back to give me a wink. She's my favorite teammate too.

I hand Miranda her purse and sit next to Alvarez. His dark brown eyes are twinkling as he tilts his cookie bag toward me.

"Thanks." I grab a peanut butter chocolate chip.

"You're welcome."

The cookie is huge. I break it in half and reach across the aisle to offer half to Miranda. I know she loves chocolate and peanut butter together.

"Ooh, yeah, thanks." She takes the cookie, breaks her half in two, offers a piece to Daphne, then leans forward to see past me. "Thanks, Alvarez." She turns her smile to me next. "You're spoiling me today, Dec. Rearranging my office, the tea, now a cookie. How are you going to top this?"

Her gray eyes are sparkling, and I sit there, grinning like an idiot, looking at her like a lovesick fool.

Alvarez nudges me as the bus pulls away to start the twenty-minute trip to the airport. I realize Miranda is waiting for an answer to her question.

"I'll think of something," I say. Brilliant. I'm a fricking wordsmith.

"I washed your thermos," Miranda says, nudging her backpack with her foot. "It's packed in there, I'll give it to you when we get to the hotel. Thanks for the tea. It was wonderful."

"You're welcome. Why did you drink the coffee at breakfast? You shuddered each time you took a sip."

Miranda's beautiful face flushes. She leans across the aisle and whispers.

"I didn't want to be rude by saying no. I want them to like me."

Is she truly worried someone is going to dislike her because she turns down a cup of coffee? Her earnest expression and the way she bites her lip, probably in anxiety, says she is.

I reach across and put my hand on her arm. I hear an *ooh* come from the rear of the bus but ignore it. Miranda glances that way, but I give her arm a light squeeze to call her attention back to me.

"Ignore them," I murmur.

Alvarez talks loudly to Daphne, and Logan joins in, to bury our conversation among the other noise. I'm lucky to have good friends like this.

"You don't have to change who you are to get people to like you," I say. "You're wonderful the way you are. Stone is a good guy. He was teasing me about the tea. It's a joke between us. He doesn't care if you prefer tea or coffee. He was being friendly and wanted you to feel welcome."

She nods and sits back in her seat. I reluctantly remove my hand from her arm. Daphne meets my eyes and gives me a subtle brow raise. She's telling me to cool it. Bedard has started a joke I'm a mind reader, and I play it off. I'm not telepathic, like they think I am, but I am intuitive and pick up on the surrounding vibes. Being this into Miranda and being obvious is going to put a ton of attention on her. I can't do that to her. It's my job to protect her, even from myself.

Alvarez and I spend the rest of the ride talking about the Spokane Sasquatch we will play tomorrow night. Since we play the same position, we share info on what we've noticed in the game films we've studied.

"Their first right wing, Ollie King, is strong on the face-offs. Their best. Great on the power play too," Alvarez says. "We will need to neutralize him."

The bus pulls into the airport and stops near the hangar for our chartered jet. I'm glad we travel in style. I know not all teams have it this good.

We spill out of the bus and walk through the building to cross the tarmac to our jet. Daphne joins us as we walk through the building to cross the tarmac to our jet.

"Ugh, baby brain. You got everything to the jet company with your passport, right Randi? I know it's a domestic flight, but since you're Irish and this is the first flight you're on, I want to make sure you're clear to fly."

"I have dual citizenship," Miranda says, "and fly on a US passport. I'm good."

"You are?" I ask.

"Yeah, my father is American, but lived in Ireland long enough to pick up the accent. When he's in the US, he sounds like he's from wherever he is. Boston, Chicago, Kentucky, you'd swear he was a native. He probably has a North Jersey accent now."

"I never knew that," I said. "I didn't have a reason to, I guess, but I always assumed he was Irish."

"Do you consider yourself American?" Daphne asks.

Miranda shrugs. "Not really. Ireland with Dec's family is the closest thing I've ever had to a home, and I'm Irish because I was born there. But honestly, I'm homeless. I bloom the best I can wherever I'm planted, but I don't have roots." Under her breath, she adds, "At least not yet."

I know she didn't intend for me to hear that, but thanks to shifter hearing, I did. My throat tightens and my eyes sting, knowing she considers the time we were together as children as she does, but also feeling she no longer has it. Every ounce of restraint in my body is being spent not wrapping Miranda in my arms and assuring her wherever I am in this world, she has a home with me. She's not ready to hear it, no matter how ready I am to say it.

As we climb the steps into the jet, I realize I miscalculated. Miranda's perky ass is at my eye level and my wolf is ready to howl. My focus has been on her being here and seeing her again, and I've ignored how freaking beautiful she is. Okay, not ignored. I'm not blind, but I haven't allowed myself to think about it. But now it's right in my face and impossible to ignore. I'm so distracted I stumble on the top step and face plant right into Miranda's fine ass.

"Oh," she cries out as she stumbles forward.

I grab her hips to hold her steady, but that unfortunately propels me against her more. This is bad. I let go, and she moves forward into the jet and turns back to look at me. She's blushing and my teammates behind me are hooting and hollering.

"Yeah, missed a step," I say. "Sorry."

Regaining my footing, I stand to my full height and look down the line of teammates behind me on the stairs. It would be easy to give Carter a shove in his smug face and send them all falling backwards like dominos. Lucky for all of us, I have a strong rein on my temper and a steely eyed glare that shuts everyone up.

I am mortified. My wolf is embarrassed. If I was in wolf form, I'd be on the floor with my paws covering my muzzle in shame. My unicorn is probably pretending he doesn't know me. Hell, I think I embarrassed my ancestors and future children, too. Of course, telling the grandkids about the time I head-butted their gran in the ass could be a fun story. I let a grin spread across my face, imagining it as I board the plane.

Stella, the chief flight attendant, gives me a warm smile.

"Declan, are you okay?" She lays a hand on my arm and squeezes gently out of concern. "Do you need ice for your knee or anything?"

I move to the side to let the rest of the team on the plane.

"I'm okay, Stella, thank you. Pride hurt more than anything."

"Well, if you need anything, anything at all, let me know." She gives my arm a squeeze one more time before removing her hand.

"My usual tea once we're underway is perfect. Miranda may want some too. Did you meet her? She's Coach's new assistant."

"Yes, I did. I'll be by with your tea."

Miranda is sitting with Brick, Logan, and Daphne in a set of four seats clustered together around a table. I take a seat next to Stone in the next cluster and am back-to-back with Miranda.

Stone nudges my arm. "*Anything* you want, Mac. I can't believe you haven't taken her up on it yet."

My cheeks burn while I shoot Stone a glare and jerk my head toward Miranda behind me. His eyes widen and he mouths "sorry" to me. I want to smack the smirks Carter and Bedard are aiming at me from the seats across from us.

From behind me, I hear Brick say, "They have blankets and pillows if you want to sleep."

"Thanks. I don't sleep when I travel," Miranda says.

"Oh no, do you get motion sickness?" Daphne asks. She's sounding maternal already.

"No, not at all. I need to stay alert."

"Why, no one is going to steal your stuff here," Brick says.

Miranda laughs. "That's not the reason. Funny story. When I was twelve, I was flying to America with my parents. It was my first time coming here and I think we were coming from Portugal?" She pauses. "Yeah, that was when they pulled me from the German school in Lisbon. They had two seats together in first class and I was back in coach."

"You didn't sit together?" Daphne asks.

"No, I was twelve." She says, like it makes sense. "First class would have been wasted on me. I had a window seat, and I was comfortable. I slept most of the flight, anyway. There was a layover in Philadelphia or Baltimore. Somewhere like that. We were to get off and take a flight to Chicago or Minnesota. I forget. I slept through the layover and stayed on the flight and ended up going to Los Angeles." She laughs like it's hilarious.

"Wait," Brick says. "Where were your parents?"

"They got on the next flight. They were used to traveling as a couple, they forgot I was with them."

"They had to go through customs," Logan says. "How do you not realize part of your group, *your child*, isn't with you?"

"I was twelve. I've gone through customs before. I knew what to do."

She says it matter-of-factly, like it's not a big deal.

"What happened when your parents realized what happened? Did they freak out?" Daphne asks.

I sneak a peek through the seats. As expected, Daphne's eyes are wide, and her hands rest on her baby bump. I bet she's thinking she'd never forget her child on a plane. I know she won't. She's going to be a wonderful mother.

"Probably not. The crew on my flight radioed the crew on theirs. They worked it out when I landed in L.A., I'd catch a flight to…" She scrunches her face in concentration, ticking off a mental list on her finger. "It was Minneapolis…and the school would pick me up. They went to their place in Florida. I was going to my next school. It wasn't a big deal."

Stone undoes his seat belt and kneels on his seat to look over the back of his seat and join in the conversation.

"You're a twelve-year-old girl. In a foreign country, separated from your parents, and they aren't walking back to coach and waking you up? They can *forget* their child is traveling with them and don't realize it until the flight crew reminds them? They arrange for you to fly back across the country by yourself and get picked up by strangers while they go off on their merry way? What the actual fuck? That can't be true."

Stella delivers my tea. I give a tense nod of thanks.

"Bring him a whisky, neat," Bedard says.

"I'm not lying. It happened." I can hear the insistence in her voice —she's getting upset and I can't stand it. "It wasn't a big deal. I was twelve, not a baby."

"What's rumbling?" she asks nervously. "The plane engine?"

"No, it's Mac growling." Bedard says.

"What? Why?" Miranda leans out of her seat and reaches back to lay her hand on my arm.

"Declan, are you okay? Do you not like flying?" Her touch is soothing. Her thumb is rubbing up and down my arm. Her hand is warm. My wolf is calming down.

"Flying is fine. I want to kill your parents."

Stella comes back with my whisky. I down it in one go. It's not as good as my family's, but good enough. Her eyes flick to Miranda's hand on my arm and back to my face.

"Would you like another?" she asks.

I shake my head. I can't drink enough to get drunk, anyway. She gets everyone else's drink requests and goes back to the galley.

Miranda pulls her hand away, and I miss the heat and contact immediately.

"Don't be like that," she says, her voice barely above a whisper. "They were busy. Everything worked out."

It's on the tip of my tongue to tell her I'm never too busy for her. I would never leave her behind. But she's not ready to hear that, no matter how much I want to say it. I'll add it to the list of things I can't say to her. Yet.

# 10

## MIRANDA

I realize I'm defensive. But when you're told you're a liar most of your childhood, when you can't trust your own memories...

I offer Stone a weak smile. "It's all right. Sorry for being defensive."

"No worries," he replies, offering me a smile. Maybe not as friendly as it was before. Crap. Have I ruined our burgeoning friendship with my prickliness?

I know my parents aren't perfect. They're busy with their practice and are in demand all over the world because they are experts at what they do. What they do is important. They keep the beautiful horses they treat healthy and safe. It's not like they were abusive or anything. Many kids have it worse than I did. Do I wish they had more time for me? Yeah, I did when I was younger. I want to have a closer relationship with them. That's part of the reason I'm back in New Jersey. But going to different schools every year, sometimes every term, helped me to be independent and resourceful. Classmates of mine couldn't handle the basics of life like booking an airline ticket or finding a job house-sitting for a professor at the local university over the holidays when the dorms would be closed at my boarding school. It worked out great. They got back the day before the dorms reopened. At most I would have to pay for one night at a hotel. If my parents had me spend the holidays with them every year, I wouldn't have learned I could do that.

Note to self: don't talk about your childhood. I know this and normally deflect questions, but I wasn't thinking. Ironically, it's probably because I need to sleep that I wasn't more guarded. Is ironic the right word? Whatever.

The flight attendant who has her eye on Declan brought me a lovely cup of tea. I shouldn't want to throat punch her. But who can blame me? Dec is gorgeous and kind. And not mine.

Everyone has earbuds in, their laptops out, or they're kicked back and napping. Getting my tablet out of my bag, I call up the local real estate listings. I can't live with Carter forever. I want my own home. I've been doing research and there are grants for first-time home-buyers I will apply for. I would be okay buying a fixer-upper with good bones but needs work. I need a functional kitchen, bathroom, and bedroom—everything else can be dealt with over time as long as the roof, plumbing, and electrical are good. I'm excited to have a project and something I can put my mark on and have control over. I haven't had that before in my life and I'm ready to be in charge of my own future.

"You looking at real estate already?" Brick asks.

I flush. Brick is being friendly, but I don't want my business out there.

Stone pops up over his seat again. I resist the urge to hug my tablet to my chest. I don't want my dream to be laughed at.

"Mac is looking too. If you're looking for a place together, I can swap seats with you to make it easier to compare."

He is such a sweet man, but I wish he'd shut up and sit down.

"Wait, you're both looking for places?" Carter asks, hurt in his voice. "What are you looking for? What's wrong with the barn? Stone, switch with Randi."

Suppressing a sigh, I get up and switch. Dealing with Carter in a mood is not on today's agenda. Dec is standing to let Stone out and let me in. He grabs my tea for me and puts it on the table.

"So, what's going on? Are you guys moving out? When did you plan this?"

Dec and I turn to each other. He raises a dark brow, and I shrug.

"We haven't," he says. "After hockey, I want a horse farm. I'm always looking to see if there are properties for sale."

"In Ireland?" I ask. That was always the plan.

"Sometimes. I'm looking in New Jersey too. What are you looking for?"

He's looking for a farm here? Would he be willing to stay here after he's done playing? Would he be willing to stay here with me?

I show him my tablet.

"I'm looking at fixer-uppers with a good size yard. I want to plant flowers and maybe get a dog. I've always wanted a dog."

"When are you planning on moving?" Carter asks.

I laugh. "Not anytime soon. I need to save up for a down payment and work for more than a week to qualify for a mortgage. This is a pipe dream. I've always looked at houses and saved pictures since I was a teenager. It's my hobby."

"Same," Dec says, nodding. Our eyes connect and a zing of awareness runs through me. For a moment I fantasize about us being a couple and looking for homes together and planning for our future. But a fantasy is all it is. I need to remember that.

Stone pops up again. I swear the man has a spring in his ass like a jack in the box.

"You guys could pool your resources and buy a property together. It sounds like you want similar things."

Bedard, bless his heart, changes the subject by talking about the team we're playing tomorrow night. The rest of the flight is spent discussing the Sasquatch and their strengths and weaknesses.

After we land and get to the hotel, Daphne and I hand out the room keys. I am rooming with Brick. Dec and Stone are in the room next to ours.

Looking around our room after we hand out all the keys, I see there is a connecting door to the guys' room. I startle when there is a knock on it. I open it to find a grinning Stone standing there.

"Hey neighbor, this feels like home, huh?" he asks.

"I don't have to share a bathroom here," I say as I step back to let him in.

"There's no getting rid of you, is there?" Brick says with a sigh when she sees her brother.

"Nope. Mom wouldn't let me leave you in the woods."

My lips quirk. I wish I had something like this in my life. When I was a kid with the Mackenzies, I kind of had it, but with so many of them there were plenty of targets for their teasing and I usually faded into the background. By the time I thought of a zinger, the moment had passed.

Declan comes to the door and peeks his head in. "Their room is like ours and like the rooms we stay in whenever we stay at one of these hotels. They're part of the Clardmore chain, and we get a deal."

"Using your family connections to ingratiate you with the team?" I tease.

"Need to work with what I have." He winks at me.

I saw him in the bathroom without his shirt on. He's working with a lot.

Both of his black brows rise and a slow smile spreads across his full lips like he read my thoughts. My flaming cheeks are probably a dead giveaway.

"We're going downstairs for dinner. Do you want to join us?" Dec asks.

I look at Brick. I don't know what is normal for road trips. She's the athlete and I don't want to disturb her routine.

"Sounds good. It's too cold to go somewhere outside."

We lock our rooms and take the elevator downstairs. It's the four of us in the elevator, but Declan is at my side. He's so close enough I can feel his body heat. I wish I could snuggle into him and steal some of his warmth. Except for when I snuggled under the flannel sheets Dec loaned me, I've been cold ever since I arrived in New Jersey.

The elevator doors open, and Dec's hand lightly touches my back as he motions for me to exit before him. His touch sizzles up my spine and to my scalp. I glance in the mirror as we pass to see if my hair is standing on end from the electricity. Amazingly, it's not.

We cross the lobby to the steakhouse, and I worry about being underdressed. Then I realize I'm walking in with three professional athletes who are guests of the hotel, one whose family owns the whole chain. I guess I'm good in my slacks and sweater.

The hostess greets us warmly and asks if we want to be seated near the rest of the team. We agree and get a table near the dozen players and staff already here. Liam is with Logan, Daphne, and Bedard.

"What's our per diem?" I whisper to Brick. I don't know why I bothered. I'm around shifters who all have superior hearing.

"No per diem, get what you want, Randi," Coach calls out. "Well, for food, get what you want. We cover one alcoholic drink. If you want more than that, it's on you."

"Thanks," I say with a smile. My cheeks are flaming. Is everyone looking at me and thinking I'm a loser for worrying about the cost? It's not that I can't afford to eat. I don't want to put a foot wrong and get in trouble.

"You're fine," Dec murmurs.

The guys get ribeye steaks, and Brick gets grilled salmon. I choose a turkey melt. None of us get alcohol.

"You don't like steak?" Stone asks.

"I do. But I don't want something too heavy. I want dessert."

"Peanut butter pie or the brownie sundae?" Dec asks. Of course, he knows my favorites.

"Not sure."

"You get the pie. I'll get the brownie and have them hold the almonds. We'll share," Dec says.

It's silly to get misty he remembers I don't like almonds, but I'm touched. That's why Declan is wonderful. He notices the little things and remembers them.

The conversation over dinner is about tomorrow night's game against the Spokane Sasquatch and their wing, Oliver King. He's a Bigfoot shifter, so of course he's been tapped to be the face of the team. I watched some game highlights and he's a skilled player, but isn't comfortable in front of the camera, judging from the interviews I've seen.

Brick and Stone leave while Dec and I are sharing our desserts. The peanut butter pie is incredible.

"Do all the Clardmore hotels have this on their dessert menu?" I ask. If they do, I'll be gaining a couple of pounds each road trip.

Dec shakes his head. "I don't think so. Each hotel has its own special restaurant, and the menu is up to the chef."

"Oh." I try to mask my disappointment. It's a pie, nothing important, but it would be nice to have something to look forward to in each town. Something to rely on. I've always lived such a nomadic life I always search for a person or a thing or even a food to be familiar with and be able to count on it. I never find it and I've learned to rely on myself, but it would be nice to have a tradition.

As if he reads my mind, Declan puts his hand on mine and gives it a gentle squeeze.

"Every time we play in Spokane, we will come here and get pie. Even if we aren't staying here. Me and you. Okay?"

I try to swallow the lump forming in my throat. How can this man effortlessly know what I need and give it to me? My own parents are too busy to do that, but it comes naturally to Declan.

I nod and let out a croaky, "Yeah."

He gives my hand another squeeze and then takes a small bite of my pie. He is the perfect person to share pie with because the end crust is my least favorite part, but he loves it. Ever since we were little kids, we shared pie like this. His siblings thought we were weird, but it worked for us and that's what mattered. I reach over and get a bite of the brownie sundae. I'm glad we're sharing.

"You're the only person I've ever shared food with," I say. Way to be random, Miranda.

Dec cocks his head. "What do you mean? You had breakfast with us this morning."

"It's been years, I think since graduation, I've shared food with someone. Of course, I've eaten meals with people, had pizza, but eating the same portion and sharing is something I never do. You're it."

I watch as he puts his bite of pie crust between his lips and drags the fork out of his mouth. There's a bit of peanut butter filling on his upper lip and I'd give my left kidney to kiss it off. His blue eyes are contemplative as he chews.

"You're the only person I share food with, too. I never thought about it. I guess it's our thing."

A warm glow spreads in my chest at the thought of having a "thing" with anyone, but especially with Declan. We finish our desserts and go back upstairs. Some of the team members bring gaming systems and players hang out in the rooms and have game nights. From the little I've seen, it seems like the Devil Birds are a cohesive unit. No wonder they have a winning record and are one of the top teams in the Paranormal Hockey League.

"You must be exhausted," Dec says as we walk into my suite. The connecting door is still open and from the collection of players gathered in there, his suite must be one of the game rooms.

I shrug. "My body clock is all messed up. I slept well last night. I'll probably get a few hours tonight, but most likely I'll watch TV for hours before I doze off. I'm used to functioning on not much sleep while I'm traveling and then crashing when I get back to wherever I call home that month."

"Would you mind some company?" Dec asks.

"That would be great. I'm going to change into something more comfortable. Be right back."

I go into my room and change into a pair of knit shorts and my favorite t-shirt to sleep in. When I glance in the mirror as I'm putting

my hair into a loose braid, I remember it's one of Dec's shirts from
Cornell. The high school I graduated from and Cornell both share the
"Big Red" slogan for athletics, so we swapped shirts on Christmas a
few years ago as a joke. He probably never wore his. He's much
broader and more muscular now, it probably wouldn't fit. But I wear
the one he gave me all the time. It's soft and faded with time and
washing and the hem has come out in spots, but I love it. I debate if I
should change, but decide to stay as I am. He's probably not even
going to notice.

Entering my room, I debate whether to leave the door open or
close it. Leaving it open seems like the best choice. I don't want
anyone to think there's something going on. What's the saying?
People with nothing to hide, hide nothing? Dec has grabbed the extra
pillows and blanket from the closet and is sitting on the bed with his
back against the headboard. Handing him a bottle of water and
chips, I walk around to the other side and climb onto the mattress.

I pull the blanket over me and hold it up as an invitation for Dec
to get under it, too. The few times I could visit him at Cornell, this is
how we'd spend our time, snuggled under a blanket, looking at real
estate listings for horse farms and daydreaming of the farm he'd
have someday. Sometimes we'd watch superhero movies, and I'd call
him Superman because of his resemblance to the actor playing the
role. He'd blush and seem more like Clark Kent than the Man of Steel.
But with all the muscles he's packing now, it's not a stretch to think
he's made of steel.

Since it's the week between Christmas and New Year's, the pick-
ings are slim for programming. We end up watching some romantic
Christmas movies. Well, Declan ends up watching them. Jet lag
catches up to me and I drift off not long after the first one starts. I
wake up a few hours later to the theme song for *Murder, She Wrote*.
Dec is asleep, lying on his back with one hand resting on his chest.
His long, black lashes kiss his cheeks, and he looks like the boy I
remember from all those years ago. There's a twinge around my
heart. I slip out from under the blanket and use the bathroom. He's

still asleep when I reenter the room. I quietly shut the door to my bedroom and turn off the lights before sliding under the blanket and laying on my side with my back to Dec. I'm not sure I'll be able to fall back asleep. I leave the TV on to watch a detective solve murders she probably committed and enjoy not being alone for once.

*The sun is warm on my face as I sit here among the daisies and forget-me-nots. This is my favorite place in the world, a refuge when I need to get away. I love playing with the other kids, but sometimes it's overwhelming. But I'm not a little kid any longer. I'm a woman. The black unicorn walking toward me across the field is not the colt I first met years ago. Now he's a sleek stallion. Such a deep black he almost shines like a hematite stone. His silver horn gleams in the sun. I've missed him. I wish I could stay here with him forever, but I know I can't. I try, but nothing ever works. He stops in front of me, as he always does. His brilliant blue eyes shine like sapphires. He's like a living, breathing treasure chest, but he may as well be in a hole twenty feet deep because he's always out of reach and I don't have a map to get to him.*

The annoyingly cheery chimes of the alarm I set on my phone go off and my unicorn is gone. Again. He's always just out of reach. Groaning, I slap my hand around until I can grab my phone and hold it before my bleary eyes. Jabbing repeatedly, I finally hit stop and make it go quiet. I let my hand flop to the mattress as I try to gather the energy to get up and take a shower. I want to roll over and go back to sleep. Maybe I'll dream of the unicorn again. It's a dream I've had since childhood. Not every night, but at least a few times a year. I had it the first time as a ten-year-old girl in Ireland. The field of wild-flowers was on the grounds of Declan's home. There used to be a gazebo there, too. When Sophie insisted on playing wedding, her favorite game because she was the wedding planner and bossed everyone around, the gazebo is where Declan and I would stand as groom and bride while Sophie or one of their brothers performed the ceremony. I always had to be the bride since all the boys were Sophie's brothers and Declan was always the groom because...I'm not sure why he was willing to pretend-marry me? He was the oldest? Whatever the reason, I'm glad he was the groom. He is the only person I ever wanted to marry. The sweet kiss he always gave me on the cheek made my heart flutter and my tummy flip. His brothers would have blown a raspberry or licked me or something else gross like that.

The ding of an incoming text has me holding my phone in front of my face. It's a text from Dec. Not going to lie—it was much nicer waking in Declan's arms yesterday morning in Spokane than waking to a text and a lonely bed in Colorado Springs, but it's better than nothing.

> Declan: Good morning. Were you going downstairs for breakfast or getting room service?

I have a stash of protein bars in my bag. I've learned to make sure I have stuff with me in case there isn't other food available. I'm about to text him to tell him I'll gobble up one of those, but my fingers hesitate above the screen. Rushing through breakfast feels like avoiding all those people downstairs, people I want to accept me, welcome me into their lives. It means I have to pretend to feel less for Declan than I do, but isn't this why I'm here? To make friends, to make a life? Forgetting the granola bars, I type:

> Me: Downstairs. See you soon.

The shower doesn't wake me up as much as I need it to. Thank goodness we will be home for a bit after tomorrow. I am going to spend as much of it sleeping as I can. If I can clear up some of the sleep deficit I'm dealing with, it will be easier for me to hide my feelings for Declan.

Walking into the restaurant downstairs alone feels weird. It's been a handful of days, but not having Declan by my side seems wrong. But Declan isn't always going to be here. He's going to go get his horse farm when he's done playing hockey. My life is going to be here. Even when Declan is gone, I'm still going to have the friends I moved here to be near. New friends I've made. I can be without Declan and be fine. I have to be.

I take the seat next to Liam and say a general good morning to everyone at the table.

Liam gestures with his fork. "That carafe has hot water."

In the middle of the table is a container with tea bags, I grab one and prepare a mug of tea.

"No shadow?" he asks.

"What?" I lower my tea bag into the hot water.

"Mac is usually trailing after you like a puppy dog. Or a guard dog. I'm surprised you're alone."

Shrugging, I pick up the menu. When the server comes to the table to deliver some plates, I order pancakes and ham.

"This is my fourth day with the team, and we are old friends. He's being nice to me. Like Carter is. Like you are. I spend a lot of time with Daphne too."

He lifts a brow. "Uh huh."

I wonder if this is what it would be like to have an older brother? Dec was never a brother figure to me. His siblings were my play-mates, but other than Sophie, I didn't have much of a connection with them. They all had each other. I was quieter and more of a dreamer than they were and didn't get involved in a lot of their adventures. I spent my time at the gazebo or in the stable with the horses and the barn cats. I've always had an easier time connecting with animals than with people. I don't know if that transfers to shifters too or not. I didn't know Dec and his siblings were wolf shifters when we were kids. Of course, Kendall is a cougar shifter like her brother, and we lived together during college, and Trevor is a wolf shifter and was my stunt partner for cheerleading, but neither of them ever shifted in front of me or talked about shifting. I've been isolated from it.

"Randi, have you been to Colorado Springs before?" Daphne asks from her seat at the end of the table.

"No, first time here," I say.

"Then you're coming with me and Logan this afternoon. We're recording a mini tour at Garden of the Gods, and you have to see it."

"Isn't it too cold for flowers?" Lindy asks. He's adorable.

"It's not flowers," Logan says. "It's incredible red rock formations. Awe-inspiring. Like nothing I've ever seen."

Daphne smiles brightly. "You must come with us if you aren't napping before the game. It will be a few hours and back in plenty of time. Morgan Development has hired us a mini coach. We have eighteen seats." She looks around the table. "You all are welcome. If there are over eighteen, I'll upgrade to a regular coach."

"That sounds wonderful, Daphne, thank you," I say.

I was going to hang out and watch more game videos, but it's not like anyone is going to ask my opinion on a play anyway. May as well see something awe-inspiring in person. I am on the verge of breathing a sigh of relief for having avoided Declan when suddenly he's pulling out the chair next to mine.

"Good morning, Dec," I say, smiling up at him. "I'm sorry to miss you. I recommend the pancakes, they were delicious." I was this close to making my escape. I can't resist him if I keep seeing him. I'm not strong enough. Rising from my chair, I say, "Daphne, I'll meet you down here in an hour."

Declan says a general good morning but follows me out of the restaurant without taking his seat. I stick with a group from the team and get on the elevator to take us to our floor. I'm in the corner with Dec beside me. Heat radiates off his body, and I want to snuggle in. I'm slowly getting used to being in the cold again and I know I'll handle it better once I'm rested. But for today, I want to snuggle and be warm. We will be back in New Jersey tomorrow, and I will sleep all day. Under Declan's flannel sheets.

Dec is at my side as we walk down the hallway. He lays a hand lightly on my arm.

"Miranda, are you upset with me about something?"

My steps falter as my head snaps his way. "No. Why?"

He shrugs and releases my arm. I miss the heat from his hand immediately.

"It feels like you're avoiding me. You went to breakfast without me." He runs his hand through his black hair and a lock falls over his brow. My fingers itch to push it back. "I sound like a petulant child. I'm sorry."

It's my turn to rest a hand on his arm. We can't have this conversation in the middle of the hallway.

"Come on, let's go to my room where we can talk." I grab his hand and pull him along behind me. I swipe my card and push the door open when the light turns green and I hear the beep. We are alone in the suite, but I go into my bedroom and close the door anyway.

I pace and Dec leans against the dresser with his arms crossed over his broad chest.

"I'm not upset with you. You're wonderful. That's the problem." I sneak a glance at him as I turn at the window and start back across the room. It's not a big room. Five or six strides is all I can take. "I can't monopolize your time. You need to focus on playing and being with your teammates, not on babysitting me."

He scoffs and straightens but doesn't uncross his arms. "I'm not babysitting you. I haven't seen you in a year and a half. I've missed you. I *want* to spend time with you."

My heart does a flip at his words. I've always wanted someone to want to spend time with me. But we must focus. I need to focus.

"I want to spend time with you too," I admit. "But my focus needs to be on my job. I need this. I want to stay here. I can't risk getting fired because we are hanging out too much. I want to be able to use my sports management degree and get a front office position with the team. And you need to focus on hockey to make money for your farm. That's why you're playing, right?"

"Yeah," he says, crossing the room in two strides and stopping in front of me. "You're not going anywhere. Even if you decide to leave this job, you don't have to leave New Jersey."

He doesn't say, *you don't have to leave me*. That's what I long to hear, or he won't leave me would be nice too. But no one ever tells me those things. Everyone leaves or sends me away. I want stability. I want to be with people I care about. I want to have a home of my own where no one can make me leave.

"Right," I say. Not because I believe him, but because I want to change the subject.

His brows furrow and he sucks in his lips. It's his thinking face. He did it as a boy, too.

"What?" I ask.

"Can I make a suggestion without you getting mad at me?"

My eyes narrow. "It depends."

"Skip the tour today and get some sleep?"

Before I have the chance to say anything, Declan reaches out and grabs my hand, cradling it in his. "Miranda, you're exhausted. You've been traveling across tons of time zones, working, and then not sleeping on the plane."

He runs a calloused fingertip lightly along the top of my cheek.

"You have shadows under these beautiful eyes, and I worry you're going to make yourself sick. Stay here. Grab a few more hours of sleep. We will be back here at least two more times this season and I promise to take you to Garden of the Gods or anywhere else you want on those trips."

This man. I can't remember the last time someone took care of me, told me to slow down. Blinking quickly so the tears springing to my eyes don't fall, I nod.

"Are you going?" I ask.

He shakes his head. "No, my plan was to stay here, look at farm listings, rest." A slight flush colors his cheeks. "Here in the hotel. I didn't mean stay in your room." His flush deepens. "Unless you want me to."

I can't suppress my smile. He's too cute when he's embarrassed. "I know what you meant. We can hang out together. Here or in your room. Whatever you want."

"Let's go to my room then. Do you need anything?"

"No, I'm good. I have my phone and my key. That's all I need. I need to change before the game, but otherwise I'm done. Let me tell Daphne I'm staying here."

I take a moment and shoot her a text. She responds with a thumbs up.

"If you're all packed up, bring your bag with you. You can change there as easily as you can change here," he says.

That sounds logical. I do a quick check of the bathroom and the drawers to make sure I haven't forgotten anything and go to grab my bags, but Dec already has them over his shoulder.

"All set?"

I nod and follow him out of my suite and down to his.

Liam and Brick are there when we walk in. I didn't think about his suite mates because I didn't see mine. I know they are Annie and Carter, but it's felt like I've had the place to myself the whole time.

"Hey Randi," Liam says when we walk in. He jerks his head toward my bags Dec is carrying. "Moving in?"

Wishing the floor would open and let me fall through, I smile weakly. Before I can say anything, Dec interjects.

"We were going to hang out and rest before the game instead of going on the tour."

"Good plan," Liam says. "You're sharing with Carter, right?"

I nod.

"He is the noisiest dude I know. I don't know how you people live with him."

Shrugging, I grin.

"Liam, I've known him longer than any of you have. I've shared hotel rooms with him. Heck, we've shared a bed sometimes when we traveled for games or competitions." I ignore the way Dec's head whips around to me. "I'm used to his noise. I can tune it out."

Brick narrows her eyes. "Have you and Carter dated?"

Oh goodness, she thinks I'm working my way through her teammates.

"Nooooo. We know each other too well to date. He's like a brother to me." My *ew* face probably says it all.

"Like Mac?" she asks.

That brings me up short. I turn to Declan to find his blue eyes intent on me. I swear he is holding his breath, waiting for my response.

"No, nothing like Declan. I've never had brotherly feelings for Dec." Turning back around, I close my eyes in humiliation. Why did I get all chatty now? I've spent years hiding my feelings and suddenly I'm an open book. Yeah, part of my plan is to share more, but there's sharing and then there's *oversharing*.

The breath he exhales tickles the hair on my neck and I shiver.

Brick's eyes widen. "Right, well, okay. You guys have fun. Come on, Coach, let's get downstairs for the tour."

Coach's head whips around to Brick. "What? I'm not going. I have work to do."

Why can't the floor open up and let me drop through?

"We're hanging out," Declan says. "I'm reading the new S.B. Hardin mystery. Or goofing on the internet."

I wonder if this is what it would have been like dating as a teenager with parents around? Having to explain what we were doing and assuring them we weren't doing anything fun. When Dec showed up to take me to my prom, the school had a whole red carpet live stream to enable friends and family to see us since it was a boarding school and most of us didn't have family there to snap pictures and give curfews. My parents didn't care. They had a big race happening in Baltimore the following week and their focus was completely on the horses under their care. Declan's family stayed up late to watch since they were five hours ahead. His mother texted and gushed how beautiful I looked and hoped we had a wonderful time. The Muffys, Buffys, and Biffs who ignored me for the two years I lived with them took notice when I showed up with Declan. He was gorgeous in his tux with his swoon-worthy accent, Cornell education, and family connections. He was polite, but he made it known he was there for me. I was the focus of his attention. That's when I knew I was falling in love with him. The six years since then haven't changed my feelings, no matter how hopeless they are.

"It's fine," I say. "Was there anything you wanted to go over together before tonight's game?"

"No, you look like you need rest, Randi," Coach says. "All I'm doing is reading some of the scouting reports for our affiliate team, the Demon Geese. See if we have any right wingers who will work. That's our weakest position."

Coach sets up shop at the table in the common area of the suite, and I take a seat on the sofa. I fire up my laptop and navigate to house listings. Declan takes the seat next to me and opens his iPad to read his book. Glancing over, I gasp.

"You wear glasses? Since when?"

OMG. This brings the Superman fantasy to a whole other level. Now it's like he's cosplaying Clark Kent with the square jaw, bright blue eyes, black hair, and black-framed glasses. I'm here for it.

"Only when I'm reading on a screen. Cuts down on the glare. I don't need them for magnification or anything like that. They are for comfort. I have perfect eyesight."

Of course he does. Goes along with every other perfect thing about him. If his eyesight truly was perfect, he'd see me as a woman and how wonderful we could be together. But when I said I'd never seen him in a brotherly way, out loud to my mortification, he didn't even respond. Not a word, not a blink. Clearly, he doesn't feel the same way. I've been sister-zoned. We could live our childhood dream of having horses and a farm. I could have my dream of having him. But I'm old enough to know dreams don't come true. I have to plan my life based on reality.

# 11

## DECLAN

THE COLORADO FANS ARE LOUD. THE FEW DEVIL BIRDS FANS PRESENT ARE A welcome sight but greatly outnumbered. The Cryptids are a tough team and playing at the Colorado Springs elevation is always a challenge. The final minutes are ticking down in the third period, and we're tied. If we go into overtime, we'll each have a point in the standings, which is great, but I want off the ice. I love playing hockey, I know I'm fortunate to be living one of my dreams, but right now I want this game to be over so I can be with Miranda.

She doesn't think of me as a brother. Does she think of me solely as a friend? Could she possibly think of me as a man? A man she desires? A man she could love?

"Mac," Carter growls from the face-off circle. On instinct, I nod to show I'm paying attention like I would to the alpha of my pack. Okay, daydreaming in the seconds left in regulation time and a face-off in our defensive zone is not a good plan. Eighteen seconds left on the clock. Ideally, we get possession of the puck and get it down two hundred feet of ice and into the Cryptids' goal in these final seconds. At the very least, we need to keep the puck out of goal and get to overtime. Carter faces off against the Cryptids' center, waiting for the puck to drop. He wins the face off and shoots the puck back to me. The whoosh of the rubber disc over the ice becomes the thwack of the puck hitting the blade of my stick. On instinct, I race down the ice toward the Cryptids' goal, my eyes fixed on the target. My long legs eat up the ice making it difficult for the Cryptids' defenders to keep up with me—that's one of my advantages. I'm not particularly fast but being taller than average, each stroke of my skates propels me further. My heavier weight also gives me more momentum which makes me harder to stop. People rarely want to be between me and wherever I'm headed because I'll plow them down. Even with superior shifter pain tolerance and faster healing, hitting someone my size at twenty-plus miles per hour is going to hurt.

It's me and the goalie, and I dimly hear the crowd counting down the final seconds. I pull my stick back and go for the one timer over the goalie's glove. It's flying like a missile of vulcanized rubber as I hold my breath waiting to hear the goal horn. Instead, I hear the ping of puck hitting the crossbar of the goal and deflecting toward the stands as the horn ending the third period blares.

Overtime. Damn it. I want this fricking game over with so I can shower and change and sit on the plane with Miranda as we fly home. I know she's been back in my life less than a week and most of that time has been in hotels and not the apartment we share, but I want to be back there, with her. I want to start building the life I've been dreaming of.

But first, we need to get through overtime and hopefully earn an extra point. I skate over to the boards since I'm not in the first group of three starting the five-minute overtime period. Before I climb over the boards to take my seat on the bench, I glance up to where Miranda and Daphne are sitting a couple of rows behind. Miranda is watching me. When she realizes I see her, she smiles and scrunches her nose in what I assume is a *you tried* gesture. I shrug and sit down, waiting for overtime to start.

Lindy is at center ice for the face-off to start overtime. He doesn't win the face-off and the Cryptids are storming our goal like they're social media influencers on the first day of Pumpkin Spice Latte Season and the net is Starbucks. Bedard is doing what he can to block them, but not block Brick's view of the action. That's the one disadvantage Brick has—she's less than six feet tall and it's hard to see around a bunch of big guys over six feet tall wearing hockey pads. Her agility helps her react in the blink of an eye, but sometimes that's not fast enough. Like this time.

The puck slips past her left pad and into the goal, lighting the lamp and signaling the end of the game. Twenty-four seconds, that's all it took. We're quiet as we undress in the locker room and prepare for the showers. There isn't anything to say. We played hard. Colorado is a tough team, and they are used to the altitude.

Guilt eats at me because I let my thoughts about Miranda distract me in the final moments of the game. If I had been paying better attention, maybe we would have avoided overtime and be flying home with two points. Not the one-point equivalent of a peewee team participation trophy. As much as I want to be with Miranda, I can't let her distract me. I need my spot on the team and the money I can earn in order to get the farm I want and ask her to spend her life with me. Everywhere else but the ice, Miranda comes first. But when I'm suited up with my stick in my hand, getting the puck in the other team's goal is all that matters.

# 12

## DECLAN

It's good to be back home. I love playing road games, but I'm worried about Miranda handling the traveling and time changes. Hopefully, being home for almost a week will reset her body clock. Obviously, she can handle the job she's been hired for. She did the same job for a year and half with the rugby team in New Zealand. They had tournaments all over the world and she adapted. She's a grown woman. I *know* all this. But I can't help wanting to care for her and protect her.

We get home right before dawn. The overtime loss to the Colorado Cryptids was gutting. We don't have any games scheduled until after New Year's, so we have a few days off. Since we have a rink downstairs, we'll still skate. Our teammates drop in a lot to use the rink downstairs too. It's easier to come out here if they live on the mainland than drive out to Atlantic City to practice on the ice at The Nest. The rink here is a synthetic surface Carter's chemical engineer mother invented years ago—not actual ice, but it's great.

Carter is sitting at the kitchen counter when I leave my bedroom mid-morning.

"Good morning," I mumble.

He raises his coffee mug in salute and continues watching a video on his laptop. A glance shows it's a cheerleading video. He helps Kendall with her cheer team that uses the gym space downstairs. Maybe he's researching a new stunt.

Brick pokes her head through our open apartment door. "Hey guys. I'm making banana bread. Any you want to contribute to the cause?"

I pull our fruit bowl down from the top of the fridge and hand her two ripe candidates. I leave the bowl on the counter. We will have to find a new place for it. Miranda isn't over six feet tall like Carter and I are. She shouldn't have to climb a step stool to get an apple.

"And Stone is making French toast," Brick says. "Do you want some?"

"He forgot to put the bread in the freezer?" Carter asks.

If one of us forgets to put a loaf of bread in the freezer before we leave for a road trip, our tradition is to make a giant batch of French toast to use it up. Knowing how much Stone loves French toast, I bet he left the bread out on purpose to have the excuse and the slightly stale bread to make a batch.

"Yep."

"We have bacon," I say as I open the refrigerator to pull out a pack.

"Does Randi like French toast?" Brick asks.

"Yeah, with cinnamon on top." I fill the electric kettle to start my tea.

Carter's narrowed eyes follow me as I put the kettle on the base I keep on the counter and flip the switch to start it heating.

"How do you know?" he asks.

My eyebrows inch toward my hairline. "I've known Miranda her entire life. We've had hundreds of breakfasts together. What aren't you understanding about this?"

"As kids. Maybe she doesn't like it now."

"It's what she cooks us for breakfast," I say. What is his problem?

"When has she cooked you breakfast? She hates cooking."

Brick is watching us avidly. She probably wishes she had a bag of popcorn to snack on.

Stone walks in. "Are you guys having breakfast with us?"

Brick slaps him in the chest with the pack of bacon. "They are. Here's some bacon."

"What's going on?" he asks in a whisper.

"They're getting territorial," she whispers back, but Brick is not a soft-spoken woman. What she thinks is whispering is a normal speaking voice for anyone else.

"Over Randi?"

"Yeah."

"Is it a wolf thing?" Stone asks.

I look over at them.

Brick rolls her eyes. "No, it's a man thing."

Miranda wanders out from her bedroom looking adorably sleep rumpled. She yawns and rubs her eye.

"Good morning." Her Irish lilt is strong, making me smile. That's my Miranda.

"You sound like a leprechaun," Carter says.

"Bite me," she says.

"Would you be magically delicious?" he asks.

A growl rises in my throat and I cough to try to disguise it.

Brick and Miranda make identical "ew" faces and laugh when they make eye contact.

"Hey, Miranda," Brick says. "Stone is making French toast for breakfast, and we have bacon. Do you want to eat with us?"

"That would be great, thanks." Miranda's lilt disappears the more she wakes up. I miss her genuine voice. The one I know is the real her, not what she adopts to fit in here. "Do we have cinnamon?"

I don't try to hide my smirk as I prepare the pot of tea I'm hoping to share with Miranda. Now it's Carter trying to suppress a growl. Good.

"Mac, is Miranda your date for the New Year's Eve party, or did you ask someone else?"

Fuck.

"What New Year's Eve party?" Miranda asks.

Carter gives me a shit-eating grin and turns to answer her.

"Oh, you don't know about it? The team is having a party at Devil's Den. Drinking, dancing, a kiss at midnight. Wanna be my date? Want to be sure I have someone pretty to kiss to ring in the new year."

There's no holding back my growl this time.

"What am I? Chopped liver?" Stone asks to break the tension. "I've been using lip balm and everything."

Miranda laughs and her questioning gray eyes flick to mine.

"I forgot about the party," I say.

"Are you going?" she asks.

"Hello," Carter shouts, waving his hand. "I asked first."

Brick lays a hand on Miranda's arm. "Most of us are going stag, hang out with us."

"Yeah, okay," Miranda says.

"Come on and make breakfast with us," Brick suggests, "before these two whip out their dicks and pee on your leg to mark their territory."

Miranda nods and wrinkles her nose before turning to walk out of the apartment.

Stone looks over his shoulder to make sure she's out of earshot.

"Get your shit together." He's usually happy-go-lucky. For him to be stern is startling. "If either of you are serious in your feelings for her, then do something about it. If you're just trying to piss the other one off, then grow the fuck up. She's a nice person and doesn't deserve to be toyed with. We need to be cohesive as a team and not distracted by petty bullshit."

"So, what's the problem?" I ask Carter after Stone shuts the apartment door behind him. "Should I be looking for somewhere else for me and Miranda to live?"

"What do you mean 'me and Miranda'? You two aren't a couple. She's here because she's *my* best friend. She didn't even know you were on the team. How close are you if neither of you knew the connection to the team?"

Okay. Score one for him. If I had my way, I'd have been talking with Miranda every single day for years, be with her every night. But I'm her best friend's brother and her friend. Not her boyfriend, not her mate, not her future. We send each other memes or listings of farms for sale with ideas of what we'd do if it was our farm, but nothing personal between our calls. We hadn't spoken since before training camp for the Devil Birds. I never had the chance to tell her about my move here and playing for the team.

"Well, I'm not leaving her behind," I say.

"Dude, there's no reason for you to leave. But you're acting like Miranda is your mate..."

"She *is* my mate," I say with a growl.

"Okay, fine." Carter holds his hands up in a placating gesture.

I do not broadcast the fact, but it's known in the wolf community I'm the next alpha of the wolf shifter pack of Scotland. Hopefully, I won't assume the mantle for many years because my father shows no sign of wanting to retire, but as heir to the oldest pack, I outrank everyone. Now pack wars are handled diplomatically rather than by force and pack Alpha is mostly a ceremonial role, but in a battle, my wolf is one of the largest and strongest. Like I am on the ice.

"But," he says, "if *my* mate suddenly showed up and moved into the room next to mine, I'd be making sure everyone knew she was my mate. I'd be claiming her."

Does he think I don't want to?

"Man, she's been here four days and is practically a zombie from not sleeping enough. It's not like I can throw her over my shoulder and take her to my den like in the old days."

Carter shrugs. "You do it your way, I'll do it mine."

"Good luck with that." I run my hand through my hair in frustration. "Seriously," I say, "she is my mate in the truest sense of the word. Since childhood. There has been no one else. There will be no one else. It's more than love, it's fate. I would do anything, give up anything, for Miranda. If I had my way, we'd be married, hopefully with a few kids already. I gave my word to our parents I'd give her time and space. I have. Now fate has brought us back together, and I'm done waiting."

"When has she made you breakfast?" Carter asks, circling back to the start of our conversation.

"When she'd visit me at Cornell. It's our thing. She'd make French toast, and I'd make scrambled eggs and bacon."

"I'm not saying this to be an asshole, but Miranda has never mentioned you in the six years I've known her."

I shrug, unconcerned. "It sounds like there are many things she hasn't told you. She gives the impression she's an open book, but she's an extremely private person."

"Are you lovers?" Carter asks.

I pause in pouring the tea I prepared into mugs for me and Miranda.

"No. Not yet." That's the best, most honest answer I can give.

Carter looks me in the eye, the most serious I've ever seen him.

"Don't hurt her. I like you, and if you hurt her, I'll have to fight you." He grimaces. "As much as I hate to admit it, you can probably break me in two."

I match his somber tone. "I will do nothing to hurt Miranda. I'd endure anything, give up everything, to keep her safe and happy. I love her."

"Does she know?"

Sighing, I add milk and sugar to our mugs. For this blend, this is how she likes it.

"I don't know."

"You haven't told her?" he asks incredulously.

"No. I didn't want to burden her." And I knew fate would bring us together again. Now it has and it's time. But it doesn't mean I can be careless about it.

Carter gets up and refills his coffee mug from the pot he made earlier.

"Dude. Maybe she would have stayed." He shakes his head like I'm insane. Maybe I am.

"She probably would have. But she needed to go. We needed to live our lives separately before we got together. It is going to work out as fate wills it."

Our conversation is over. Enough heart to heart—that's not how we work.

"Good luck with that," Carter says, echoing my earlier sentiment as he reaches out to open our apartment door. "I'm not leaving things to fate. I'm making them happen."

# 13
## MIRANDA

I TRY TO HEAR WHAT STONE SAYS TO DECLAN AND CARTER AFTER BRICK AND I leave my apartment and go to the common kitchen, but for once, he's speaking too quietly for me to hear him.

"So, you're the hot commodity," Brick says with a wiggle of her eyebrows.

Heat rushes to my cheeks, and I want to crawl under the counter. "I don't know what is going on with those two. They're ridiculous."

"Mac is all gooey for you, and Carter is territorial. He was the same way when Bedard and Kennie started seeing each other. Is he always like that?"

I shrug and watch Stone come out of the apartment, closing the door behind him. I wonder what that's about. Did they ask him to close the door, or does he think something is going to happen? I don't want to leave. I like it here. I want to stay. If there's a problem, it will be my fault and I'll have to leave. I'm tired of leaving.

Stone places a mixing bowl on the counter with a thud and turns to the fridge.

"How can I help?" I ask, desperate to end this conversation.

Stone holds up a shaker of cinnamon for me to inspect. "This okay?"

"Yeah, that's fine," I say. "Give me something to do."

The apartment door opens, and Carter and Declan come into the common kitchen. Dec places a mug of tea in front of me, the fragrant steam rising and feeling like a hug. Blinking quickly, I try to clear the tears springing to my eyes. I'm not used to someone taking care of me and thinking of me. It's overwhelming in the sweetest way possible, but I'm afraid to get used to it because when he stops, it will hurt even more.

"I forgot about the party. I'm sorry," Declan says. "Did you want to go?"

I smile. "I am going."

Dec returns my smile.

"With the group," I say to make sure there's no misunderstanding, or in case he thinks I'm expecting anything.

"Oh." His smile fades, and it's like the sun going behind a cloud. Damn it. Why do I do everything wrong?

"Do you have a dress?" Brick asks. "Or something dressy? All the girls are getting ready in a suite at Devil's Den. We can go shopping today."

I have a basic black dress that would probably work. Brick's offer feels like a hand extended in friendship, and I don't have many friends. But I hate shopping. I'd rather chew my own toenails.

"That would be great, thanks. I don't have anything. I sold or put a bunch of stuff in consignment when I left New Zealand. It's easier to get things when I need them than haul them from place to place. Traveling light makes it easier to start over."

"Why do you move around all the time?" Stone cracks an egg in a bowl to start the batter for the French toast.

How to answer this and not sound like a loser?

"Um. My parents traveled a lot for work. It was easier for me to be in boarding school to give me stability."

"But they'd move you at least every year," Dec says. "You had no stability."

I shoot him a glare. They don't need to know everything about how screwed up I am.

"Thanks, Dec," I say sarcastically. "Yes, I had to switch schools a lot because I never fit in. No place let me stay for a second year until my junior year of high school." I try hard to keep the bitterness out of my voice, but looking at the others, I'm pretty sure I didn't succeed.

His brow furrows in confusion. "That's not true."

I scoff. "It was my life. I think I'd know the truth. It's not like my parents moved me for the fun of it."

He opens his mouth like we are going to discuss this in front of everyone. Not going to happen. It's in the past and doesn't matter anymore.

"I'll finish cracking the eggs," I offer, desperate to change the subject, "if you want to get the rest of the stuff together."

The door from the stairs opens. When Stone is distracted, I grab the bowl and the carton of eggs and start cracking them.

"Hey," Kendall says cheerily as she enters, followed by Bedard. "I didn't expect everyone to be awake."

Everyone says good morning and continues with the breakfast prep and coffee pouring. It's nice to be included for once. I've never experienced feeling like I'm one of the gang like I do now. It's like the empty spaces in my heart are getting filled up. As wonderful as it feels, I'm afraid to trust it. It's going to crush me if it gets pulled away.

"Kennie," Brick says, "Randi and I are going dress shopping for New Year's. Want to go with us?"

Kennie turns wide eyes to me. "You hate shopping. Who are you and what you have you done with my best friend?"

I laugh, trying to hide my discomfort. "I need something to wear, Ken. Shopping is a necessity."

"There are dresses in my closet," Declan says.

I think I understand what he's saying, but before I can respond, Bedard claps him on the shoulder.

"Mac, we will support you in your choices, but your dresses won't fit Randi. You're twice her weight and almost a foot and a half taller than her."

Bedard's sincerity is touching, but the laughter slips out and soon I'm laughing hard enough to cause tears to stream down my face and Dec's deep chuckles join mine. When we finally compose ourselves, five expressions ranging from confusion to amusement are facing us.

"They aren't my dresses," Dec says. "They're dresses Miranda left behind when she moved to New Zealand."

My hand hovers over the bowl's edge, having stopped before I could crack it. For some reason, my heart has kicked into overdrive. "I thought you put them in consignment? You sent me the money," I peek at him over my shoulder, feeling inexplicably shy.

Dec's expression is sheepish. "That was too much effort. Go see if any of it will work."

"Wait." Brick holds up her hands in loose fists and shakes them like they were a set of my old pom-poms. I wonder if he has those stashed in the closet, too? I'll have to snoop when I unpack. "You move her dresses around with you? That's so romantic."

Not sure I'd call it romantic, but it's sweet. As is the blush creeping up his cheeks from under his beard.

Stone looks up from the bread he's pulling out of the wrapper. "I'm going to make a French toast casserole instead of individual slices. You have time to play dress up, Randi."

Kennie pulls her phone out of her jeans pocket. "Want me to text Mallory and Daphne? I think they're all at the house."

Shrugging, I say, "Sure. You all have a better idea of what is appropriate than I do. I'm not good at this stuff. I have a black knit dress I use for everything."

Ken's fingers fly across her screen. "They'll be here in five minutes. What size shoe do you wear?"

"US seven and a half."

More typing. Ken grins and glances up. "Same size as Daph. If you need something, she's got you covered."

"Um, okay..." Sharing shoes isn't something I like to do, but whatever.

Bedard opens the apartment door to let in Mallory and Daphne. They must have been on their way because it hasn't been five minutes.

Daphne hugs me, hard. "Yay, we'll get you ready for the party, like fairy godmothers."

Then she bursts into tears. While laughing. "Sorry, hormones." She pulls a pocket pack of tissues from somewhere around her boobs. At our stunned looks, she pulls a *What?* face. "I don't have pockets, but I've got these puppies." She cups her boobs. I swear they've grown a cup size since last night. "And they're going to be useful."

Declan stands. "I'll show you where the dresses are."

We follow him into our apartment, and I lead the way into my bedroom.

"Oh, this is nice," Daphne says. I didn't make my bed yet, leaving Dec's Scottie dog sheets visible. "Scotties, I love them. I think Birdie needs a puppy."

She rubs her belly, and I swear it grew along with her boobs overnight.

"Are you sure Birdie is the only one in there?" I ask in what I hope is a diplomatic way.

Declan is behind Daphne, frantically shaking his head no and doing a "cut" motion across his throat.

An unholy growl comes from sweet Daphne, and I take a step back.

"Yes. I am carrying one huge baby. Huge because I was stupid enough to fall in love with a giant." She spins around and pokes Dec in his chest. "When you get your wife pregnant with your humongous spawn, you better spoil her and bring her ice cream and brownies and French fries. And watermelon. Even in December."

Declan's eyes connect with mine. "Anything she wants, I will get her. I'll do anything for her."

It feels like he's making a promise to me, not reassuring Daphne. I know that's not true. I'm not his future wife or mother of his children-to-be, no matter how I wish that were the case. He doesn't think of me that way. I'm his sister's best friend. And his friend.

Opening the door to the closet, I turn on the light and walk in. Other than a quick glance my first night, I haven't explored it. That was my plan for today as I unpacked.

"Wow." Daphne turns a full circle to take in the shelves, drawers, racks, and bench. This closet is larger and nicer than any bedroom I've had since leaving for my first boarding school.

"You're a very tidy man, Declan Mackenzie," Mallory says. "Can you teach your coach your ways?"

"Thanks." Dec blushes again. My heart melts a little bit each time he gets that embarrassed little boy look on his face. I flash back to all the time we spent at the gazebo and our play weddings, and I wish we could go back to those simpler times.

He goes to the section of our shared close where he stores his suits and grabs a bunch of garment bags. Walking to my half, he hangs them on a rod. "Here are the dresses."

The moment he steps away, Mallory and Kendall swoop in on the bags like seagulls going for French fries, and start unzipping the bags.

Dec comes back with some shoeboxes and small tubs.

"And the shoes and bags."

Brick and Daphne open those and start pulling everything out and placing them on top of the counter area in the center of the closet.

I turn and am mesmerized by his sparkling blue eyes. He has a soft smile on his face, watching our friends enthuse over my fashion choices.

The closet is huge, but with him standing across from me, looking at me like he never wants to look anywhere else, it shrinks. I press my back against the shelves, trying to find room. I shake my head and look away.

"I can't believe you kept all this stuff and moved it around with you."

"It's a couple of garment bags and some small boxes, not a big deal." He reaches out for my hand and my tummy flips. "Come see what else I have."

I follow him around a corner—this closet is big enough it has separate chambers within it—and slides open a mirrored door. I gasp when I see what this closet holds.

"Oh my goodness, I thought this was gone." Tears spring to my eyes.

"What?" Daphne comes rushing—well, her version of rushing—into the area we are. The others trail after her.

I sniff and reach into the closet to pull out my favorite thing from high school.

"He has my hockey gear," I say, pushing the words out around the lump in my throat. "From high school."

"You play hockey?" Brick asks.

I nod. "I was a forward on my high school team."

"Two-time state champion," Dec says proudly.

"I played two years. They've won more years than that."

"You were a cheerleader and a hockey player? You're badass," Mallory says in awe.

Shaking my head, I correct her. "I wasn't a cheerleader until college. Wickham didn't have a hockey team. I had to try something new."

"Wait, you hadn't cheered at all until Wickham?" Kennie says. "I knew you didn't do all-star cheer, but I assumed you cheered in high school."

"Nope, I studied the *Bring It On* movies and the competitions on TV. I'm a quick study and good at athletic things."

"I've known you for over six years but it's like I don't know anything about you. How is that possible?" The hurt look on Kennie's face is the last thing I want. I hug her.

"Ken, I don't like talking about myself or my past. I deflect. It's not personal. I'm not trying to hide things. There's no point in talking about them."

She returns my hug with a sniffle thrown in for good measure.

"We gotta get you on the rink downstairs," Brick says.

"But first we need to go through your dresses," Mallory says.

Stone calls out from the main kitchen, "First you need to come eat unless you want to starve."

My stomach growls and makes the easiest decision of the day.

"Coming," I call back. If our faces are full of food, no one can ask me questions and I can't be expected to answer them. Activate the French Toast Forcefield. Tastiest deflection shield around. Maybe the maple syrup can reattach some of the bits of armor that have come loose. I know eventually I will have to shed it in order to make the true connections I want, but I'm not ready for it to fall away completely yet. I'm willing to stop deflecting as much as I have in the past, but it doesn't mean I'm ready to deal with a bunch of direct hits with nothing to shield me. I'm working on being braver, not foolhardy.

# 14

## DECLAN

GIGGLING DRIFTS OUT OF THE CLOSET AS MIRANDA SORTS THROUGH HER dresses to see if she has something for tomorrow night. Coach and I are playing foosball against Stone and Carter. Stone gets one in our net and does an obnoxious dance. I put up with it because his breakfast casserole was delicious.

"What's up with you having her dresses?" Carter asks. "That's weird."

"She was packing up before going to New Zealand and wasn't taking them with her. She didn't have time to take them to the consignment store. I said I'd take care of it. I sent her a check and shoved them in my closet because I didn't feel like dealing with it either."

"Why didn't she leave them with me?"

I can't believe he's pouting over this.

"I don't know. I was there, and you weren't."

I'm not trying to be an asshole, but part of me has a hard time forgiving the way he and Kendall abandoned Miranda. If I hadn't been at her graduation, she would have walked across the stage in silence and had no one there to congratulate her and tell her they were proud of her. She spent much of her life alone. I couldn't let her go through something else by herself if it was in my power to be there. I want to be there for all her moments if she'll let me.

That must have struck a nerve because he spun his handle hard enough the ball went airborne, and it was Bedard's lightning-fast reflexes that kept it from flying across the room.

"Fashion show time," Kendall calls out as she walks into the room.

"Ken, no," Miranda whines. "It's ridiculous. They don't care."

"Yes we do, Randa Panda, strut your stuff," Carter says as he turns away from the foosball table to face the door.

My breath catches in my throat when Miranda walks out in a gorgeous green floor-length gown with a beaded lace bodice. When she spins around and her skirt flares, I see how the back of the bodice dips to show an expanse of creamy skin. I swallow hard.

"Liam, isn't this gorgeous? This is what I want for our brides-maid dresses," Mallory says, bouncing on her toes where she has wedged herself between me and Coach at the foosball table.

Miranda's laugh tinkles like wind chimes. "This is a seven-year-old prom gown. I don't think you're going to find it unless you hit the thrift stores. Or get someone to sew something similar."

"Wait, you still fit in your prom gown? How?" Daphne asks. "Of course, I'm not sure I can fit in what I wore yesterday, let alone a decade ago."

"It fits differently than it did back then. I'm leaner in some places, curvier in others," she says, running her hands along the curves I'm dying to touch.

"You're even more beautiful now than you were then." My voice rumbles from deep in my chest, next to my heart. Shocking myself by saying out loud the words I think every time I see her. She's always more beautiful to me than she was the moment before.

I clear my throat and fiddle with the knobs on the table, watching my foosball players dance a jig. I know my face is burning.

"OMG, that is the dreamiest thing I ever heard. Where are the tissues? I used my pack up." Daphne is sniffling and looking around for something to wipe her eyes with. Stone, ever a gentleman, rushes to the powder room and comes back, handing her a roll of toilet paper.

Brick waves her finger between me and Miranda. "Did you two go to prom together?" Miranda nods.

She turns and lifts her skirt going back into our apartment, and I realize she's barefoot. She was wearing three-inch heels with the gown back then and with a foot difference in our heights at the time, her dress wasn't dragging on the floor.

"Here, check this out." Miranda returns from our apartment, opening a frame and handing it to Brick. All the girls gather around as a collective "Aww!" goes up along with assorted "You were babies" and "Wow."

"I remember this picture. You and Trev were going to his first Barrister's Ball." Kendall is pointing to the other picture in the frame. Miranda and Carter are in formal attire. This time, her gown is a deep red with thin straps and Carter is in a tuxedo. They aren't doing the prom pose, but they are side by side with their arms around each other and his hand is resting on her hip. Their smiles are genuine and relaxed. Nothing looks like a forced pose done at the direction of the prom photographer.

Kendall passes the photo across the table to Carter, and he studies both pictures before handing it to Stone.

"I bet you had more fun at your prom, huh, Randi? I was a lousy date. Left you to go home with Serena Kincaid." Carter looks at her and I can see the remorse in his eyes. "I'm sorry, Miranda, I haven't been the friend you deserved."

She slips out of my hold and walks around the table to hug Carter. He lifts her up and I see her bare toes peek out from under the hem of her skirt.

She whispers, but my shifter hearing can pick up every word she says.

"It's okay, Trev. You've never let me fall and I can trust you to catch me. I love you."

My brain knows she means it in a friendly way and not romantic, but my heart feels like it had a dagger shoved in it.

"I love you, too." He pecks her on the cheek as he lowers her to the floor.

She pulls out of his embrace, laughing. "Good. Now never call me Miranda again. It creeps me out. It's okay Declan calls me Miranda."

"I still call you Daisy in my head." The words slip out before I realize I even thought of them. When tears well up in her eyes, I think I've made a huge mistake, but when she throws her arms around my waist and burrows into my chest, I decide maybe I did okay. I wrap my arms around her.

"What's up with the daisy thing?" Stone asks.

Sniffling, Miranda, my Daisy, pulls out of my arms and takes the roll of toilet paper from Daphne, rips off a bunch, and blows her nose. I can't help it. I chuckle. It's just so...her.

"When I was a little girl, around eight years old, I was out in this field of wildflowers at Dec's home in Ireland. It's my favorite place in the world, full of forget-me-nots and daisies, and there was an old gazebo there. I was crying because my grandfather called me his daisy. My mother was a beautiful Irish rose, and I was a common daisy. I wanted to be beautiful too, like my mother or like—" She points at me."—his sister Sophie. They are both petite, beautiful, and perfect. Like porcelain dolls. Always tidy. I was all knees and elbows and freckles with my crazy dark hair and unruly curls. When I wasn't in the wildflower field, I was playing with the dogs and cats or in the barn with the horses and I'd have dirt smudged on my cheek. I was always a mess."

With Miranda standing here in a gown looking like a goddess at a foosball table, I think back on the little girl from that day and my heart flips. Two sides of a beautiful coin. And I've been blessed to see them both.

She's trembling in my arms. From what I've seen, she doesn't share much about her past with her friends. It's her choice to tell them what she wishes. I will support her either way. I give her a gentle squeeze that I hope conveys my intention. Miranda raises her head and our eyes lock. I give her a gentle smile and maybe it's my imagination, but it feels like her trembling lessens. She takes a deep breath, and maintaining our eye contact, continues, "Declan finds me and sits next to me on this dusty stone wall bordering the field and asks me what's wrong. Of course, I blurt everything out. And he stayed. I was always told by my parents I talked too much, and no one cared about my nonsense. Stop being dramatic. But Declan stayed and listened to me."

"Do you remember what I said?" I ask. Lost in her serene gray eyes. The clouds there before have been chased away.

She shrugs. I guess she needs a reminder. I take her hand. The one without the wad of snotty tissue in it.

Taking a deep breath, I look at my teammates and friends. The tips of my ears are probably glowing red from embarrassment but if this is what Miranda needs, I will do it.

"Okay, I'm paraphrasing because I like to think I can speak more eloquently as a man than I could as a ten-year-old boy, but the sentiment is the same. And I'm Irish—we're a poetic people, at any age."

Our friends give supportive chuckles and smiles bolstering my bravery. If Miranda can lay her soul bare, I can too. Looking deeply into my Miranda's eyes, I share my memory.

"Roses are beautiful, but daisies, tulips, daffodils, and dandelions are too. They are all beautiful in their own way. Some are flashy, like roses and lilies, drawing your attention to their blooms and scents. Some are delicate and rare, like orchids. Some last for a brief while in spring, like tulips and daffodils. But some, some are constant and determined and bring an unexpected bit of color and beauty. Those are the daisies and dandelions. They aren't going to call attention to themselves, they don't have to be coddled. They don't bloom briefly and then fade. In a rocky field, you aren't going to find a rose. You know what you'll find? A daisy. Walk along a lane and suddenly there's a daisy in your path and it makes you smile because it's there, an unexpected treat. People like roses because of how they look, but they love daisies because of how they make them feel. Daisies are my favorite flower."

Miranda looks at me like I've hung the moon and I'm about to lower my head and give her the kiss I've been longing to give her for years.

"Pass the toilet paper." Stone's request is like a record scratch on one of the most beautiful moments of my life. I don't care if he's my teammate and friend. I'm checking him into the boards the next chance I get.

I glance around and all our friends, every one of them, has toilet paper wadded up in their hand and are wiping their eyes and noses. Not mockingly.

Brick clears her throat. "I think you should wear this one tomorrow night, Randi."

Miranda nods in agreement as she glances up shyly at me. "Yeah, I think so."

The girls go back into our apartment and to the closet. Carter comes around the table and starts pulling at the sleeves of my t-shirt. I twist away.

"What are you doing?" I ask.

"Looking for your heart. It's on one of those sleeves. Dude, I didn't realize what you were telling me earlier. I get it now." He holds out his hand for me to shake, and I take it. "Good luck. She deserves to be happy. So do you."

# 15

## MIRANDA

I TAKE A SIP OF CHAMPAGNE AND CLOSE MY EYES AS IT SLIDES DOWN MY throat. It's lovely.

"I assume you didn't have champagne when you were getting ready for prom?" Kendall says from the pedicure chair next to me. We are at the spa at Devil's Den, getting primped and polished for the party tonight. Turns out it's more than a simple party. It's a gala. Season ticket holders and community leaders will be attending, eager to mingle with the players.

"No. I didn't have friends to share it with, either."

She looks at me in confusion. "What do you mean?"

I look at my glass, wondering if it was high octane because I'm sharing things I never do. I've spoken more about my past this week than I ever have. I know it's not the champagne—it's Declan. Most of my life has been in separate parts—the real me Declan knows and the curated version of me I show everyone else—and now they are melding together. I want to stay here and be able to trust the relationships I'm building are true. For that to happen, I have to lower my defenses and let people in. I have to risk getting hurt and it petrifies me.

"I didn't have friends. Anywhere. You were the first friend I had since Declan and Sophie when I was a little girl. I hated school." I blink rapidly to hold back the tears.

Kendall smiles kindly at our attendants. "Can you give us a few minutes, please?"

I watch them walk away, grateful for Kendall's request. I'm not comfortable talking about this at all, let alone in front of strangers.

"You know I've learned more about you this past week than I did in four years of living together? Was I self-centered and didn't ask? Did I make you feel like you couldn't share? I'm sorry."

"Oh, Kennie, no. You did nothing wrong. I don't talk about my past because I don't want to make people feel bad for me. And I don't want to let people know how screwed up I am. I don't know why no one wanted to be my friend. I tried. I think I'm a nice person."

"You are," Kendall assures me.

"I was incredibly lonely," I whisper. "The first school in England, everyone pretended they couldn't understand me because my Irish accent was too strong. I was ten and alone. Being without my parents wasn't anything new, but I didn't have Declan or Sophie. I spent all my time in the barn with the horses and made the equestrian team. I used to ride. I loved it. My dream was to go to the Olympics. The day before my first competition, my parents pulled me out of school and sent me to a German immersion school in Portugal."

I stretch out my leg. "This fair Irish skin wasn't used to the Portuguese sun."

"Oh, honey." Kendall rests her hand on my arm. It feels good. Kennie is a toucher and until we roomed together at college, I hadn't realized how deprived I'd been of simple human contact. I loved cheering and dancing with Trevor because I was touching someone. Not in any kind of sexual or romantic way, of course, just basic human contact and connection.

"Prom night was the first time I'd been hugged out of my hockey gear in eight years." It feels shameful to admit that. "You know hockey hugs after goals are a thing?"

Kendall nods.

I swallow hard. "I'd get them when I scored, but they weren't personal. Declan hugging me when he saw me before prom was the first genuine hug I'd had since he hugged me when I left Ireland for boarding school."

"How are you not a sociopath?" she asks.

Her question startles a laugh out of me. "What?"

"There are studies where children who have been deprived of affection and stability like you were often grow up to be sociopaths and serial killers and generally horrible people. And you're not. It's amazing."

"Are we sure I'm not?"

"Did you have friends in New Zealand? Were you happy there?"

I look across the spa where Brick and Teagan are getting facials, thinking about how to answer.

"I had people I was friendly with," I answer slowly. "People seemed to like me, but I was more aloof. I knew I wasn't staying, so there was no point in getting attached. I enjoyed being there. It's beautiful, but it wasn't going to be my home. I learned a lot I hope to use here."

I wiggle my toes. I don't want to talk about this anymore. This is a day to be happy and thinking about my past makes me sad. I don't want those shadows intruding on the light of today. The new year is about me finding my home, my tribe. The past can stay there.

"Should we call the attendants back? What color polish are you picking?" I ask.

---

"Okay, close your eyes," Abby, Kendall's friend and co-worker, tells me. I do what I'm told, and she swipes the eyeshadow across my lids. When she steps back, I blink at the transformation. My eyes, normally a boring steel gray, look almost silver with the dramatic shadow.

"Oh my goodness, how did you do that?" I say in awe.

She shrugs. "I'm a raccoon shifter. Smokey eye is my birthright."

Kennie giggles next to me as Abby works her magic on her. Not that Kennie needs magic. She's beautiful in an ice-blue gown that hugs her curves and perfectly matches her eyes. Bedard is going to lose his mind when he sees her.

I finish putting on mascara and lipstick and appraise myself in the mirror. I hope Declan thinks I look pretty. This past week since we've reconnected, it seems like there is a bond that wasn't there before. I've always been attracted to him, and he's always been kind to me, but I never got the feeling he saw me as anything other than a friend. Now there seems to be an...awareness...between us that wasn't when we were younger. Maybe the stars are finally aligning for me, and I'll find the connection to someone I've always longed for.

I slip into my gown, and Mallory zips it up for me. My eyes mist over when I remember I had to go ask the cleaning lady of the dormitory I lived in to zip me up when I was dressing for prom. I wasn't included in the primping with the other girls. No giggles and gossip, no shared hopes for the evening. I was alone, dressing myself in a gown I got in the clearance section of a bridal boutique in town. The moment I saw it I prayed it would fit and I could afford it because the shade of green reminded me of Ireland and the fields of clovers I'd scour with Sophie and her brothers trying to find four-leaf clovers. I never found one, but I still felt lucky to be there with them.

"What are you doing for jewelry?" Daphne asks with a slight smile on her lips.

I bite my lip in consternation. "I didn't wear any for prom and I don't have anything. I'm not a jewelry person."

"Huh," Daphne says. "You should at least wear a necklace."

"Yeah, you need a necklace," Brick chimes in. "Let's see what we can find..."

"No, I don't need anything, I'm fine." I appreciate how kind they are, but I'm okay with how I am.

"Oh, look," Kennie says, holding up a small gift-wrapped box. "I wonder what's in here?"

We've been friends long enough I know not to trust her innocent air. She's up to something. I confirm my suspicion when she hands me the box. There's a slip of paper taped on top of the green and white striped wrapping paper. I flip it open, and my eyes get misty when I read the message.

*Saw this and remembered hunting for four-leaf clovers with you. I hope you'll wear it. -Declan*

I slip my fingernail under the tape and reveal the small wooden jewelry box with a Celtic knot inlay in a lighter color wood. It's beautiful, but nothing compares to what I find when I lift the lid. On a delicate silver chain is a pendant in the shape of a four-leaf clover with the leaves a gorgeous green gemstone—I can't believe it's emerald, it's probably colored glass—and around the clover is a round filigree frame in silver in a Celtic knot design. It's beautiful and reminds me of happier times.

"Oh my, how gorgeous," Teagan exclaims. She is wearing a glittery black gown that skims her body. "Lift your hair. I'll put it on you."

I turn around and lift my hair off my neck so she can place the chain around my neck and do up the clasp. I've left my hair down with the sides pulled back with exquisite silver combs Mallory lent me. For once, my curls are cooperating and falling in tidy ringlets down my back. After she fastens it and I let my hair fall, I touch the pendant where it sits at my collarbones. I can't believe Declan remembered our childhood games and thought to get me something both beautiful and meaningful. I'm already hopelessly in love with him. He doesn't need to do things like this to make me fall even harder. I'm afraid to hope gestures like this mean he has similar feelings for me.

A knock on the door of the suite we're using to get ready signals the guys are here to escort us. Other than Daphne, Mallory, and Kennie, we're all single ladies. It's a group thing and not specific dates. Declan is by far the most handsome of the single guys—all the guys—easily eclipsing Carter, Stone, and Alvarez. A shiver flows through me when his gorgeous blue eyes slowly sweep over me, from head to toe. The smile curving those lips I'm dying to kiss stirs butterflies in my tummy.

"You got it. I hope you like it," Dec says when he walks over to where I'm standing by the sofa in the suite's seating area.

I reach up to caress the pendant and his eyes follow my movement and then glance down to the swell of my breasts, visible thanks to the v-neckline of my gown. Nothing excessive is showing, but the maturing my figure has done from teenager to woman has changed how the dress fits. If the slow blink and faint blush are anything to go by, Dec likes the changes.

"You look beautiful," he says, his voice tinged more with the Irish lilt I'm used to from growing up, rather than the Scottish brogue he most often sports since his time in boarding school. The butterflies in my stomach take wing and there is no stopping the smile spreading across my face.

Reaching up to brush the lapels of his black suit, I say, "You're looking very dapper yourself, Mr. Mackenzie. I love the tie." His tie is the Mackenzie family tartan and the green of it matches the green of my gown perfectly, like we are meant to be together. He wore a black tuxedo for prom and was the best-looking guy there, but this is a whole other level of gorgeousness.

Daphne walks over with her cell phone at the ready. "I need a picture of you two. There will be a blue carpet and a step and repeat downstairs for more formal pictures. You *have* to recreate your prom photo and let us show them side by side on the jumbotron at a game. We'll get prom pics from all the team."

"Great idea, Daph," Teagan calls out.

"Don't forget about me," Carter exclaims. "Randi and I need a picture together too since we went to one of my Barrister Balls together."

"If Mac and Carter get pictures with Randi, I want one too," Stone says with a mock pout. At least, I think it's pretend.

In the end, I get my picture taken with everyone on the team, including Brick. Daphne, Mallory, and Kendall make their guys do prom pose pictures with them too. Logan holds Daphne's belly, looking smug. Can't blame him. Daph is gorgeous in a midnight-blue floor-length gown with an empire waist highlighting her Birdie bump and chiffon ruffles at her shoulders. She is radiant. I love seeing her happy and loved. I hope I have that someday, too.

We walk into the ballroom and I'm in awe of how elegant it looks. I realize it's not a single ballroom, but a series of them with partitions open to create a massive space. Casino games are dotted throughout, inviting guests to gamble for fun with proceeds going to the charities tonight's gala is supporting. There's a stage with a dance floor, tables for dining, bars and food stations, and what looks like a lounge area at the far end of the space.

Teagan waves to get everyone's attention. "Don't forget we have the player auction where the winner will get to spend half an hour with you. Please remain in the ballroom for your allotted time. If you choose to rendezvous outside of the half hour, that's your business. But for those thirty minutes, you are representing the Devil Birds, and we want to keep it PG. You can play blackjack, dance, eat. Karaoke is down the other end." She points to the lounge area. "Whatever. Make sure they have a good time, but don't do anything that makes you uncomfortable. If there is a problem with anyone getting too handsy or inappropriate, signal for security. They're in black suits with gold ties and have earpieces. They'll take care of it."

"There's an auction?" I ask Dec.

He grimaces. "Aye, we are to stand on stage like stallions at stud and get bid on. I offered to write a check to buy my freedom, but Teagan won't let me." The plea in his blue eyes makes it obvious what he's going to ask of me. "Please bid whatever you must to win me. Here's my credit card." He shoves the card into my hand, then clasps his hands behind his back so I can't give it back.

I know Declan is trying to save money to buy his farm. I don't want him to waste it on this. As I slip his card into my clutch, I think about the balance on my credit card left over after I wrapped up things in New Zealand before I left and my flight here. I can bid around two thousand dollars, but it will be every penny I have available to me. It's absolutely worth it in order to have time with Declan. Hopefully, the bidding won't go too high, because the thought of another woman getting to spend time with Declan tonight is too dire to consider.

"I'll do the best I can," I promise.

They open the doors for the guests, and soon the ballroom is full of men in suits and women in gorgeous dresses. There is an air of merriment, and the champagne is flowing. Because Dec is taller than average, he's easy to spot in the crowd as he meets fans and poses for pictures. An advantage of him being almost seven feet tall is, all the women who would try to kiss him on the cheek can't reach him. I feel a jolt when his eyes meet mine over the crowd. When he gives me a sexy wink and a half smile, it's more than a jolt. It's like I stuck my finger in an electrical socket while standing in a bathtub full of water. It's a pulse throughout my body, concentrating on my abdomen and nether regions. I want this man. I've always been attracted to him, but this is the first time I've felt a bone-deep desire like this.

The players get time off through the night to eat away from the fans or spend time with their dates. When it's Declan's turn, he beelines for me.

"Have you eaten yet?" he asks.

I shake my head.

"Would you like to join me?"

"Yeah," I say, suddenly feeling shy.

He takes my hand and tingles run up my arm.

We fill our plates with lobster, filet mignon, and other delicious things that are thankfully not the haggis we would have if we were celebrating Hogmanay in Scotland.

We take seats with Brick, Crosby, Daphne, and Logan.

"Isn't this spread incredible?" Brick asks, as she enjoys her shrimp cocktail.

"It is. Miranda is thrilled it's not a Hogmanay feast," Declan says.

Logan smiles knowingly. "Not a fan of haggis, Randi?"

I shudder at the thought.

"What's haggis?" Daphne asks.

"You don't want to know," Declan and Logan say in unison, causing me to choke on the sip of champagne.

Daph looks at me, and I shake my head, agreeing with the guys she's better off not knowing the truth about haggis.

"The auction is next," Brick says. "I hope whoever bids is okay playing blackjack."

"Same," Crosby says. "What about you, Mac?"

He shrugs. "Depends who wins. I'd be okay doing karaoke or dancing."

"I didn't think you could dance," Brick says.

My head whips around to Dec because I know he's lying.

"No, I said I don't dance. I can dance, but I usually choose not to." He bumps me with his shoulder. "I'll dance with Miranda if she wins me."

I bump him back. "Are you saying I have to pay you to get you to dance with me?"

"Eh, maybe you can convince me to give you a freebie."

"Be careful, Randi," Logan says. "The first one is free to get you hooked."

Yeah, like I need any help with that.

Teagan pokes her head in the side room we're inhabiting.

"Finish up, guys, and get backstage. The auction is about to start."

We separate from the players, and Daphne shows me where to get a paddle to enable me to bid. Logan is taking pictures, and we choose seats at a table bordering the dance floor. The plan is for everyone to be on stage and the player up for bids will come down off the stage and join their winner for the rest of the auction. Once everyone has been claimed, then they will go do their thing. Teagan will act as auctioneer while Coach and Jake, the third owner of the team and its General Manager, will be the bid spotters. Mallory and Kendall join me and Daphne at our table with paddles.

"Who are you bidding on?" I ask Mallory. I assume Kennie is going to bid on Bedard.

Mallory sighs and rolls her eyes. "My brother. He made me promise he goes for at least as much as Stone."

Shaking my head, I chuckle. Carter is such a goof, but he's cute and charming in his own way. I'm sure there will be a bidding war.

Teagan starts the auction and Colby Alvarez is the first up for bid. He's a skilled player, but not a star. He gets a few bids, and his highest bidder is a lady in a server uniform at the dessert station. The other players all get bids. Stone ends up being bought by a group of ladies for four thousand dollars.

Bedard is next and Kennie immediately raises her paddle and yells out, "Ten thousand dollars!"

The room is silent except for Alvarez's "Damn, girl," said in his Texas drawl. At that, the room erupts in laughter and applause. Bedard comes off the stage and sweeps Kennie into his arms and gives her a thorough kiss that leaves her breathless and quite a few folks in the audience whistling.

It's Carter's turn, and he struts the stage, engaging the crowd and urging them to bid. It's going great until the bidding stalls at four thousand dollars. Apparently, tying with Stone isn't good enough, he has to earn more.

"Mallory," he shouts from the stage. She rolls her eyes and heaves a sigh as she raises her paddle. "Four thousand and one."

Teagan points at her, laughing. "We have four thousand and one dollars. From his sister. Any other bids?"

Stone calls out, "That's lame. My sister didn't have to bid on me."

Brick responds, "Because your sister was raising more money than you."

The group of couples she's sitting with sends up a cheer. Combined, they bid five thousand to win her.

"Going once...going twice..."

"Four thousand and two," comes from the back corner and Mallory sags in relief.

Trevor goes to join the male couple and I grin when I realize they were teammates of ours on the cheer team at Wickham. Neil and Byron started dating as students there and I'm happy to see they are still together. Trevor points to me and the guys wave excitedly. I wave back. I'll have to catch up with them. But first I need to win Declan.

I checked the app for my credit card, and I have an available balance of almost two thousand dollars. Dec is worth more than that, but I pray everyone else has spent their money. No way I'm using the card he gave me.

"Our last player up for bid is Declan Mackenzie, left wing. Let's start the bidding at one hundred dollars."

Dec's blue eyes dart around the room, following the flurry of bids. In seconds, the bid is fifteen hundred dollars, and I want to be sick. There's no way I can do this. He looks at me beseechingly and I bid the exact amount I have available to me. I shrug and mouth. "That's all I have."

"Two thousand dollars," comes from the table next to mine. An older woman in a leopard print gown and heavily teased black hair is waving her paddle hard enough to kick up a breeze.

Everyone's staring and my face burns as tears sting my eyes.

"Aren't you going to bid?" Daph asks.

I shake my head. "I'm tapped out."

"I saw him give you his credit card," she murmurs.

"I can't spend his money."

"I can!" She grabs my paddle. "Three thousand dollars!"

"I don't have that kind of money," I whisper hiss.

"Don't worry, he does," she assures me.

"Four," comes from the woman I now call Spot.

"Five!" Now it's Mallory waving my paddle.

"Ten!" Spot again.

Kendall gets a steely glint in her eyes. Oh, no.

"Fifteen." Kendall's bid causes gasps to go around the room.

Spot starts to raise her paddle, but a lady at her table grabs her arm as another yells in a thick North Jersey accent, "Give it up, Diane. You're making a fool of yourself."

Yeah, Diane, listen to your friends.

Teagan speeds through the closing spiel and slams her gavel. "Sold to paddle eighty."

The smile Declan gives me causes my heart to race and my face to flush. He stalks to me like the wolf he has inside him, and even though I am his prey, I am more than willing to be caught.

"Thank you," Dec says when reaches our table. He's speaking to everyone, but he is focused on me.

Declan grabs my hand. "The clock is ticking. Wanna do karaoke?"

"Yeah, sure." Honestly, I will do anything, *anything*, he wants. Karaoke is our thing. We always did it when I visited him at Cornell. Music is something else bonding us.

Hand in hand, we weave through the crowd.

Carter yells, "When you're done, you owe me a dance."

I wave with my free hand to acknowledge him.

The karaoke is in a lounge area as far away as possible from the band to enable the singers to be heard.

We look to see if our song is available and, when it is, add our name to the list. There is one singer in front of us and we listen to their version of "Toxic" by Britney Spears. They are having fun and that's what matters.

I've never sung in front of people I know. Why did I think this was a good idea? Oh, yeah, Declan is holding my hand. As long as he does that, I will try anything. We applaud the singer before us and climb the stage. With our connection severed, the nerves claw at me again.

"Hey," he says, looking at me with concern. "We don't have to do this if you don't want to. You never have to do anything you don't want to. I thought it would be fun."

He takes my hand again, and the butterflies flitter away.

"I'm okay," I say.

But when I face our audience and see Daphne, Mallory, and Kendall, along with their guys, smiling back at us, the butterflies return in force.

"Miranda, look at me. We've done this dozens of times. Doesn't matter who is out there, we are singing to each other. Okay?"

I nod, and Dec gives the thumbs up to start our track and the opening chords of "500 Miles" come out of the speaker. We almost always choose songs by Irish or Scottish artists and this fun song by The Proclaimers is a favorite of ours. We've worked out a duet version, and it usually gets the crowd clapping and singing along. This time is no different and by the time the song is over, a huge smile has spread across my face and I'm laughing with Dec. He gives me a big hug and spins me in a circle as our friends clap and cheer. When he puts me down, we turn and bow to the crowd—it's bigger than when we started singing—and leave the stage.

"You've sung together before," Kennie says, as she gives me a hug.

I get hugs from Mallory and Daphne while the guys do high fives and bro hugs with Dec.

Carter gives me a long hug. When he turns me loose, he holds me at arms' length, and I swear his eyes look misty.

"You never sang with me. All those parties and karaoke nights at cheer comps, you never sang a note. Why?"

Oh no. His feelings are hurt, and a pouting Trevor Carter is a Carter needing to be placated. I think it's from being the youngest child. Dec's youngest brother, Seamus, is the same way.

"I dance with you, Trev. I was going to go on a TV dance show with you. Dancing is our thing." Please, let Dec keep his mouth shut about all the times we've danced together. He must have seen my desperation because, other than raising his eyebrows, he doesn't react. Bless him.

"Can we dance together tonight? It's been years since we've danced together."

"Of course. I'd love to." It's amazing the different expressions a pair of raised eyebrows can make. Before, they were saying, "Okay, fine, I'll go along with it." Now, they are saying, "Oh, hell no."

My eyebrows aren't as chatty, but my eyes are telling him, "Suck it up, Buttercup. It's a dance, and he's my best friend."

His eye roll and sigh say it all—*fine, go ahead, but you're dancing with me too.*

I can't wait.

# 16

## DECLAN

Holding Miranda's hand, looking into her smiling face and happy gray eyes, with our friends cheering us on, is like a glimpse into the future I desperately dream of. I can picture us at the altar, exchanging vows to love and honor each other until death do we part, our family and friends watching. It's what I've wanted since I was a teenager and realized she is more to me than my sister's best friend. She is my world. I kept my promise not to pursue her until she finished college, and I didn't interfere with her going to New Zealand. I trusted the universe would bring us back together when it was the right time. That time is now. She's meant to be mine, and tonight is the night to tell her how I feel. The new year is going to be the start of our forever.

My wolf wants to howl watching Carter and Miranda dance to a fast song. It's like a mishmash of a jive and a swing dance. They dance well together. I'm sure doing something choreographed would be incredible if this is what they can improvise. I know she's a wonderful dancer. We've danced together countless times. Most of it was as kids when my mother was teaching us all how to ball-room dance. We can all do the basics. My sister Sophie and her twin,

Ian, stuck with it to make it a profession and follow in Ma's dance shoes.

I approach the stand and slip the bandleader some cash to play a request. I've been patient. It's my turn to dance with Miranda and I don't plan on ever letting her go.

Their song ends and I approach them.

"My turn," I say, extending my hand. The tingle when Miranda takes it races up my arm directly to my heart.

"Hi," she says when I take her into my arms as the first strands of the band's cover version of "Perfect" by Ed Sheeran come from the stage.

"Hello." I lower my head to place my lips at her ear. I can do the fancy spins and turns Carter did, but all I want to do is hold Miranda close to me and relish her body against mine. Humming along with the song as we sway, I echo the line about her looking beautiful tonight. She shivers, but the way her breath hitches tells me it's not from being cold.

"It's like this song is about us," I murmur.

"Wha...what?" She stutters, and I think she's holding her breath.

Okay, Declan, it's now or never.

"We were kids torn apart, but now we're together again."

Her hair brushes my cheek as she nods.

"And I love you."

Her breath comes out in a whoosh that tickles my neck. She turns her head, and we are face to face, inches apart.

"You do?" she whispers. Her beautiful gray eyes are wide in shock.

"I do." *I do.* I can't wait to say those words for real someday, to bind our lives together like our fates already are. "I have loved you for years. I've been waiting for you to come back to me."

Her grin splits open wide, and her hands on my shoulders tighten, as if she never wants to let me go. "I love you too. I always have."

We stare at each other. Holy shit. I lower my face and finally,

*finally*, kiss her. This is something I've been wanting to do for almost a decade. Her lips are soft against mine and she is trembling. Or maybe I am. I know it's an innocent peck to anyone else, no tongue, no roaming hands, but to me this is a fantasy come true. I could do this for the rest of the night—the rest of my life—but I don't want an audience.

Reluctantly, I pull back. My brain is so muddled, I blurt out the first thing that comes to mind. "Stay or go?"

"Go," she says.

"Upstairs or home?"

"Home."

"Need anything?"

"You."

Okay. Taking her hand, I lead us from the ballroom. It's minutes before midnight and I already know the coming year is going to be the best ever.

"What about your phone or a coat?"

"My gown has pockets." She blushes when she glances up at me as I push the button for the elevator. "And I was hoping you'd keep me warm."

The doors open and it's empty. We have it all to ourselves. I hit the button to take us to where we cross to the parking garage.

I step close to her and put my hand on the wall above her head and lean down.

"I can do that. It will be my pleasure."

Her blush deepens. "Mine too."

As my watch ticks to midnight, I start the countdown. "Five... four...three...two..." I lower my head and Miranda whispers, "One."

Our lips meet, and this kiss is even better than the first one. We have around fifteen floors to go, and I use the time to deepen the kiss. Miranda opens her lips and I slip my tongue in. I can taste the champagne she drank earlier, but that's not what is making me light-headed. Neither is the descent of the elevator. It's about being able to finally express my emotions to her and not keep the fact I love her a secret. I can't believe she loves me too. This is more than I dreamed of ever having.

As the elevator slows its descent, we break our kiss and grin at each other. Miranda reaches up to rub her thumb across my bottom lip. I take a nip, causing her to giggle.

"Happy New Year," she whispers.

"It will be," I promise.

The doors open and we make our way through the crowd in party hats, all cheering and hugging. Paired with the noise of the slot machines, it's a cacophony. Stopping, I slip out of my suit jacket and drape it over Miranda's shoulders before we go through the doors to the parking garage. She holds it in one place with one hand as I take her other again.

"You smell good." She rubs her cheek against the lapel and breathes deeply.

As a shifter, I know how important scent is, especially your mate's scent. It's imprinted on your brain. Knowing Miranda finds my scent pleasing does strange things to me. Wonderful things.

I unlock the passenger door to my Suburban and help her into it. I make sure her skirt is fully inside before closing the door.

"Can I flip up the console to make it a bench seat?" she asks when I get behind the wheel.

"Miranda, love, you need to stay on your side because if you're next to me, I'm pulling off on the side of the road and we're making out like a pair of teenagers."

"And...?"

I huff out a laugh. "And I'm almost seven feet tall and it's January. I want to be alone with you where we can be comfortable and warm. No worrying about frostbite or being interrupted."

"No one is coming home?"

I shake my head. "I think everyone has rooms."

I don't know what we talk about—if we even talk at all. What I remember of our drive home is holding her hand, giving it brief little kisses at stoplights, and stealing glances. Pulling up to the barn, I shut off the engine and we sit there in the darkness. I'm not sure what to do. Of course, I know what I'd *like* to do. I've been fantasizing about this for years. But will the fantasy live up to the reality? Is what I want the same as what Miranda wants?

"Are we going to go in?" Miranda asks.

Giving what I hope sounds like a suave chuckle and not the sign of nervousness it is, I say, "Yeah, I guess we should. Wait there. I'll come around and help you down."

After helping her down from the passenger seat, we stand in the light of the almost full moon. I brush my knuckles along her cheek.

"You are so beautiful," I whisper.

On a sigh, she murmurs, "Kiss me."

And I do. There, in the moonlight, I kiss her with all the love, devotion, and passion I've been feeling for her for years but haven't been able to express. Our lips cling, our tongues dance, and our bodies press against each other. When she shivers, I know it is partly in reaction to our kiss, but it's also below freezing outside, and she must be cold.

"Let's get you inside and warmed up." I take her hand and lead her to the entry door leading upstairs. The moonlight is enough to illuminate the stairs through the window at the landing, so I don't bother turning on any lights. Hand in hand, we enter our apartment, and I stop, unsure what to do next.

"Do you want something to drink? Are you hungry?" I ask.

"No, we ate at the party, remember?"She gives my hand a light squeeze. "Are you okay?"

I run my free hand through my hair. "Yeah, I'm fine." I should tell her the truth. Sighing, I admit, "Honestly, I don't know what I'm doing. I've never done this before."

Tilting her head, she eyes me curiously.

"What do you mean? You've never brought anyone here before?"

"Yeah, but I mean any of this." I gesture between the two of us. "Our kiss on the dance floor? That was my first one. You're the only woman I've wanted to kiss. I was waiting for you. I know you must have kissed other guys and done stuff. It's just...you're it for me."

At first, I think the way her eyes are glistening is a trick of the moonlight. But then a tear slips down her cheek and I know it's not. She reaches up and places a hand against my cheek and gives me a sweet smile with her trembling lips.

"It was my first too. I haven't been attracted to anyone else like that. Haven't wanted anyone other than you to touch me. I wasn't waiting—I didn't think you'd feel the way I do, but I wasn't looking because there was no point since no one else is you."

"So, we're the blind leading the clueless?" I ask.

She giggles. "We aren't clueless, we're...inexperienced. We'll figure it out. The rest of the human race has, no reason we can't."

"We can wait. I don't want to rush you," I say. I'll die, but I'll do it.

"Wait for what?"

"Until we're married."

Her breath catches. "Married?"

I kiss her gently and brush her hair behind her ear. "Miranda, I want to marry you, have babies with you, make a home with you. I want everything with you."

"That's all I've wanted, too," she says, with more tears streaming from her eyes. "I want to belong somewhere and be with someone who loves me and won't send me away. I want that someone to be you."

My heart breaks. I hate what her parents have done to her.

"Please, Declan, make me yours." She slips my jacket off her shoulders, and she glows in the soft moonlight.

I've never seen a greater temptation. "I...I wasn't planning on this. I don't have any condoms."

I could go looking for some, I live with a bunch of men—and Brick. Someone must have some in their nightstand or in the bathroom, but I don't want to invade their privacy like that.

"We're both clean, obviously. I've been on the pill for years to keep my cycle regular. We should be okay. And if we aren't, well, then we have a head start on a family?"

My heart skips a beat at the thought of Miranda carrying my child. Resting my hand on her bump the way Logan does with Daphne. Having the connection of creating a person with the woman I love. I'm trying to restrain myself from wishing her pill doesn't work. We have years to work on that. I can be patient.

"Are you sure? I don't want this to be something you regret."

"I will never regret loving you, Declan."

At her declaration, I scoop her into my arms and carry her into my bedroom, bridal-style. In a way, this feels like our wedding night. In my heart, I've already vowed to love, honor, cherish, and protect her until the day I die and for eternity beyond that. We are married in our hearts. A piece of paper and the blessing of a parish priest isn't going to change anything.

She's standing before me in her gorgeous gown. Ever since her prom I fantasized about unzipping it and watching it fall to the floor and now that dream is coming true. As she loosens my tie, I slowly lower the zipper on the back of her dress and watch as the bodice sags. I press a kiss where her shoulder meets her neck as the strap slides down. Her pulse is hammering against my lips, and I give a tiny nip eliciting a gasp from her. I soothe the spot with my tongue. My wolf is begging for me to give her a claiming mark the way it was done generations ago, but we don't do that anymore. The thought of marring Miranda's beautiful ivory skin permanently is something I can't do, no matter what my wolf wants.

Her nimble fingers are undoing the buttons of my shirt and pulling it from the waistband of my slacks as I run my hands along her shoulders to finish pushing the straps down. I was expecting a gentle "whoosh" of satin, instead there was a definite thud.

"Crap, your phone. I forgot. I'm sorry."

I bend to get it and get a gander at the black lace panties covering her most intimate area. I forget what I'm doing and stare at the scrap of lace and breathe deeply. I can smell her arousal, and it's driving me crazy.

Tearing my gaze away from her panties, I fish her phone out of the pocket of her dress, so it doesn't get stepped on and stretch to put it on my dresser. I do the same with my phone. Everyone I want to talk to is right here. Miranda rests her hands on my shoulders and steps out of her gown, kicking it to the side with a strappy silver high-heeled shoe. It's a piece of footwear, but I damn near swallow my tongue seeing it on her foot. I never thought I had a foot fetish, but seeing the strap buckled around her dainty ankle makes me want to go for a swim in the pond like Mr. Darcy did in the *Pride and Prejudice* movie we watched one rainy weekend at Cornell.

My eyes travel from the delicate rhinestone buckle, up her toned, trim legs, past the triangle of temptation, her flat abdomen, to firm breasts I consider a perfect mouthful encased in matching black lace and stop at where her hand is nervously fingering the four-leaf clover pendant I gave her.

"Are you okay?" I ask.

She nods emphatically. "Aye." The lilt sneaking into her one little word makes me smile. That's my Daisy girl. "But you're wearing too many clothes."

"Well, I guess we have to fix that, don't we?"

I reach to unbuckle her shoes and hold her hips to keep her steady as she steps out of them. Without the extra inches, I'm now level with her belly button and press a kiss there, too. The way her skin breaks out in goosebumps gives me a thrill of satisfaction knowing I am affecting her as much as she's affecting me. I untie my shoes and take them off, along with my socks. She's so delicate, standing in front of me in her bra and panties. She's not short, not like Kendall or my sister, but I'm tall enough that the top of her head doesn't pass my shoulder. For a moment, a flash of panic flows through me that I'm too big and I'm somehow going to hurt her or crush her.

Thankfully, sanity asserts itself and reminds me of the couples I know with significant size differences—my parents, Bedard and Kendall, dozens of basketball and football players. It will be okay.

I straighten and remove the emerald cufflinks from my wrists and add them to the pile on the dresser, along with my watch. Miranda slides her hands up my chest to my shoulders to push my shirt off. I help by shaking my arms and she grabs one sleeve. As she pulls it off my left arm, the moonlight hits my wrist.

"Hey, what's this?" Miranda grabs my arm and angles it toward the window. "You have a tattoo?"

"Um...yeah." I don't know if she'll be able to tell what it is. Maybe she will think it's a random blob.

Leaning in to study it, she turns her head one way and then the other.

"Is it a daisy?" she asks.

"Aye."

She shoots me a grin, but her eyes glisten as she rubs her thumb gently over the tattoo. "I love it when you talk Irish to me."

"Oh, yeah?"

"Yeah."

I murmur some phrases like, "I love you, I think you're beautiful, and I can't wait to make love to you," in Gaelic as I kiss a spot under her ear, making her whimper. I continue with kisses on her shoulder and drag her bra strap with my teeth. Bra. Yeah. We gotta get rid of that. I reach behind her for the clasp to set her lovely breasts free. I may not have experience, but I know the basic mechanics of how a bra works. There's supposed to be a clasp there.

"Wait. Hold on," Miranda says, stepping out of my arms.

My stomach sinks. I'm screwing this all up and pushing her too far, too fast.

"It's a front clasp." She reaches up and flicks open the clasp. The two sides part, and I swear I hear angels sing as her creamy mounds are exposed for my gaze. They are perfect, firm and high. Not big but proportionate to her figure.

"Wow." I shut my eyes with a groan. Way to be articulate, you idiot.

Her giggle has my eyes popping back open. She's rocking from foot to foot and about to cross her arms and hide this beautiful sight from my view. We can't have that.

"Hey, no hiding." I reach out and gently grasp her hands, pulling her against me. Her nipples are hard as she nestles against my chest. I love being skin to skin with her.

She's trembling.

"Miranda, my love, are you okay? We can slow down or stop. I don't want you to feel rushed or do anything you want to do. We go at your pace."

"If that's the case, Declan, then why are we standing here and why do you still have pants on?"

I chuckle and undo my belt with trembling hands. She puts her hands over mine.

"Dec, we're in this together. If *you* want to slow down or stop, we can. This has to be right for both of us."

Somehow, I fall more in love with this woman. How could I not?

"Miranda, I want you so much I can barely see straight. But I'm nervous. I'm afraid I am going to hurt you. What if I'm terrible at this? What if you don't enjoy it? What if you regret being with me? I want it to be perfect."

She brushes my hands off my belt buckle and finishes the job for me. Her deft fingers unbutton and unzip my pants and push them over my hips until they fall to the floor. I step out of them and kick them to the side.

"Wow," she breathes, echoing my earlier sentiment. She's looking at my cock in my boxer briefs and it's so hard I'm shocked it hasn't poked a hole through the cotton. "Can I see it?"

I'm grateful the lights are off because the blush no doubt rising on my cheeks is hidden.

"Okay," I say, pulling my briefs down. This can't be normal.

Aren't we supposed to be doing more kissing and touching and less talking? We should be on the bed now.

"But now I'm naked and you're not. That's not fair." I rest my hands on her hips and slip my fingers into the waistband of her panties. "May I?"

Her response is a sharp intake of breath and a rapid nod. I lower them down her legs, dropping to my knees as I go. At the sight of her neatly trimmed black curls, I realize I am probably not going to survive the evening. I am going to die a virgin. No way can I caress and kiss and make love to this beautiful woman and not have a heart attack. Maybe I'm already dead and I'm in Heaven. I could believe that.

"Declan," Miranda says. "I know we're supposed to be romantic and all sorts of good stuff, but I'm freezing. Can we get under the covers, please?"

"Of course." I stand and reach around her to pull back the comforter and sheets on my bed to let her slide in. She scoots over to the other side to make room for me too.

"Oh," she says with a sigh. "The flannel feels good against my skin and your bed is cozy. I can't believe I'm here with you." She rolls to her side and snuggles next to me. I extend my arm inviting her head to rest on my shoulder. I lower my head to kiss her and it's like a match set to the fuse of a firework. We ignite and explode in a flurry of feelings and movement. Our hands roam each other's bodies. Our mouths kiss, suck, and nibble everywhere we can reach. I can feel how wet Miranda is for me.

"Please Declan. I want you. Now." She opens her legs wider, allowing my hips to nestle against her.

"Are you sure? I don't want to hurt you."

"It will be fine. Please. Make me yours."

That is all the encouragement I need. I take my cock in hand and rub the head against her slickness. Placing it at her opening, I slowly push in. All the Saints in Heaven, I swear I'm going to die. She is wet and warm and tight. I'm going to embarrass myself here. I'm ready to blow. Just from having a couple of inches in her.

"Fuck...," I moan.

"Yeah, kind of the point," she says breathlessly. Even at a time like this, she's got jokes. No wonder I love her.

"Are you okay?" I ask.

"I will be. Please. Please Declan, I want you. All of you."

I push in further. And then pull back out most of the way. I thrust in again. And again. This is incredible. How do people ever do anything other than make love? I think this is my new favorite thing. I thrust a couple more times and a tingle starts at the base of my spine. Oh no, not yet. I don't want this to end yet. I try to hold back my release, but I can't. I give one last thrust and then I'm shuddering, releasing everything I have into Miranda's incredible body. Happy New Year to me.

# 17

## MIRANDA

I HOLD DECLAN'S BODY, STILL TREMBLING FROM THE AFTERSHOCKS OF HIS orgasm, against mine. His weight is comforting, not crushing. Wow. I can't believe what we did. I had sex—made love—with Declan Makenzie. He loves me, he wants to marry me and have children and make a home. I will finally have a home I won't have to leave. Tears slip from my eyes, and one must drip onto his face tucked against my neck because his head pops up.

"Oh, Miranda, I'm sorry. Please don't cry. I'm sorry." His beautiful blue eyes are sad and breaking my heart.

"What? What's wrong?" I ask.

"You're crying. Did I hurt you? I'm sorry I didn't last longer."

Oh, this dear man. I pull his face to mine and press a kiss to his lips. He sighs and kisses me back and slowly lifts his head. His eyes are a little less sad. That's a win.

"You didn't hurt me. I'm crying because I'm happy. I never thought I'd have this with you. This is everything I've ever wanted. I love you. This was perfect."

The skeptical look on his face makes me giggle.

"It was perfect," I insist.

"You didn't come."

"We were both virgins. The first time is awkward for everyone. Anyone who says differently is either lying or a character in a romance novel."

We both start laughing and Dec rolls to my side. Uh...

"Next time we do this," I say.

"There's going to be a next time?" Dec says hopefully, nuzzling my ear and kissing a spot behind my ear I didn't know connected to my girly parts. I tilt my head to give him more access.

"Yes. Oooh, that feels good. But not tonight. Yeah, feels good." I close my eyes and enjoy the sensations. I roll to face him and remember what I was talking about.

"Next time, we should use condoms or figure out better logistics."

"Miranda, love, we're in bed, naked. Why the hell are we talking logistics?"

"Because, my dear Declan, I'm lying in a wet spot and your *stuff* is leaking out of me and I'm sticky and icky."

He looks confused, but the light dawns. "Oh, *oh*. Um, yeah."

Jumping out of bed, gloriously naked, he rushes to the bathroom, and comes back with a wet washcloth and a towel.

"Okay, here's the plan." He turns on his bedside lamp and sits on the edge of the bed.

We had done everything by the light of the moon, and to have more light is jarring. All of those muscles and taut skin were touching me moments ago. I peek at his cock. Even soft, it's impressive. Not that I have anything to compare it to, but...yeah...wow. It twitches and I startle.

"If you keep staring at him, he'll wake up," Dec says.

When my gaze darts to his face, he winks.

"Here's a cloth in case you want to wipe off or whatever. I figured we could take a shower and then sleep in your bed?"

I nod.

"How about you go start the shower and I'll join you in there?" I ask. I know we just had sex, but to do this with him here is way too intimate.

He gives me a sweet smile. He gets it. "Okay. See you in there."

Being in locker rooms all the time must have made him comfortable being naked. Of course, if I looked that good without clothes, I'd strut my stuff too. He pushes the door partially closed to give me privacy and I quickly take care of what I need to. I'm not as comfortable walking around naked as Declan is. I need to wrap up in the towel to enter the bathroom.

The shower is running, and steam is filling the room.

"Be right there," I tell Declan. "I'm gonna go in there," I say, gesturing toward the toilet room.

Handing me the soap when I join him in the shower, he says, "If you wash my back. I'll wash yours and your front. And everywhere else."

Giggling, I take the soap and motion for him to turn around. I run the bar between my hands to get a lather going. I inhale the crisp, clean scent that reminds me of my favorite field after a fresh rain. And then run my hands over his shoulders and down the glorious muscles of his back. I can't believe all of this is mine. I'm free to touch it, caress it, kiss it, and have it next to me in bed, holding me from now on. I'm afraid my alarm is about to go off and prove all of this was a dream. But, for now, I'm going to enjoy this. I want to remember it for the future.

Once I'm done with Dec's back, he takes the soap and winks.

"Your turn, my beautiful Daisy."

My heart melts at the use of my childhood nickname. The shower is equipped with rainfall shower heads. The warm water is streaming over both of us. Before he can get started soaping me up, I grab his left arm and turn it over in order to clearly see what is there on the inside of his wrist, normally hidden by his watch band. It's a small white and yellow daisy bloom.

My throat tightens, and I cough to clear it. "When did you get this?" I ask over the sound of the water raining down on us.

"After you left for New Zealand. I wanted to have you with me."

"Wanna know one of the first things I did when I got to New Zealand?"

When he nods, I hold up my right wrist, showing him the small tattoo of the blue bloom of a forget-me-not flower. The blue is the same shade as his eyes.

"I got this done to remind me of you. Your eyes are the same shade of blue and it reminds me of the field we would play in as kids. Those were the best times of my life."

"Your life thus far," he says. "There will be even better days ahead."

He pulls me to him and kisses me deeply as the water streams over us.

"Miranda, love," he says. "I want to make you feel as good as I do. Will you let me?"

My eyes widen, unsure how this is going to work. I've pleasured myself in the tub plenty of times. But, well, I know what I'm doing.

"Oh...okay," I stammer. Of course I want an orgasm, what woman doesn't? But I don't want any broken bones or concussions for either of us. No orgasm is worth that.

His low chuckle is sexy. Okay, every last, *glorious* inch of him is sexy. But the vibration of his chuckle against me, well, it's almost as good as Mr. Buzzy living in my nightstand drawer.

"Trust me," he murmurs as he presses a kiss behind my ear. I shiver at the sensuality of it.

"Mmm..."

Recognizing my murmur for the agreement it was, he guides me back to sit on the wide shower bench. This shower is incredible. It is huge, with more than enough room for a giant like Declan to move around easily. The rainfall shower heads are mounted high enough for him to stand under them. There are jet nozzles built into the walls if you want to direct the stream to aching muscles, and there's a handheld sprayer Dec grabs and fiddles with to get a strong pulsating stream flowing from it.

He kneels in front of me with the water streaming over him and catching on to his long, dark eyelashes, making them spiky over his mischievous blue eyes. With a wiggle of thick, dark brows, he uses a hand to nudge my legs apart, opening wide and exposing my most intimate part. I know we made love earlier, but that was in the shadows. I feel too exposed with him *looking* at me. I keep things trimmed and tidy down there but maybe I'm too furry? He's a shifter, though. Maybe I'm too bare?

Maybe he sees the apprehension in my eyes because the sweetest, sexiest smile appears on his kissable lips and the blue of his eyes darken with what I'm pretty sure is desire.

"I'm admiring the view. You're beautiful. Everywhere."

I remember I need to keep breathing if I'm going to live long enough to enjoy whatever he has planned. My inhale is shaky—from anticipation, not trepidation—and I try to exhale slowly. That effort is a lost cause when he runs the handheld sprayer up the inside of one leg, stopping just short of the goal, and then back down, repeating on the other leg. I'm quivering at the sensations the strong pulse has on my sensitive inner thighs. I can't wait to feel what it does to my clit.

As if reading my mind, he starts the trek up my leg again and this time hits the target. I yelp at the jolt of pleasure shooting through me at the contact of the pulsating jet. I've been shortchanging myself all these years, limiting myself to the tub and toys. Of course, my rentals never had state of the art handheld shower heads either. When I finally buy a house of my own, that will be one of my first purchases.

Again, his low chuckle causes things to tighten and flutter inside of me.

"You like that, Daisy?"

I nod, gasping for breath. He turns the head to another setting and the pulsating stream is another rhythm. If I knew Morse code maybe I'd know it was spelling out something like, *I own your pussy*, because it does. The pressure and pulse on my clit are making me writhe and squirm and use the Lord's name in ways our parish priest back home would frown upon, but I don't care. I'm about to shatter when suddenly the stream of water disappears. I whimper because I was *so close* to coming.

"Can't let the shower head do all the work, can I?" Declan asks as he scoots forward on his knees after turning off the shower head and leaving it to dangle. Speaking of dangling, his cock is hard and long and bouncing against his belly as he moves. Wow. I'm glad I didn't get a good look at him before we made love because I would have been even more nervous. I assume we are going to have sex again but Declan surprises me by dropping his head and giving my clit a long lick. He pulls my hips forward, perching me on the edge of the wide seat and wiggles his shoulders under my thighs. He licks, nibbles, and sucks my clit and upper thighs, holding me in place so he can feast on me. Judging by the mmms, grunts, and groans, feasting is definitely what he's doing. I'm helpless to do much of anything other than lean back against the tiled wall. I should probably be thinking practically about if our roommates are here and can hear me, but I can't. The rasp of his tongue is magical. His hot breath on my center causes shivers to rush through me. His wet hair I'm grabbing to help keep him right where he is licking me, is slick and soft. I have always loved the slight curl he gets in the back. After tonight I never want to sleep without Declan at my side again. Any thoughts of road trips, hockey, or even my own name fly out the window when he releases his hold on one of my hips and pushes inside with one long, thick finger. His cock was bigger, of course, but it didn't curl to hit that spot.

"Oh yeah, right there." I realize I'm chanting those words aloud, not thinking them as he pumps first one and then two fingers inside me. Curling to hit my g-spot while he continues to lick and flick my clit with his magical tongue.

I will never be able to go get an ice cream cone with this man without spontaneously orgasming watching his tongue lick it and wishing I was the sweet treat. I'd giggle at the thought but suddenly I'm coming like never before. It's like riding a giant wave and you've reached the crest and now you are coming down the other side with the water crashing around and stealing your breath.

"Oh my god, Declan. Oh, oh," I cry, trembling as the waves of ecstasy wash over me. I think I'm crying but with the water raining down on me, I'm not certain what are tears and what is the shower. I have never felt like this before. Connected to someone but also like I'm floating away. It's incredible. I can't do anything but gasp, trying to catch my breath. With a last kiss to my upper thigh and a self-satisfied smirk, Declan gently lowers my legs until my feet touch the tiled shower floor and stands. His cock is at eye level, and I reach out to return the favor, but he steps back.

"I'm okay," he says, his voice gravelly and a bit breathless too. "It's going down. Watching you come apart was the sexiest thing I've ever seen, and I popped my cork when you did." He looks down, maybe embarrassed to admit to his lack of control, but it makes me love him more. That a man as big and strong as Declan is comfortable enough, trusts me enough, to be honest and vulnerable with me lets me know I am safe with him. I can trust him with not only my body and my heart but with my dreams too. I have a home. Declan Mackenzie is my home.

Eventually, we both are fully clean and I'm grateful Carter invested in a high-capacity hot water heater. Declan gently towels me dry after our shower, and then carries me into my room and carefully places me on the bed because my legs are still wobbly after my mind-blowing orgasm. Walking into our shared closet, he grabs me a pair of panties and the Cornell t-shirt I like to sleep in and helps me put them on. He pulls on a clean pair of boxer-briefs. When we are under my covers and I'm wrapped in his arms with my head resting on his chest, I silently thank everything in my past that has brought me to this point. I have never felt safer or happier. Happy New Year to me.

# 18

## DECLAN

This is how I want to wake up every day for the rest of my life. Miranda's back is nestled against my chest and I'm spooning her. My morning wood is snug against her delectable rear, her head is pillowed on my arm, and my hand is resting on her boob. Yeah, I think this is one of the most perfect ways to start the day. The one thing that would make it better is if we were finally married and on our own farm. I wonder if she still likes to ride horses? As a girl, it was all anyone could do to keep her out of the barn. Any chance she had to ride or be around animals, she took.

She braided her hair before bed, leaving the back of her neck available for me to nuzzle and place gentle kisses on. Her sleepy sigh and wiggle don't help with my morning wood, but it makes my heart happy.

"If this is a dream," she says, her Irish lilt strong in her sleepy voice, "don't wake me up."

I move my hand off her boob and around her belly, giving a gentle squeeze.

"If it's a dream, we are both having it."

She wiggles in my embrace until we are face to face. She is beautiful with her gray eyes clear and shining, the smattering of freckles across her nose she usually hides with makeup on display, and the sweet smile on her face belongs to me.

"Best dream ever," she says, pulling my face down to kiss her.

Our kiss grows more fervent, and our hands start roaming. We won't go all the way, but no reason we can't have a hearty make-out session to start our morning off right. Maybe I can bring her some of the pleasure I enjoyed last night. My wolf gives a sharp bark in the back of my mind, but I ignore him. He's been bugging me about Miranda for years and now we finally have her, I don't know what his problem is. However, when he gives a deep growl—his warning growl—I tear myself away from Miranda's sweet kiss just in time to hear the bedroom door open.

"Hey, Miranda, surprise! JESUS MARY and JOSEPH!"

"GET OUT," I shout at the intruder as Miranda ducks under the covers.

Well, that took care of my boner. I can hear the commotion in the living room and sigh.

Miranda peeks out from under the blanket, her cheeks blazing and her eyes wide. "Was that...was that your sister?"

"Aye. I don't know what the hell she's doing here."

I can hear her and Carter talking but can't concentrate enough to make out what they are saying beyond Carter saying she's crazy—he's not wrong—and she can't go barging in like that.

Sophie is supposed to be in England or Ireland or wherever. Not in New Jersey and not in my apartment. How did she find her way here? Even with the address and GPS, it's not easy to find the barn, let alone get inside. She knew this was Miranda's room.

I slide out of bed and walk into the closet to put on a pair of gray sweatpants and a white t-shirt.

"Let me go see what is up with her," I say.

Miranda nods. "I'll be out in a moment."

I'm about to open the door when I change my mind and return to the bed. Bending, I press a quick kiss to her lips, pulling back before

I'm tempted to linger and let the circus on the other side of the door continue.

"I love you, Miranda. Always have, always will."

Her eyes are glistening with unshed tears as she gives me a wobbly smile and swallows. She can't say the words because she's trying not to cry. That's okay. I know she feels the same.

I exit the bedroom and hear voices from the common area and head that way. Aw, crap. Everyone is here. Well, all my roommates, my sister, Kendall, Coach, and Mallory. Logan and Daphne walk in. So, yeah, everyone. All eyes turn to me, but it's Sophie who marches up to me and pokes me in the chest.

"What were you doing in bed with Miranda?"

Each word she snarls is punctuated with a poke. She has a bony finger I never noticed before. Of course, my little spitfire of a sister usually has no reason to be poking me.

Heat floods my cheeks. Everyone here can probably figure out what we had done and were hoping to do again as soon as possible.

"Alexander Declan Mackenzie, you answer me." She stomps her foot.

"Your name is Alexander?" Stone asks.

"Aye, after our father," I say, looking over Sophie's head.

"Declan," she says warningly.

I look back down at her and sigh. "Sophie, what are you doing here? Aren't you supposed to be in London or Dublin or somewhere not here? How did you get here? How did you get in?"

"Don't worry about that. What is Miranda doing here? She's supposed to be in New Zealand. What's she doing in bed with you?"

"Sophie," Carter says, "when a man and woman love each other—"

"Shut up, Trevor," Sophie and Mallory shout in unison. Must be something sisters learn to do in sister school or whatever.

"What's going on?" Daphne whispers to Mallory. Why she bothers whispering in a room full of shifters who can easily hear her is beyond me. She tilts her head toward Sophie. "And who is she?"

"Sophie is my younger sister," I say. "I'm not sure why she's here."

"Don't worry about why I'm here. Why were you in bed with my best friend?"

"OMG, you're together?" Daphne bounces excitedly while holding her baby bump with both hands. "Yay!"

Sophie gives her a look like she's daft and turns back to me. I love my sister, but she's pissing me off.

"I was in bed with my girlfriend, not that it's any of your business. Why would you barge into someone's bedroom when the door was closed? Ma would make you weed her garden for that."

Our mother doesn't believe in spanking her children. If we were to be punished, then it would be mucking stalls or weeding her gardens.

"I wanted to surprise my best friend."

"You certainly did," Miranda says with a laugh, walking out of our apartment. "Sophie, I'm so happy to see you!"

She rushes over and gives my sister a tight hug, winking at me over Sophie's shoulder. Miranda is four or five inches taller than Sophie, her black hair a sharp contrast to Sophie's blond. Even their personalities are opposite. Where Miranda is calm and serene, Sophie is energetic and in your face. They balance each other.

"I thought you were in New Zealand?" Sophie says while they are still hugging.

"I was. My contract ended, and I got a job with the Devil Birds. Started last week. What are you doing here? Visiting Dec?"

She pulls out of the hug with Sophie, and I see what's she's wearing. She's put on black yoga pants and has a pink hoodie with a black unicorn head on it and the words "Feeling Horny" emblazoned across it. I damn near swallow my tongue.

Sophie notices her shirt too and turns to me with a smile. "You told her? Great!"

"Told me what?" Miranda asks. Her forehead wrinkles in confusion as she looks at me.

"About the unicorn," Sophie says.

The look of confusion on Miranda's face deepens as she looks down at her shirt and then looks back up, and I see the others in the room trading glances.

"What about the unicorn? I've always loved unicorns since I was a little girl. Especially the black ones. That's why I got this shirt. It's one of my favorites."

"She's always had unicorn trinkets," Kendall says. "She didn't have a lot of personal stuff in our room in college but she had her unicorn collection."

Sophie looks at me, and I shake my head. I haven't told anyone. I guess that's about to change.

"You have to tell her," Sophie insists.

"Tell me what?" Miranda asks, caution creeping into her voice. I hate to hear that. Today is supposed to be a wonderful day. The first day of the rest of our lives together. There's no room for caution or worry. Damn it. Why does this have to happen now?

I glance down and see Miranda is wearing thick socks. Good enough. I grab her hand and head for the door leading downstairs. "Come on."

"Okay." She keeps up with my long strides. "Do I need shoes or my coat?"

"No, we won't be outside long."

As we descend the stairs, hand in hand, me leading the way, she whispers, "Dec, I'm scared."

Me too. But I say, "Don't be. Everything's fine."

I pray with all my heart I'm not lying to her.

# 19
## MIRANDA

I FOLLOW DEC DOWN THE STAIRS, SOPHIE AND THE OTHERS FOLLOWING US. What in the world is going on? What is Sophie doing here? It doesn't seem like Dec was expecting her. A feeling of dread settles in my stomach. Today started off perfectly. The future I dreamed of was in front of me. I knew it was too good to be true. I don't know what Dec is going to say or show me when we get outside, but I'm betting it isn't good. It never is.

Opening the door, he leads me outside. Then he turns to me and gently squeezes my hands before letting go. The kiss he presses to my lips is brief, too brief. What if this is the last kiss he ever gives me? My stomach is churning.

He strides away, his long legs taking him about fifty feet from the patio. Suddenly those legs transform from gray cotton to sleek black with a fringe of black hair above glistening black hooves. Where Declan stood a moment ago now stands a strong black unicorn stallion with a flowing mane and tail. Proud and regal, his twisted silver horn reflects brightly in the sun. It's beautiful but also looks like a deadly weapon. He rears up on his hind legs and...yeah.

You know the phrase "hung like a horse?" Anyone who ever used that phrase never saw a unicorn. Wowza. This is no My Little Pony. This is a warhorse, something from mythology or a nightmare. Or my dreams. I can understand why the unicorn is the national animal of Scotland. They are right to brag. He tosses his head in a way seeming to call me to the edge of the brick patio where he's trotted over. I approach cautiously, knowing he won't hurt me, but still unsure. The chill of the bricks seeps through my socks, but I don't care. Looking in his eyes, I know this is still Declan and I have nothing to fear. He is stunning. And huge. I haven't been around horses in years, but he seems larger than any horse I've ever seen. He's leaner than the Clydesdales I've seen but still gives an aura of strength and size. Standing next to him, I can't see over his back. He towers over me. I'm guessing he is over sixteen feet tall when he rears on his hind legs. He is magnificent.

With a toss of his head, he snuffles and bumps my arm with his muzzle.

I pet his velvety nose and sigh.

"No rainbow mane or glittery hooves, but I guess you're okay."

Letting out a huff, his giant head nuzzles my shoulder, and his tongue rasps my neck. With a laughing shriek, I skitter away. That will teach me to tease him. The gentle breeze stirs his glorious, wavy mane. He looks like he should be in a shampoo commercial. Even in this form, his beautiful blue eyes, fringed by long, dark lashes, shine with a fierce intelligence.

Then it hits me. He's real. I'm not dreaming. We aren't in a field of daisies and forget-me-nots, we are in a yard ringed by oak and pine trees. We aren't children, we're adults. But we've done this before.

"You're real," I whisper. "You've always been real. It wasn't a dream."

The trembling starts, and I can't stop it.

Suddenly, Declan is back to himself and is pulling me into his embrace.

"Hey, Miranda, darling. Are you okay?"

He's looking at me with such concern, brushing tendrils of hair back from my face. Tears flood my eyes. Shaking my head, I pull out of his arms and rush across the patio.

"Miranda, wait," Dec calls after me.

I'm on the verge of sobbing and the gasping breaths I'm taking have me afraid I'm going to pass out. I sit in one of the chairs Bedard likes to sit in.

Dec kneels in front of me and takes my hand. "Daisy, you're scaring me. What's wrong?"

"I thought you were a wolf shifter? You're a unicorn? How? They don't exist."

"Obviously they do."

"No. I'm dreaming again. This is all a dream. I'm going to wake up and none of this has happened."

"What? No. This is real." He lays my hand against his cheek and turns his head to press a kiss against my palm. "I'm real."

I shake my head. "Bears and wolves are real animals. Unicorns are not."

Dec has the nerve to wink at me. "With enough practice, I promise I can be a real animal."

I want to laugh. I want to accept this and move on, pretending none of this has happened. But I can't.

Rising to his feet, Declan gives my hand a gentle tug. "Let's go back inside. It's cold and I don't want you to catch a chill."

Nodding, I get up and follow him. Our friends are in the rink area, waiting for us.

Kendall comes over with a mug of tea from the kitchen off the gym. "Sit down, you've gone pale. You're almost see-through."

I sit on a bench at the side of the rink, and she hands me the mug. I take a sip. It's passable. Not as good as the tea Dec makes me, but I appreciate the effort.

I look around at all the faces full of concern, and it's both comforting and overwhelming. My friends are nosy. I know this. But

I don't need them to witness me fall apart and try to put myself back together.

Brick, bless her, must realize how I'm feeling because she suggests they all head upstairs, but no one moves. I guess we're going to have an audience. Whatever. If everyone hears it now, then I won't have to explain anything later.

"So, you're not a wolf shifter? You're a unicorn?" I look at Sophie. "You're a unicorn too?"

Sophie shakes her head.

"I'm a wolf. And a witch."

Dec rests his hand on my knees, and I turn to face him.

"I'm a wolf shifter," he says, "but in the shifter community there is a special..."

"Class." Trevor completes Declan's sentence.

Nodding, Dec continues. "Class is a good word for it. It's rare, but certain shifters can shift into unicorns besides their normal animal. I'm one of those shifters."

This is crazy. I accept shifters in general, but to have two is inconceivable. Does someone else have a whole zoo in them?

"Do you have special powers?" I ask.

"I can't shoot lasers out my eyes or breathe fire. But in a way, it comes with special powers. In the future, I will have a seat on the Unicorn Council. It's kind of like the United Nations of the shifter community."

What the hell? This is ridiculous. I must still be dreaming. I pinch my arm. Hard. Nothing changes.

"Randi, it's really happening," Kendall says.

I nod. My hands are shaking too much to hold the mug of tea. I put it on the bench next to me. A little sloshes out, and I'm shocked I didn't drop it.

Trevor scratches the stubble on his jaw, staring at Declan before turning concerned hazel eyes to me. "Each of the major shifter classifications and species—wolves, lions, tigers, gorillas, bears, raptors, horses, foxes, and others have a unicorn—one of their own who shifts to a unicorn besides their main animal."

"How do you get to be a unicorn?" I ask. "Is it random?"

"It's hereditary," Dec says. "Through my mother's family. My maternal grandfather is the current unicorn for the wolves. Once I turn thirty, I will be eligible to take my seat when my grandfather abdicates his. It's a ceremonial thing now that shifters are public and human laws govern, but historically they would handle disputes between groups of shifters. Like if wolves and bears were fighting over a territory." He takes a cautious step toward me. "You don't care about any of this, do you?"

I shake my head. "You're real."

"Aye, why would you think I wasn't? You saw me when we were kids. That's how it was discovered I was a unicorn. I hadn't shifted before then, but your powers called me."

"My...my powers?" I don't have powers. What the hell is he talking about now?

"Your powers as a witch," Sophie says, like it makes perfect sense.

I jump to my feet and walk away.

"What powers? I'm not a witch."

I pace. Being active helps things make sense. It's been that way since I was a girl.

"Yes, you are. You're a fauna witch, like your mother," Sophie says.

That stops me in my tracks, and I look at Sophie in shock.

"*My mother is a witch*?" I reach up to run my fingers through my hair, but I forget I have it in a braid, and I end up with them jammed in. "What's a fauna witch?"

"You have an affinity with animals," Dec says. "That's why you were amazing with horses and always had the dogs and cats following you. Even the ones who hated everyone else loved you. It's like Ma with her flowers but with animals. And shifters."

"This is crazy. You all are teasing me. It's January first, not April first. This isn't funny. What is this, some kind of hazing?"

"Miranda, no." Dec stands and walks towards me with his arms open to embrace me, but I back away and hold up my hands to stop him. Hurt flashes across his face, but he stops.

I wrap my arms around my stomach. "When we were kids. That day in the field. You were a unicorn, and we were both there and I rode you and we played. It really happened? I fell asleep leaning against your flank and when I woke up, I was alone. It wasn't a dream?"

"Aye, it happened. Why do you think it didn't?"

I laugh bitterly. "Because for the past fourteen years, I've been told I'm a liar. That I make up tall tales for attention, and your parents were tired of it. It was time for me to go away. Every school I went to asked my parents to remove me because I didn't fit in with the other kids because of all the lies I told. I never told a single lie. I'd be locked in my room when I was with my parents until I admitted I lied." I laugh mirthlessly. "*Those* were the only lies I ever told—that I was lying."

I take a few gulping breaths. I'm ashamed to admit this, but I need to.

"I'd get bread and tea and a bucket to relieve myself in until I admitted it. If I protested, then the lights would be turned off. When I'd admit it, they'd hug me and tell me I was a good girl but should stop lying. I'm not a liar, I swear." Tears stream down my face.

Daphne is crying with her head against Logan's chest, cuddling the bump Birdie is making in her middle. I take a quick glance around and see a mixture of shock and sympathy on everyone's faces. Except for Declan. His face is full of rage and he's snarling. Is his wolf about to appear?

Sophie says something in Gaelic I don't catch. It's been too long since I've been around it and I was never fluent anyway. Whatever it was, it seems to calm Declan down. He closes his eyes and takes some deep breaths, causing his t-shirt to tighten around his chest. I get distracted by the play of muscles outlined under the cotton.

"It happened," he says, quietly. "It was the first time I shifted. Puberty is when it starts for most shifters. You were there in the field, upset because you had a spat with Sophie or something. I hated seeing you upset. Apparently, your powers were burgeoning too, and your emotions called out to my unicorn, and I shifted."

"I'm not a witch, I don't have any powers. I can't make you shift. Like I can point and say 'shift.'" I fling my hand out and there's a loud honk. Everyone gasps and I turn my head. Where Brick was standing is now a pissed off Canada goose.

"Holy shit," Coach says.

Stone giggles and jumps back when the goose tries to peck his knee.

Suddenly, I'm lightheaded and slumping against the wall.

"Oh my god. I broke Brick!" I yell before I break into hysterical sobs and fall to my knees.

That breaks everyone out of their shock, and suddenly it's pandemonium. Brick shifts back to her human form and stands there with her arms crossed. She's fully clothed and I realize Dec has clothes on too. How the hell can you go from being an animal to back to being a fully clothed human?

"It's shifter magic," Bedard says, apparently reading my mind. "Something with wearing natural fibers and magic. Scientists are studying it."

I tune him out and through my sobs I say, "Brick...Bridget, I'm sorry, I didn't mean to do that. I don't know how I did that. I hope I didn't hurt you. I don't know how I made you a goose when you're a moose. I'm sorry."

I'm flailing as I apologize and Trevor comes behind me, pulls me on his lap, grabs my hands and puts them in the pocket of my hoodie.

"Let's put those away. They're dangerous," he says.

I know Trevor's trying to make a joke to lighten the mood, but the truth is, my hands are dangerous. I randomly pointed at someone and turned them into a goose. That's not normal.

Brick heaves a sigh. "It's okay Randi, you didn't break me. You compelled a shift. I *am* a goose shifter. Our parents have a mixed marriage. Mom is a Canada goose shifter and dad is a moose. Very Maine. The kids can take after either parent. I let people assume I'm a moose because who is going to take a goose goalie seriously? Especially a female one."

"That's how it is with me and my brother," Logan says. "I'm an eagle like Dad and he's a cougar like Mom."

"I'm way more afraid of geese than moose," Daphne says.

This is all fascinating, but it's not addressing the fact I have magical powers I know nothing about and can't control. That's a big problem. Oh my god. I can't catch my breath. I know I'm hyperventilating, but I can't stop it.

"Randi, breathe. Calm down." Trevor is running his hand up and down my back, trying to soothe me. I'm trying, but it's difficult. It takes all my effort, but I calm down for a moment.

"Daphne, leave," I say between my sobs. "What if I hurt you or Birdie? I'm dangerous."

I watch both her and Logan's faces go pale. They hadn't thought of that. Judging by the way Trevor's hand stalls while rubbing my back and the gasps from around the room, no one else did either. I don't know if it's possible. I know absofuckinglutely nothing, but I can't take the risk.

I turn in Trevor's lap and bury my head against his chest and start crying again. I never fully stopped, but now it's less sobbing and more whimpers and tears. What am I going to do?

"Who are you calling?" Sophie asks.

My head pops up. Is someone calling the cops on me? Can I go to jail for this? They don't burn witches at the stake anymore, do they? Maybe ones who can't control their powers?

I try to scramble out of Trevor's hold and escape, but he tightens his grasp.

"He's calling the cops, I'm going to be burned at the stake. Let me go," I cry.

"What? No." Declan drops to his knees next to me and tries to take me into his arms. Trevor won't let go of me and I'm clinging to him like a koala. Dec stops trying.

"Miranda, love, I'm calling my mother. She will know what to do. She loves you. You know you can trust her." He shows me his phone screen with her contact info up. I think for a moment and then nod. He hits the button to make a video call.

"Declan. Happy New Year." Nora Mackenzie sounds happy as she answers. Her tone changes. "What's wrong? Are you hurt?"

"Hey, Ma. I'm okay. Sophie's here, she's okay too. I need your help. Miranda is here, and she just found out she's a witch. She made one of my teammates shift accidentally. She's upset."

"What do you mean, *she just found out*? She's twenty-four years old. How could she not know? Put her on."

Dec turns the phone toward me. I think he expects me to take it, but my hands are not leaving my pockets.

"Miranda darlin', what's wrong?" Nora's face, an older version of Sophie's, fills the screen. I can see care for me I've never seen in my own mother's eyes, and my already shattered heart breaks into more pieces.

"The unicorn was real. It wasn't a dream. I wasn't lying. I'm a witch and I don't know what to do. I'm scared." I whisper the last part because it's the hardest to admit. I'm terrified. I *know* I didn't have these powers before right now. I can feel them, and they weren't there before.

"What?" she asks. Then realization dawns on her face. "Sit tight, my lamb. Try to get some rest. I'm on my way. Alex and I are in Chicago. We will fly to you. Let me talk to Declan again. It will be okay. You will be okay. I love you."

Dec turns the phone back to himself and steps away. Sophie joins him and talks to their mother too. I don't pay attention to the conversation. Nora said she loves me. She meant it. I could see it. My own mother has never told me that. Maybe one of those broken pieces has fused back together. But as one piece is repaired, a dozen other cracks spread like a spider web.

When I woke up this morning, I thought I finally had a home, a community, people who loved me, people I could be my true self with. Now I know I had none of those things. My closest friends kept secrets, huge secrets from me. I have powers that can hurt people I love. I can't believe I was dreaming of a future, thinking about building a life on the shakiest of foundations. I was considering following Declan wherever he wanted to go and put his dreams ahead of mine as long as we were together after one night of great sex and some claims of love. I'm never going to learn. Suddenly exhausted, I close my eyes and rest my cheek against Trevor's chest. He's the one man I can trust. He's never dropped me. I'm safe with him. Why can't he be the one I'm desperately in love with? His steady heartbeat is comforting as I drift off to sleep.

# 20

## DECLAN

MA DISCONNECTS THE CALL, BUT BEFORE SHE DID, I HEARD MY FATHER IN THE background calling the pilot of their private jet to arrange the flight here. They will get here in a few hours. I'll pick them up from the local airport. I hope she can help Miranda. She's asleep in Carter's arms. Part of me is glad she's calmed down, but a larger part of me is disappointed she's not in my arms.

Carter rises effortlessly, holding Miranda as if he's done it countless times before. Maybe he has. I shouldn't be jealous, now is not the time for jealousy about their friendship to rear its head. But damn it, I can't help it. I should be the one holding her. I should be the one she turns to for comfort.

He walks to the stairs. "Can you get the door?" he asks Stone.

Brick goes first, presumably to get the upstairs door. We all trail behind, a quiet procession of people trying to deal with everything happening. He carries her into our apartment and lays her on her bed, pulling up the covers. The bed we spent the night together in. I check the time on my phone. I can't believe how much has changed in less than two hours. It's like my life has gone from perfection to shit in the blink of an eye. Or the intrusion of my sister. That reminds me—I need answers.

Miranda is still sleeping, but I'm not concerned. She was like this as a girl. She'd be upset by something, cry her heart out, and then fall asleep. It's like her mind and body needed a break and a chance to reset from the turmoil. There were quite a few times when we were kids she'd be upset by something with her parents or a horse she loved being sold, and she'd go to our gazebo to cry it out and then fall asleep among the wildflowers. I'd lay there next to her and watch the clouds float by, content to be near her. I didn't realize then I was falling in love. We were children. Adult love wasn't a thought in our heads yet. But it was there in my heart.

"Here, eat something," Stone says as he slides a turkey sandwich in front of me. "Everyone else, help yourselves."

Feeding people is Stone's thing. He's a bearded, burly guy like most of my teammates, but he has a Betty Crocker heart.

"Thanks." I pick up my sandwich. He used his special cranberry mayonnaise made from cranberries his family grows. It's my favorite.

"Are you going to tell me why you're here, Soph?"

"You don't know?" Coach asks.

"Him and Miranda left before midnight. They missed it," Mallory says.

"Missed what?" I ask.

Coach chuckles. "Sparky, show him the video."

Mallory pulls her phone out of her back pocket, pokes and swipes, and hands it to me. "Hit play."

I do and watch as the last bits of confetti drift down over the crowd of revelers. Teagan wishes everyone a happy new year when Coach takes the microphone.

"Happy New Year everyone. Before you go back to celebrating, we have one more thing to do. Where's Carter?" He appears to be looking through the crowd. "There you are. Come on up here."

Carter makes his way through the crowd and joins Coach on the stage. He's smiling and waving to the crowd, but his confusion is obvious.

"You're our first line center and my future brother-in-law." There are some hoots and hollers from the crowd. "You showed us you can dance earlier tonight." Now there are cheers. "So, I dare you to show the nation you can dance. You have been chosen to compete on the upcoming season of Celebrity Dance Dare-Shifter Edition."

Carter stands there in shock, his eyes wide and scanning the crowd. A camera crew has joined them on stage.

"Meet your partner, Sophie Mackenzie!"

Sophie walks across the stage, smiling and waving, and Carter still looks in shock.

"Trevor, it's wonderful to meet you. I hope you have your dancing shoes laced up because together we are going to win the Platinum Paw. Are you with me?"

"You're my partner? How are we going to train with me playing?" Carter asks.

Sophie nods, smiling like she's in a toothpaste commercial. Not her normal smile at all.

"We'll go over the details later," Coach interjects before smiling at the crowd again. "The Devil Birds are such a big, happy family that even your dance partner is part of the family. Sophie is your line mate, Declan Mackenzie's, sister. Mac, come on up."

Teagan murmurs something the mic thankfully doesn't pick up. Coach nods and continues speaking.

"You will train together and compete on national television to bring home the Platinum Paw trophy. We gotta start filling our trophy case at The Nest. Show 'em how it's done."

The crowd cheers and the video ends. I hand Mallory back her phone.

Rising, I wrap my little sister in a hug and lift her until her feet are off the floor.

"Soph, how wonderful! You're performing as a pro? I'm so proud of you."

She hugs me back and kisses me on the cheek before I set her back on her feet.

"Thanks, Declan. I'm excited to get out of the troupe and see how the US show works. It's a much larger production than the UK version. Almost as big as the main show Ma and Ian are on."

I explain to my friends, "Our mother is a former championship ballroom dancer. She's the lead judge for the original Celebrity Dance Dare in the UK. Sophie's twin brother is one of the pro dancers on it and has won twice. He's a wolf shifter too, but his partners are usually human, not paranormal folk unless they are big name A-list celebrities."

"You volunteered for this?" I ask Carter.

Carter rolls his eyes. "No, I was voluntold in front of the crowd."

Sophie huffs out a breath. "Well, you weren't my first choice, but I know Dec won't do it."

Oh boy, Carter has already gotten on Soph's bad side. Heaven help him.

"As part of the PHL marketing campaign," Coach says, "each team has a player on a reality TV show. Oliver King from the Sasquatch is going on Bigfoot Finds a Bride. Someone from the Aliens is going on Secret Singer."

"I still don't know how it's going to work to learn dance routines in addition to hockey practice and games." Carter looks like he sniffed a dozen dirty jockstraps.

His sister rolls her eyes. "Trev, you have a dance studio downstairs. You help Kennie with her cheer team. With Randi here, you'd probably be dancing or stunting with her all the time. You can find the time to work with Sophie and kick ass in the competition."

"She's traveling with us too," Coach says. "The way our schedule falls, you won't miss any games for the live shows. It's perfect."

"Yay." Carter circles his finger in the air with mock enthusiasm.

I shoot him a look. I don't care if he's my friend, he's not going to disrespect my sister. Before I'm able to say anything, Sophie is toe-to-toe with him with her finger poking his chest. She's so short she's poking at her nose level.

"Listen boyo, this is my opportunity to make a name for myself, and you're not going to screw it up for me. Do you hear me?"

"Hey Kennie, there's another tiny but scary one around now," Coach says to his sister with a wink.

We all laugh when Kennie scratches her nose with her middle finger.

Soph stops poking Carter's chest and grabs the front of his shirt and gives a yank. "Show me the dance studio."

They disappear downstairs. Poor Carter. My sister is as stubborn as a mule and when she wants something, she isn't letting anyone or anything keep her from her goal. He's going to be dancing his ass off regardless of what he wants.

Going into my bedroom, I strip the sheets and start the laundry. I stand there with my hands braced against the washing machine, my head hanging. What the fuck am I going to do? If Miranda didn't know she's a witch and thinks my unicorn is a dream, what else has been kept from her? What else have her parents brainwashed her into believing? Because that's what they did from the sound of it. Locking that sweet little girl away with the bare minimum until she admitted to what they wanted to hear. How could you do that to a child? To someone you loved?

I think back to when I first shifted to my unicorn. I was shocked by the form I took. I knew I was a wolf shifter and part of growing up and my body maturing was I was going to start shifting. I wasn't prepared to see hooves where I expected to see paws. I knew about the Unicorn Council from my shifter history lessons, and I knew Grandpa Robertson was the Unicorn for the wolves, but I wasn't expecting it to pass to me. It doesn't automatically pass to the eldest male. It could have gone to any of my siblings. Or it could have gone to another branch of the family tree.

"Hey," Bedard says. "It's going to be okay."

My laugh is without humor. "The woman I love discovered she's a witch, I knew, and didn't tell her. I know her. She's going to think I lied to her. She's going to run."

"Why would she run? She has a job, her friends are here. You're here."

"She is used to being nomadic."

"But is that what she wants? It's what she's known, but it doesn't mean that's what she'd choose."

That brings me up short. All the times she moved as a kid she had no say in it. Her parents were calling the shots. When she was old enough to decide for herself, she settled at one high school and then spent four years at the same university. She went to New Zealand because her plans here changed with Kendall eloping and Carter choosing a pro hockey career over practicing law and being a sports agent. She was going to stay. And she came back. Last night—okay, early this morning—she was crying happy tears because of our future having a home and a family. Of being settled. She doesn't want to go. All the more reason I need to make sure she knows she's safe here, that she stays here. With me. Or without me, if necessary.

"You should shift and go for a run," Bedard says. "It's New Year's Day, it's a wolf tradition, right?"

It is. If I was with my family, we'd shift and go for a run around our estate in Scotland. We always spend New Year's and celebrate Hogmanay there. We run on New Year's Day to burn off the last of the alcohol we drank. As shifters, especially shifters of Scottish and Irish heritage, we have a high tolerance for alcohol, but we do our best to get drunk anyway.

"I don't want to leave Miranda. I don't want her to be alone when she wakes up."

"Kendall and I will be here. I don't know Randi as well as you do, but I think she needs some space to process things and decompress. I know how it is when the woman you love is hurting and you are powerless to fix it. You were there for me then, and I want to be here for you now. Go run, clear your head. I shouldn't say it's all going to be okay because I don't know, but I know it's not going to make it worse."

He's right, I know. But everything in me wants to be near her, to comfort her. What I want doesn't matter though. It's what is best for my dear Miranda that is important now.

Nodding, I sigh and push away from the washer. "Yeah, you're right. You promise you'll be here if she wakes up before I'm back? I don't want her to be alone right now. I'm worried about her."

Bedard claps me on the shoulder. "I'll be here. Kendall won't be going anywhere. She's dealing with guilt over how she got wrapped up with her ex and neglected their friendship. She won't do that again." He grins. "And you know where Kendall is, I am."

"Aye. Thanks." Now it's my turn to sigh. "Let me go see what the terrible twosome is up to. I can't believe they will be teamed up to dance together. I'm not sure which one I feel sorrier for. They are going to drive each other crazy. Sophie is an adorable little tyrant and Carter won't take anything seriously. It's going to be like oil and water."

"Or matches and kerosene," Bedard says.

I peek in at Miranda before I go downstairs. She's still sleeping peacefully, curled on her side with her hands tucked under her cheek. My heart swells with love for her. I hate that I accidentally hurt her. If I had any clue she didn't know about her powers, I would have spoken to her about it. Helped her learn about them. My mother would have taught her if her own parents wouldn't. It's her choice if she uses them or not, but at least she would be the one choosing. Too much of her life has been out of her control. I never want her to feel powerless again.

I guess it's ironic because I feel like I'm ceding my power to her, but she's always had it. I love her and as my fated mate, my goal in life is to make her happy and keep her safe. If it means I have to let her go at the expense of my desires, it's what I must do. But I pray I don't have to.

I go downstairs to find Carter and Sophie. Hopefully they are getting along because trying to dance with someone you don't like is challenging. I've watched enough episodes and heard the gossip from Ma and Ian that it was obvious which pairings couldn't stand each other. It was fun watching them grit their teeth and dance, but when it's my teammate and my sister, it's different. Carter needs to focus on the game and Sophie needs this chance to prove she's good enough to be a full-time pro and not get moved back to the troupe.

"You have a dance background." Sophie's voice pierces through walls, clear as day. "You know you must wear the proper gear. You wouldn't play hockey without your pads. You're going to wear Cuban heels on the show."

Grinning, I walk toward the dance studio at the back of the gym space. Carter's cousins participated in cheerleading and dance when they were younger. When the barn was converted from unused stables and added on to, they put in stuff for the other kids in the area to give everyone a safe place to hang out.

"Hey guys," I say as I enter the dance space. I recognize Sophie's fists on hips, head tilted back, glaring at a man pose all too well. I'm rarely the recipient, but our brothers are. We are about three seconds from a foot stomp or a shin kick, depending how pissed off she is. Carter is smiling down at her. This will not end well for him.

"I'm going to shift and go for a run in the woods. Want to come with me? Bedard and Kendall are staying with Miranda. She's still asleep. I don't know if Coach and Stone are joining us. It's New Year's Day, may as well keep with tradition even though the rest of the day has gone to shit. I need to do something before I go crazy."

Soph spins on her heel and walks over to where I stand at the edge of the blue tumble mat and wraps her arm around my middle. Carter can thank me for saving his shin later.

"Declan, I'm sorry I messed everything up for you. I didn't mean to. I'm an idiot. Please forgive me?" She looks up at me with her tear-filled blue eyes. Of course, I forgive her. She's my baby sister. I'll forgive her almost anything. She's impulsive but not malicious.

I return a hug and kiss her forehead. "Soph, there's nothing to forgive. Well, never burst into someone's bedroom like that again. But we didn't know Miranda was in the dark about everything. If I'd known, I would have done things differently."

My cheeks heat at the smirk spreading across Sophie's face.

"Okay, I'd still do things as they happened, but we would have talked about it. I never brought up my unicorn or her witchiness, because why would we talk about it? You know we don't talk about it in normal conversation any more than we talk about clipping our toenails. It's simply part of us."

"Ew, do not compare my powers to foot hygiene, thank you very much. And, as a dancer, we talk about clipping toenails more than you'd expect."

Shaking my head, I go back to the original subject. "Shift. Run. Want to?"

Sophie looks at Carter questioningly.

And he shrugs. "The woods here are great to run in. A river runs at the back of the property. My family owns most of the land around here, it's not a problem. The farm across the street is vacant. The kids are looking to sell, I think. It's not listed yet."

What kind of farm is it? I know Carter's extended family has a Christmas tree farm and some produce farms growing blueberries, corn, and other stuff. Is it big enough for horses? A family? I'll have to ask him about it, maybe I can make an offer to the family before it goes on the market. My horse farm was always a future thing but now that I know Miranda loves me too, it's a now thing. The plan was to go back to Ireland, but New Jersey is fine too. If this is where Miranda wants to put down roots, I will find us a farm. I was hoping to save more money before buying something, but I can get a mortgage. My wolf is ready to find us a den.

Soph shrugs and I refocus.

"Okay, let's go," she says. "My wolf hasn't been out to play in a while. She'll be happy to stretch her legs. And I need to see what your wolf looks like and how you move, since at least one dance will require us to incorporate your 'wild side.' If you don't screw up and get us kicked off before then."

Carter's spine straightens and he plants his hands on his hips. His nostrils flare and he sucks in his top lip. This is the first time I've seen my happy-go-lucky landlord lose his temper.

"You don't have to worry about me being the reason we get kicked off. Make sure you choreograph good enough dances and I'll dance them. You do your job, I'll do mine, sweetheart."

Oh no. This is going to be ugly. You don't challenge Sophie and expect to escape unscathed. And she hates being called sweetheart like that. He's my friend. I should save him.

"Great," I say with faux cheer. "Carter, go see if Coach and Stone want to join us. We'll meet you out back."

He can be a fool, but he's not stupid. He nods and leaves the studio to go upstairs.

"I wouldn't have hurt him, Declan. I need him to be healthy enough to dance," Sophie says.

"And I need him to be healthy enough to play hockey. Please don't hurt him. He is silly sometimes, but he's a good man. He's not stupid, and he cares more than he shows."

"Whatever. I need to put up with him for two months. I can endure anything for that long, even your idiot teammate."

"Where are you staying? We're a full house here."

"I'm staying at Devil's Den. It's enough I have to dance with the man. No way would I want to live with him too. I don't know how you can stand living with people you work with."

I shrug. "I like them, and the rent is insanely reasonable. I can save more of my salary for a farm. It's good for me to live with people. It's too easy for me to be alone."

"If you lived alone, I couldn't have busted in on you this morning."

"If I lived alone, I wouldn't be with Miranda."

Her sigh betrays her exasperation. "Miranda, Miranda, Miranda.

She's all you talk about. Trevor too. Are you sure there isn't something going on with those two? She seems more into him than you."

"She loves me," I say, barely restraining a growl. "They are friends. That's it. They were cheerleaders together in college."

"He was a cheerleader? Like shaking pompoms?" There is a touch of scorn in her voice that raises my hackles.

"Have you seen what they do? It's incredible. The strength and balance required by both of them is amazing. And the trust. Miranda put her safety and her life in his hands. The way she'd be tossed in the air and the flips she did and then get caught securely. It's an incredible amount of trust and connection to have with someone. But nothing romantic."

"Whatever," she says, reminding me of the moody teenager she was not too long ago.

"Come on. Let's get outside."

She picks up her phone and walks into the tumble gym. "Be right there," she calls over her shoulder.

I exit the door in the weight room to the backyard of the barn. Carter joins us with Coach and Stone.

"Run back to the river?" Coach asks.

"It's a few miles round trip," I tell Soph when she walks up.

"Sounds good," she says.

We shift into our animals—me, Carter, and Sophie as our wolves, Coach is a tawny cougar, and Stone is a gigantic bull moose with a massive rack of antlers—and start running toward the tree line. Carter gives a happy yip and Sophie howls. Howls reach our ears from the surrounding farms. Carter's family is celebrating too.

Stone slows down as we enter the woods and I realize with his antlers he needs to go more slowly to make sure they aren't knocking into the pine and oak trees. He gestures with his massive moose muzzle to go ahead at my own speed. I race ahead and catch up easily. We're individual but together, our strengths filling in for others' weaknesses like when we're on the ice. What Coach said in the video about us being a family is true. And I want Miranda to be a part of it. But will she? Alone and asleep and scared...will she ever be able to join us?

When we reach a clearing in the woods outfitted with a fire pit and chairs, Coach slows and shifts back, and we all follow suit. We take seats on either side of the cooler and Coach opens it up to see what's inside.

"Beer?" he asks, holding up a bottle of the IPA he favors.

"Yeah, thanks." I reach out to take it. I tip my head back to take a long sip. It's not going to make me even tipsy, but it's nice to have something to calm the racing thoughts in my mind. I stretch out my legs and kick them up the edge of the unlit fire ring. I hear rustling behind me and turn around to see Stone make his way into the clearing. He shifts and takes a chair on the other side of Coach, accepting the offered beer.

"So, this is quite the mess you find yourself in," Stone says as he lifts the bottle to his lips.

"Aye," I say with a sigh. "I'm hoping she wakes up and recognizes it was all a misunderstanding. I wasn't keeping secrets from her. I would never keep something like that from her."

We sit in silence for a few minutes. I can hear Sophie and Carter running back toward us. Carter stops when he enters the clearing and Sophie leaps on him, ready to tussle. She sees us sitting there and suddenly gets off him, sitting on her haunches primly and wrapping her tail over her feet. If she had a crown, she would have lifted a paw to make sure it was on straight.

"Good run?" I ask. She nods and looks at Carter. He shifts and walks to the cooler.

With a huff, she shifts as well and takes the chair across the fire pit from me.

"Beer, soda, or water, Princess?" Carter asks her.

Princess? Does he have no sense of self-preservation?

"Water is fine. Peasant."

Coach chokes on his beer and I sigh.

He hands her the water bottle and takes the seat next to her. He crosses his leg, resting his ankle on his knee and jiggling his foot. Sophie side-eyes his foot. When he starts whistling tunelessly, I mentally start counting, curious if I'll reach ten before she explodes. Carter somehow knows every button to push with my sister. This will be fun. I know she's my sister and I should be concerned, maybe, but Sophie can handle herself and it will be fun to watch Carter's tail be tweaked.

Stone is the brave one to speak first.

"So, you and Miranda?" he asks, tipping the lip of his beer bottle toward me.

"Yeah."

"Good. You two are right for each other," he says.

Sophie huffs.

"What?" I ask, knowing she's going to say something to piss me off. It's been that kind of day.

"Nothing," she says. I look at the rest of the guys. We all have sisters. We know the answer is never *nothing*.

I take another sip of my beer. I know her. She won't be able to keep her mouth shut. I can wait her out.

She rises and starts pacing between our chairs. "I know you think she's the one for you and you'll have your happily ever after. I want that for you, Declan. I really do. But it's not with Miranda. She likes to move around too much. She's not going to want to settle down."

She reaches up, undoes her ponytail, finger combs her long blonde hair and puts it back up. This is what she always does when she's agitated.

"Look at all the schools she went to. The second she finished university, she was gone. Then she shows up here. Who knows how long this will last before she's off to someplace new and leaves you behind like she's left everyone else behind?"

"What are you talking about? Who has she left behind?" Carter asks.

"Me!" Sophie cries, spinning to face him. "We talked about going to boarding school together and picked out our dream school. Then she gets the chance to go and leaves without me."

"She didn't choose to go away to school," I say.

"Yes, she did. She could have stayed with us, but she was tired of the village school and wanted to go to school in England where she could ride her precious horses. Mother wouldn't let me go and even though we had promised we'd go together or not at all, she went anyway."

I rise from my chair now to pace.

"Sophie, she was a ten-year-old little girl. What makes you think she had any say in the matter?"

"Her parents told me so. They knew I was heartbroken and tried to comfort me. They told me they tried to convince Miranda to stay after Ma put her foot down about me going away, but Miranda was insistent. She wanted to go there and ride for their equestrian team and make it to the Olympics. They gave me tea and biscuits while I cried. They took time away from packing to care for me. Then Miranda didn't even stay at that school to compete. She wasn't going to get to ride the horse she had her heart set on and raised a ruckus. They had to kick her out. When she went to the school in Portugal and refused to take part in class, they had to find another school for her."

"Soph, she was put in a *German* language immersion school in *Portugal,* and she didn't know *either language.* How the hell was she going to learn?"

I can't believe it when she stamps her foot like she's still a ten-year-old. I'd take another swig of my beer, but it's empty. Coach realizes and hands me a fresh one over his shoulder as I pace behind him.

"Thanks," I say as I hand him my empty bottle.

"Well, she knew English for all the schools in America and couldn't stay in any of them either." She stops in front of me and lays her hand on my arm. In a gentle voice, she says, "Declan, you know I love Miranda like a sister, but you can't rely on her. She's going to break your heart. I don't want to see you hurt."

I know she means well, but her ire is misguided. Miranda was a child. She had no say in where she went to school.

"She went to the same high school for her final two years and university for four. How do you explain that?" Carter asks.

Sophie turns to face him. "Her mother finally put her foot down and refused to let her flit around. She had to make the best of it where she was or they were going to pull her out of school, have her live with them, make her do an equivalency exam, and get a job."

"How do you know this?" I ask. This doesn't sound right to me.

"Her mother told me. We keep in touch. She's heartbroken over how Miranda treats them. Never returns their calls or emails. Didn't tell them she was moving to New Zealand. Didn't invite them to her college graduation. She cut them off."

My blood is simmering, but before I can erupt, Carter jumps up.

"They are complaining she didn't invite them to her graduation when they didn't tell her they were moving to Argentina? Can't be bothered to tell their child they are moving to another continent? She goes to California for Christmas to discover they've been gone for months. And she told them about graduation. I was sitting next to her on the couch when she emailed them the information. They never responded."

She twirls her ponytail around her finger. She's always done that when she's agitated.

"There are two sides to every story," she says. "We'll get to the bottom of it when her parents get here."

My wolf lets out a low growl, and I don't bother to try to hold it in.

"What do you mean 'when they get here?'" I ask, my voice low. I have a sinking feeling in the pit of my stomach.

She shrugs. *Shrugs.* "I texted them to let them know what was going on. They will be here in a few hours."

Coach tilts his head in confusion. "You texted Miranda's parents she discovered she's a witch and they are coming from Argentina in a matter of hours?"

"No, they live in New Jersey. I visited with them this week before I came here. Near some racetrack. Mammoth?"

"Monmouth," Carter says. "When did they move there?"

"I don't know. A bit over a year ago."

"Does Miranda know?" I ask.

"That they are in New Jersey? Yes, I assume that's why she's here. She regrets treating them callously and wants to make amends."

"So, as soon as she graduates and leaves the country, they suddenly move within an hour of where she spent the past six years? For twelve years they couldn't work it out to be in the same place she was so they could live together, but suddenly they can be here now? And *she* has to make amends? You don't think that's fucked up, Sophie?" Carter asks. It was exactly what I was thinking but couldn't say without many more expletives and maybe punching something.

"Are they coming here?" Coach asks pointing toward the house and barn.

"No. I have a suite at the Devil's Den. I said I'd meet them there. Can someone give me a ride back there?"

I don't want to leave Miranda except to meet my parents' plane and drive them back here. Carter looks pissed. I don't know if the two of them in the confines of Carter's little sports car is a good idea.

"I'll drive you," Stone says.

"Thanks." She turns to me. "I assume Ma and Dad will stay there too?"

"I already reached out to Teagan, and she has a suite ready for them," Coach says.

"Thank you," I say sincerely. I was focused on taking care of Miranda and didn't consider the logistics of where my parents would stay.

"Ready to go?" Stone asks.

Sophie nods.

We shift and run through the woods back to the barn. I'm eager to see if Miranda is awake, but I'm dreading the arrival of her parents. They seem to have Sophie fooled, but I'm not as gullible as she is. I know Miranda is nothing like Sophie says. I'm shocked Sophie thinks what she does. It doesn't make sense at all. Something isn't right here, and I'm going to figure it out.

# 21

## MIRANDA

I SLOWLY AWAKEN. I KNOW I'M IN MY BED, ALONE, LIKE I'VE ALWAYS BEEN, but I shouldn't be. Declan should be next to me, holding me, loving me. I know last night wasn't a dream and today was a nightmare, but maybe it will get better. Stretching, I get out of bed and walk to the window. I slept two hours, but I can easily sleep another six and it still won't be enough.

There's movement in the woods and I realize it is my friends. I know the moose is Stone. I assume the cougar is Liam because Kendall hates the cold, and she wouldn't be out running in January. The wolves must be Declan, Sophie, and Trevor. I've never seen any of them in their wolf forms, but I know them. The dark gray wolf must be Trevor, and the one with more silvery fur must be Sophie. Of course, my friend would be sparkly. The beautiful black wolf, bigger than the others, has to be Declan. His muscles bunch and flex as he runs, his tail flowing behind him like a flag. I wonder if his eyes are blue like they are when he is his unicorn. A unicorn. I can't believe for all these years I was called a liar when every word I said was the truth. No one stood up for me. Or told me I was a witch. My mother is a witch and never told me. Why? Does my father know? Does he care? Horses are all he cares about. He only noticed me was if I was on the back of one, and then it was still all about the horse.

How could I have spent all these years with no clue to my powers? I was not turning people into their animals. No making things levitate, no telling the future. If I have powers, they are the most boring ones ever, or they were dormant until today. Does losing your virginity strengthen powers? Is it something I can Google? I can't imagine asking Nora. Sophie is a witch, I could ask her, but Declan is her brother and that's weird. Talking to anyone about my sex life is weird. Gah.

Everything was easy this morning. Now I'm confused. I still love Declan, but he kept stuff from me. Important stuff. Life-changing stuff. Why? Are there other things he's kept from me? More than my witch powers. Important information about him. What does it mean to be on the Unicorn Council? Does he have to live somewhere special? Is this something he passes down to our children? Are they going to have their futures dictated from birth? I don't want that for my children. Children. I can't believe this morning we were talking about a future, and now the past has called that into question. Right?

They've reached the back door. They'll be back up here soon. I should go out and deal with things. I look longingly at my bed. I could feign sleep for a few more hours to buy myself time, but I should face things. Or I could leave. Leaving is always an option. I'm good at starting over. But I don't want to. I want to stay. I want to put down roots. I want to belong. Looking down at my hoodie, I cringe. I love this shirt and it makes me smile. Even though my parents insisted I was lying about seeing a unicorn, I knew it existed in my dreams at least. Shirts like this and my little collection of trinkets were my way of making my dreams real and my parents could kiss off. But knowing what I do now, I don't know if I can ever wear it again. Changing into jeans and a gray sweater matching my mood, I sit on the edge of my bed to put on my sneakers when there is a light tap on my door and a murmured, "Miranda?"

"Come in," I say.

Sophie opens the door and pokes her head in. "Hey, I didn't know if you were still asleep or not."

"I've been awake for a few minutes. Come in."

She leaves the door open, and I can hear Dec in the living room. The sound of his deep voice is soothing. It wraps around me like the tartan blanket he loaned me for my bed, and we slept under last night. I run my hand over it, wondering if we'll sleep beneath it together again tonight.

"Earth to Miranda." Sophie waves a hand in front of my face.

"Huh?"

She rolls her eyes and lets out a huff. "Daydreaming like always. I said your parents will be here soon. Stone is driving me back to the hotel. Pack a bag. We need to get there before them."

"What?" I cry.

In a flash, Dec is in the doorway. His forehead is furrowed, and I think I see concern in his beautiful blue eyes. "Miranda, what's wrong?"

"Why are my parents coming here? Who called them?"

Sophie tilts her head and looks at me like I'm crazy. After today, I'm pretty sure I am. "I did. You're having some sort of crisis. It makes more sense for *your* mother to be here than *mine*."

"You're in touch with my parents?" I haven't heard from them other than a text telling me they moved to New Jersey after I left for New Zealand. I texted them and sent emails while I was over there but didn't hear back. I chalked it up to them being busy. Once I'm settled here, my plan was to let them know I was here and suggest meeting up. This week has been crazy with the travel and jet lag, and I hadn't had a chance to do anything yet. I want to show them the life I've made for myself. How I can take care of myself and not be dependent on them. Make them proud of me.

"Of course. We talk on the phone, I visit with them. I was with them before I came here. We exchange birthday cards. I called Doreen before I went for a run."

Birthday cards. Phone calls. Visits. They have more of a relation-ship with Sophie than they've ever had with me. Why can't they do that with me? I know Sophie is more vivacious and fun than I am. Even so, I'm their daughter.

"And you knew they were in New Jersey? Is that why you came back?" Dec asks me from the doorway.

Before I can answer, Sophie puts her hands on my shoulders, and the connection I've always felt with her zings. The concern I'd expect from my best friend is shining in her eyes.

"I'm sorry I called your parents," she says. "I thought it's what you'd want. I'm trying to help. They've always been kind to me. Surely there's a reason you didn't know about being a witch. I want to figure this out as much as you, Miranda. Let's do that, okay? Then you can come back here"—she rolls her eyes—"and play house with Dec. Blech." I giggle at the face she makes. She grins back. "C'mon, let's get your bag packed." She gives my shoulders a friendly squeeze before stepping back.

"Why does she need a bag? What's going on? Miranda?" Declan walks farther into my bedroom. He's running a hand through his hair, and I try to ignore how sexy the flexing of his biceps is.

Before I can answer, Sophie does.

"Her parents and, for some strange reason, our parents, are coming to town because she's upset. It makes sense for her to be where they are. It's not like they want to trek out here. She works across the way. It makes sense for her to stay with me. I'm sure she'd be more comfortable. Right, Miranda? I assume your bag is in the closet?" She walks into the closet and calls out, "You never even unpacked, let's go."

I hear a long zip, and Sophie emerges from the closet I share with Dec, pulling my suitcase behind her.

"Ready?" she asks.

"Wait a minute, what is going on? Miranda, you don't have to go." Dec takes my hand and laces our fingers together. "Daisy, don't leave me." The desperation in his voice breaks my heart.

"Declan," Sophie says with a huff of exasperation mixed with sympathy, "don't be dramatic. It makes sense to have everyone in the same place. It's a night or two, not forever."

Dec's phone dings, and he checks it. "They are about to land." He looks up at me.

"Then I suggest you go get them," Sophie says. "Meet us at the hotel. Ready to go, Miranda?"

Dec's thumb brushes across my knuckles, and my tummy flips. "Come with me and then we'll all go to the hotel. Let's talk about this."

Sophies lets out a huge sigh, rolling her eyes so hard I'm surprised she isn't dizzy.

"Ugh. Could you be more dramatic?" she asks. "You two can be apart for an hour and survive. Declan, you go meet *our* parents who dropped everything to come here from Chicago in under three hours. Miranda will go meet *her* parents, who also dropped everything to come here. We will get this straightened out, and then we can all move on."

This is all happening too fast. I need time to think. My mind can't move as fast as Sophie's whirling around the room.

She grabs my wrist and drags me toward the door. "Miranda, come on. I know you don't want to be rude and leave your parents waiting."

"Okay, Soph," I say. I know she's trying to help me, but I'm annoyed at myself for falling back into the passive habits I had as a child. Sophie was always the more forceful one of us and it was easier to go along with her than fight it. Same with my mother. Same with a lot of people. Hell, they aren't childhood habits, they are habits I've had my whole life. I need to break them. But not today. I need to get through today and then I can work on all my other faults. I want to stay with Declan but until I know what the hell is going on with me being a witch and being told I was a liar all my life when I know I'm not, I can't deal with him and with my emotions. I'm not sure I can trust my feelings. I'm not sure I can trust him. But I want to.

I stand on tiptoes to press a quick kiss to his lips. I want to say, "I love you," but it's new, and it's awkward to say it in front of Sophie when she's in this kind of mood. "I'll see you at the hotel, Declan. Thank you."

Sophie grabs my arm and pulls me behind her out of my bedroom, calling, "Can one of you get Miranda's bag?"

Carter grabs it and follows us. I'm surprised he hasn't said more. Stone leads the way downstairs, with Sophie following him. Everyone else must be in the other apartment. It's weird to be leaving like this. It is reminiscent of all the times I've switched schools. It was like this, someone coming in, saying it was time to go. Packed in a hurry and out the door. No time for goodbyes. Not that I had friends to say goodbye to. But this isn't goodbye. I'll be back. I guess it makes sense to spend the night with Sophie to get maximum time with my parents. I want to spend time with my parents and reestablish our relationship, but I'm sure they will leave in the morn-ing. They're busy. I want both Declan and my parents to be in my future. I'll have to learn to balance it. This will be the first test. They are within a couple of hours. We can drive up and visit them when we have home stretches.

"Hey, wait a second, Randi," Carter says when we reach the land-ing. "You don't have to go. You can stay here. I'm sure Mallory and Liam can put your parents in one of the guest rooms. Same for Mac's mom and dad. Even his she-devil of a sister."

I give him a quick hug. He can be a twit sometimes, but he has a generous and loving heart.

"Thanks, Trev. This is for the best. I need to work out some stuff with my parents and for myself. Anyway, I wouldn't wish my parents on your sister."

"Randi, you haven't met our parents yet. I'm sure yours aren't any worse than ours."

"Thank you, Trev, but I sense a big family blow-up coming, and I don't want to force my family drama on anyone else." Besides, my friends here already have the wrong idea about my parents. Every time I shared stories about my childhood, they reacted with shocked eyes and open mouths. If I'm going to try to change things with my parents, I don't need to be around those negative vibes. And if I can't change things, I don't need them to see me shattered.

Declan comes bursting out the door, ready to rush down the stairs. He stops short when he sees me and Carter on the landing.

"Miranda, you're still here," he says with relief clear in his voice.

"Go ahead," I tell Carter, "I'll be down in a moment."

Declan comes down to join me on the landing. "Miranda, let me come with you. We'll face your parents and whatever happens together. Please don't push me away."

I grab his hands and hold them to my heart. I hope he can feel how hard it is beating. For him.

"Declan, I have to do this myself. I need to speak with my mother and figure out what is going on. Everything I thought I knew about myself is wrong. You kept things from me." He starts to protest but I press a finger to his lips to silence him. "I'm not saying you did it on purpose. But you knew things about me I didn't know about myself. Who knows what else there is?"

He kisses my fingertip and pulls his head back. "Okay, you need to speak with your parents. But you don't have to stay there. You go see them, maybe have dinner, and then come home."

I shrug. "Maybe that's how it will work out. But I don't think it will work out that easily. You know my mother, she's…difficult. It will be easier to be there and deal with her. The sooner things are resolved, the sooner we can get on with our life. Please, let me handle this."

Turning and jogging down the stairs, I wipe away a tear. I take a deep breath to steady myself before pushing through the door. I can do this. I've done hard things before. It's talking to my parents. I'm not thirteen years old and friendless in a new school being told about the facts of life by the cleaning lady who found me sobbing in the girls' restroom convinced I was going to die when I got my first period.

Sophie and Stone are already in Stone's truck. Taking the passenger seat, I close the door.

"Let's go," I say.

# 22

## DECLAN

Watching Stone's truck pull away with Miranda and Sophie in it is wrong. Miranda should be at my side. In my arms.

Carter claps me on the shoulder. "Come on. Let's collect your parents and then see what's up with Randi's folks. What's the deal with them?"

I unlock the doors to my Suburban and we get in. As we bump down the dirt driveway, I think about how to respond to Carter's question. "Her mother runs the show. She's beautiful and very charismatic. Charming. Flirtatious. Her father is quiet and does whatever Doreen says. Paul is great with horses. I think he prefers them to people. They are both vets, but the impression I get is Doreen charms the owners and trainers, and Paul does the hands-on work with the horses."

I turn onto the paved road taking us through the woods to the main road to the airport.

"I haven't seen her parents in about nine years. When Miranda was starting her last two years of high school, we all met up in New York City. They made me promise I wouldn't try to date Miranda until after she graduated from college. I guess it was

obvious I was interested in her." I direct a smirk in Carter's direction. "It's probably for the best they made that rule. If I had my
way, we would have gotten married the second she turned eighteen, if she loved me too, and everyone would have been very
young grandparents."

Carter laughs. "Yeah, I can see the wisdom in that. It's been less
than a week you've been together here and you're already sleeping
together. No surprise what would have happened with teenage
hormones raging."

I glance over at Carter. "When you guys were at university, were
there any signs she was a witch? I've always known she had powers,
but today is the first time I'm actually feeling them from her. I don't
know if it's because we have...a deeper connection now or not?"

"No, I didn't have any idea she was a witch. I didn't get those
vibes from her." Carter turns and rests his back against the door. "I
don't hang out with a lot of witches, but I was with Randi all the
time for years. Physical contact too. No jolts, no sparks. Nothing.
With other witches I've known—" He must catch the side eye I'm
giving him because he changes course with a sheepish grin. "Okay,
*been with*. Generally, you kind of feel that...I don't know. A low grade
energy hum. Do you know what I mean?"

I think about what he said and nod.

"Yeah, I do. I grew up with witches. I'm used to the energy and
don't even consciously notice it. But I know I haven't felt it with
Miranda at all until today."

"Dude," Carter says. "If you say something like your magic peen
gave her extra strength with witchy powers, I'm gonna have to
punch you."

Chuckling, I shake my head. "No, trust me...I...yeah, no super-
powers coming from me."

I sigh. I don't know what to say. I kinda wanna talk to someone.
But this is awkward as hell.

"It was the first time for both of us and I don't think it went as
well for her as it did for me. And for me, it went too quickly."

Heat rises in my cheeks and I risk a glance over to see if he's laughing at me. To my surprise, he's not.

He's nodding his head. "Wow. Okay. I wasn't expecting that. A virgin at twenty-six? You weren't kidding about being a unicorn." He laughs. "With you both being virgins, I'm not surprised it wasn't fireworks and marching bands. I think everyone's first time is kinda awkward and maybe a little disappointing for the girls. But, given the happiness Miranda was exuding before all the shit hit the fan, I think it went well enough. And with more practice, it definitely gets better for both of you." He clears his throat. "If you ever need condoms or...whatever...there's stuff under my bathroom sink. You know until you stock up or whatever."

Now my face is blazing, and another glance shows a pink tinge to his cheeks too.

"Thanks, dude."

We have about fifteen more minutes until we reach the airport, and a thought occurs to me. Hitting the button on my steering wheel, I call Teagan to see if there's a room available for Miranda's parents.

"I'm interested in hearing what Teagan thinks once she meets Miranda's folks," Carter says. "She's excellent at reading people."

I nod as I pull into a short-term parking spot near the terminal. This is the same airport we use for our team flights and I'm familiar with the layout.

"Yeah," I say. "I'm curious, too, about my impression of them now I'm an adult."

Before I can get out of my truck, I see my parents appear from the terminal with their bags in tow. I give a quick beep to get their attention and restart my engine to pull around.

"I love that your parents pull their own bags even though they are worth close to a billion dollars," Carter says.

"They are very down-to-earth." I shrug as I pull up to the curb where they are waiting.

Carter jumps out and takes my mother's bag to put in the back. I get out and hug Ma first because my father is putting his bag in the back and shaking Carter's hand. I hug Dad as Ma hugs Carter, saying she enjoys watching him play.

My parents sit in the back seat even though Carter offers the passenger seat to Dad. I pull away from the terminal and set course for Devil's Den.

---

Teagan looks up as we approach the front desk at Devil's Den and smiles, but it's not her usual friendly, confident smile. It's the smile of a woman who is either on the verge of a breakdown or a felony charge. Miranda's parents must be here already.

"Hello," she says. "Welcome to the Devil's Den. I'm Teagan Penhall, and it's lovely to meet you." She holds out her hand and I introduce my parents as they shake hands.

My parents tell her to call them Nora and Alex, and she tells them to call her Teagan. With that out of the way, she tilts her head to motion us to walk down to a spot away from her employees and comes out from behind the check-in counter.

"The Quinns are already here," she says, "and we have given them a suite on the fourteenth floor. Sophie's suite is there too, at the other end of the hall. Do you want your suite on the same floor or away from them?"

I can tell from her tone her vote is to be on a different planet than the Quinns, and I agree wholeheartedly. My parents look at each other and have a silent conversation of lifted eyebrows and eye rolls until Dad sighs and nods.

Ma smiles and lays a hand on Teagan's forearm. "Oooh, I love this. Merino wool?" Mom pets Teagan's cranberry colored sweater. Teagan nods. "Very nice. Anyway, it would be best if we have a room as close to the Quinns as possible. Next door or across the hall. We have a lot to catch up on."

I'm not picturing tea parties and giggling. My mother is every inch a lady, but I pity anyone who tries to push her or hurt someone she loves. She loves Miranda like she's one of her own kids. Depending on the foolishness my brothers get up to, sometimes she loves Miranda more.

Teagan's eyes widen slightly. She's picking up on the steel behind the velvet of my mother's words. If we were talking about anyone else, I'd almost pity the Quinns, but we're not and I don't.

"How is Miranda?" I ask as she leads us over to the bank of elevators taking us to my parents' suite. That's all I care about. Her parents can take a long walk off one of the shorter piers lining the Boardwalk as far as I'm concerned.

"She seems to be shell-shocked. I think her parents being here is throwing her for more of a loop than discovering she's a witch."

When we get off the elevator on my parents' floor, I automatically turn left.

"The suite is this way," Teagan says, turning right.

"Miranda is this way." I don't need a room number, her scent lures me. Now that we've mated, her scent is even stronger to me, my soul is connected to her. My parents can get settled without me. I need to see Miranda.

I knock on the door I instinctually know is Sophie's. Miranda is behind that door, and I need to see her. I knock again.

"Miranda!"

"Declan, are you daft?" Sophie asks as she opens the door. "You don't need to bellow."

"Dec?" Miranda asks from over Sophie's shoulder. "What are you doing here?"

I gesture behind me with my thumb. "Dropping my parents off. Your parents arrived?"

Miranda nods, her gray eyes tired. "Aye. My Dad isn't staying. You know he doesn't enjoy being away from the horses."

Can't say I blame him. I'd rather be with horses, too, but that dream must wait until Miranda is ready to settle down and go back to Ireland. Or wherever she wants to be. I don't care where we are as long as we're together.

"Can I come in?" I ask.

Sophie rolls her eyes. "Come in, but don't be gross."

I enter and look over the room. It's a small suite. I'm not sure if it is one or two bedrooms. I could get us another room if necessary if she's determined to stay here to be close to her mother.

Miranda takes a sip of tea and sits in the armchair of the seating area. No embrace or kiss. Is she letting Sophie make her feel awkward about our relationship?

"Could I have a cuppa, Soph?" I ask as I take a seat on the sofa, as close to Miranda as I can get.

"I don't have any, sorry," Sophie says.

I look pointedly at the mugs both she and Miranda are holding.

"My mother gave it to us," Miranda says, a note of apology in her voice.

"What did your parents say? Have they cleared everything up?" I ask. Please let them have explained everything so Miranda and I can get back to planning for our future. I know that's selfish and I'm not proud of that side of me, but I've been patient for years. I don't want anything to slow us down now we're finally together.

Sophie gives an impatient huff. "They've been here an hour, Declan. Be patient."

After all the years I've waited for Miranda to be mine, I think I've been patient enough.

The light knock on the door delays me telling my sister to butt out. Probably for the best. With a huff, Sophie walks over to the door and wrenches it open.

"Sophie," Ma sweeps her in a hug as she crosses the threshold. "Miranda," she exclaims as she releases Soph and moves to hug Miranda, who has risen from her chair. Her eyes drift closed as Ma hugs her tightly and my heart clenches as a single tear trails down Miranda's cheek. Dad hugs first Sophie and then Miranda when Ma finally releases her.

"It's been too long, sweetheart," Dad says, pressing a kiss to her cheek. He reaches out a long arm—I get my height from him—to pull Sophie back in for a hug. In his Scottish brogue he says, "Having both of my girls together is the best way to start a new year."

My Dad is not the most demonstrative of men, but he has always made sure we've known we are loved. That he easily shows his love for Miranda too makes me appreciate him even more.

There's another knock at the door and since I'm closest, I open it to reveal Carter. I step back to let him in, and he says hello to everyone like he hasn't already seen all of us today.

"What are you doing here?" Sophie asks.

"Sophie Eileen, don't be rude," Ma chides her. "Trevor, come in. I apologize for my daughter, she was raised better."

He gives the smile that always charms the ladies. "No worries. I'm getting used to Sophie. For the next two months, we will be the best of friends. She's getting her hostility out of her system early, before she falls in love with me."

His wink makes Sophie give a low growl. I don't know if it's a wolf's growl or an angry Sophie growl. They sound alike.

"Dance? You're partners for the show?" Dad asks.

"Aye," Sophie grumbles.

"Anyway," Carter says, "to answer your question. I'm here for Miranda. For support. She's my best friend. Where else would I be?"

"Aww...thanks Trev." Miranda gives him a hug and kiss on the cheek.

What. The. Hell? She hugged and kissed every person in the room but me. I'm the one she's in love with, but she hasn't touched me or given any indication of her feelings for me. How have things changed so much between us this quickly? If it has, does it mean what she told me last night, the promises we made, the dreams we shared, mean nothing?

The knocking at the door deters anyone from saying anything more. Ever gracious, Sophie stomps over and opens the door. Miranda's parents are on the threshold. We should have used the ballroom from last night.

Sophie's smile is huge as she steps back to let them into the suite. I glance over at Miranda and her face doesn't betray any emotion. I know she's already seen them, but if someone didn't know better, they'd think Sophie was their daughter based on the greeting. The years haven't brought many changes to the Quinns. Paul is still lean, standing around six feet tall. There is more gray in his brown hair and it is thinning. When I step forward, he shakes my hand and murmurs, "Hello." Miranda has his gray eyes.

Doreen is a beautiful woman at fifty-something years old. Her hair is still the same black as Miranda and her green eyes remind me of a house cat sizing up a juicy mouse she wants to pounce on. She has a dainty build, but there is no doubt she is physically strong from her work with horses. She is the type of woman who would be equally at home in riding breeches and boots, as she is in an exquisite gown. Miranda laments she doesn't have her mother's timeless beauty, but she doesn't realize Doreen's brittle manner detracts from any physical beauty she possesses. Anyway, I think Miranda is stunning whether she's in a gown or an old t-shirt. Sixty years from now, when we are both old and gray, she's always going to be the most beautiful woman in the world to me.

I turn away from Paul and face Doreen Quinn.

"Declan," she says, tilting her face toward me and presenting her cheek like I'm going to kiss it.

"Hello Doreen." I step back. Her green eyes flash with anger because I didn't fawn over her like most men do. Too bad. Miranda is the Quinn woman I'm kissing, no one else. Carter introduces himself and shakes both of their hands, rejecting Doreen's proffered cheek as well.

"Miranda," Paul says in an American accent. I'm shocked because he's always sounded as Irish as my mother. I guess I know where Miranda gets her changeable accent from. "I need to get back to the racetrack. The horses need me."

I think it's more he needs the horses. He strikes me as the type of man more comfortable with animals than with people.

"I'm sorry we don't have more time to spend together, but I hope you do well."

With that, he steps toward Miranda, and she meets him halfway, opening her arms to hug him. She quickly drops them when he holds his hand out to shake. It is damn awkward. Miranda recovers quickly and shakes his hand. On what planet does a man shake his daughter's hand? My dad isn't a big hugger, but even if he shook Sophie's hand, he would use his grip to pull her in for a hug as well.

"I understand," Miranda says. "Thank you for coming down, Father. I appreciate it. I hope the horses are well." She turns to Doreen. "Mother, I hope you have a safe trip home."

"Oh no," Doreen says, her Irish lilt sounding harsh. "I'm not leaving. You need me here, this is where I will be. You're my daughter."

Am I projecting the flash of alarm flitting across Miranda's face? Everyone says goodbye to Paul as he leaves. I don't know why he bothered to come down. Maybe Doreen didn't want to drive.

"Get your bag, Miranda," Doreen says as she follows Paul out of the suite. "We'll get you settled in my room,"

"I'm going to stay with Sophie, Mother," Miranda says.

Doreen stops and looks over her shoulder with her cat-like green eyes slightly narrowed.

"Miranda," she says with a note of sharpness to her voice. "I came down here to spend time with you, not to stay in a hotel room by myself. If you don't want to see me, say so and I will leave with your father."

Carter and I share a look saying *good riddance*. However, Miranda says, "Of course, Mother. I'm sorry. Let me get my bag."

I go to grab Miranda's bag to carry it for her, but Doreen says, "She can carry it herself, Declan. She's built like a hockey player. She's not helpless."

Miranda flushes a deep pink as she picks up her bag. Of course, she's not helpless, but she deserves care and consideration. I would do this for my mother or my sister. For Carter's sister. Hell, I'd do it for everyone. Except for Doreen. She can carry her own damn bag. Goodness knows she's given Miranda more than enough baggage to deal with.

As I go to follow Miranda out of the room, Sophie says, "Really, Declan? Can't you allow Miranda and her mother a moment alone? You don't need to be joined at the hip or the lip or any other parts."

Now it's my turn to flush. I don't remember when my sister got this nasty edge to her. Being the girl with five brothers, she's always given as good as she's gotten. But now there's a meanness and cruelty to her remarks and I don't like it.

"Sophie," Ma exclaims. "They're in love. Of course Declan wants to be with her. You'll understand someday."

"Not anytime soon," she scoffs. "Dance first and only. I don't have time to be distracted by love or hormones or whatever they have going on."

"You're a charmer," Carter says, and my dad chuckles. Earning them both scowls from Sophie.

"Miranda, come along," Doreen commands. Before I even have a chance to give Miranda a hug, or a kiss, or have a private word with her, she is out the door and closing it behind her. I worry that closed door is a statement about our relationship.

# 23
## MIRANDA

I'm not sure why I'm following my mother down the hall. I should be with Declan. But here I am with my bag, following her to her suite. We enter and mother points to a bedroom.

"You can put your bag in there."

I do as she says. I always do as she says.

"This is a nice suite," I say, looking around the space. Mother sniffs and tosses her long, black hair over her shoulders. There are no traces of silver in it. I don't know if she colors it or if there's a chance I may be similarly lucky as I age.

"It's adequate, but it's on a middle floor. They couldn't have given me a room on one of the upper floors? And the view. It's not even a direct view of the ocean. I have to look at an ugly pier."

I look out the window. Yes, she can see The Nest. But she also has a beautiful view of the Atlantic Ocean. And she's not paying for this room, she should be happy for anything she has.

"Yes, mother," I say. "That pier is where I work, where the rink and offices for the team are. Stores and restaurants, too, if you would like to explore them."

"I'm sure there's nothing there I would want," Mother says. "Here, have some more tea."

I turn to see her holding out a mug to me.

"Thank you," I say. "But I'm not thirsty. I had a mug of tea not too long ago."

Some quiet voice in my head keeps screaming: Who cares about tea? I'm a witch. Why did you never tell me? Why don't I know? But something else streaming through me lowers the volume dial on it. I can't hear it. But I know it's there. I know I want answers to these questions, but...I can't seem to get them out. She won't want to talk about that. And I try to always do what she wants.

Mother sets the mug of tea on the counter with a thud.

"Really, Miranda? Must you always be so ungrateful?" From seemingly out of nowhere, she has a tissue she's using to dry her eyes. Not that I see any tears. "I have important things to do at home, but I dropped everything to come down here for your little crisis."

She does air quotes around *crisis*.

"And what is this crazy claim you are a witch? Do you need attention that desperately?"

"I'm not *claiming* I'm a witch. Declan and Sophie told me I *am* a witch. Back when we were kids, I saw a unicorn. It was Declan. My witch powers made his unicorn come out. I don't know. And then earlier today I pointed at someone while saying, 'shift,' and she shifted into a goose." I point to show what I did to Brick. "I made her shift into a goose. I have magical powers I know nothing about!"

Mother sighs as she takes a seat on the sofa and gestures for me to sit in the chair across from her. I take my tea and sit down.

"I can't believe you are this gullible. You did not turn that woman into a goose. You do not have any magical powers. Yes, I am a witch. But my powers did not get passed down to you. You are ordinary in every way, like your father. They were playing a trick on you, making you think you had powers."

She shakes her head sadly and gives me a look full of pity. Well, if she is capable of pity. I have another objection I can't quite grasp. It's in me, but it's not breaking the surface.

"Now I'm here trying to take care of you, and nothing I do is good enough. All you ever do is reject me. I don't know why you can't love me?"

It's like I've been punched in the stomach. Ungrateful. Reject her. I don't love her. I must have landed in an alternate universe. She's claiming ownership of all the things I've wondered about for myself.

"Mother, of course I'm grateful. Thank you for coming here. It's wonderful we live close together now. That's one of the reasons I moved back here." Experience has taught me it's best to placate her.

I take a sip of the tea. It's cooler than I like but I drink it anyway. It's the least I can do after my mother went to the trouble to make it for me. It's the same tea she made me as a child, and drinking it brings a sense of comfort. She wouldn't send me birthday cards or call me, but she'd send packages of her tea. This tea was essentially the one sign of nurturing she's ever provided me. When I was upset or, more often, had displeased her, she would give me this tea. After drinking it, I would inevitably apologize for whatever she thought I had done wrong and she would thank me, nodding with approval. She never gave me a hug or a kiss or said *I love you,* but I lived for those nods and her acknowledgement she knew I was trying. When I was at school, I'd drink it a few times a week, stretching it out to maintain some semblance of a relationship with my parents. Once they moved to Argentina the tea stopped coming. I guess I wasn't worth the international postage.

"So, you're sleeping with Declan now?" she asks.

I choke on my tea. I was not expecting to have this conversation with my mother. Ever. But here she is. And here we are. So, I guess this is what we're talking about.

"Um," I run a finger around the rim of my teacup. Round and round. It's mesmerizing.

"Please, Miranda, don't mumble," she says.

Heat rises in my cheeks as I snap back to our conversation. "Yes, Mother. Declan and I are in love. He wants to marry me."

Mother scoffs. "That's what he said to get you to open your legs for him. I don't see a ring on your finger."

I tuck my hand behind my back even though it's pointless. "It's new."

"We raised you better than this, Miranda. I thought you had more pride in yourself." She clucks her tongue. "Are you going to whore yourself to the entire hockey team? I assume you've been with Trevor as well."

I gasp. "Mother, no. Trevor is my best friend. There has been nothing like that between us." I blink rapidly to hold back my tears because I know they will anger Mother. "What Declan and I have is special. I am most certainly not a whore. I was a virgin until last night."

"Hmm," Mother says in a disbelieving tone. "Well, now he's gotten what he wants. I hope you don't expect a proposal now. Declan and Sophie have always ganged up on you. Don't you remember from when you were a child? All the McKenzie children were always being mean to you, and you would run off and cry." She sighs and shakes her head. "You were always needy. And yes, Declan shifted into a unicorn because he could not control himself. They tried to blame you because it was easier to blame the poor little human girl no one would believe."

Mother leans forward to put her hand on mine. I can't remember the last time she reached out to me first. At least, in any sort of comforting way.

"That's why we took you away from there. You weren't safe."

"What?" I press my fingers into my temples, hoping to nudge the confusion clouding my mind into some sort of clarity. "What do you mean, I wasn't safe? The Mackenzies would never hurt me."

Mother pats my hand and leans back. I didn't know it was possible for a pat to be condescending. It is descending, right? Or is it comforting? Is physical closeness so foreign to me I can't tell the difference between comfort and condescension?

All those muffled voices in the back of my head are trying to scream something at me. Something along the lines of *that's condescension you twit*, if the sound could get through the fog.

"Like I said, you are gullible and naïve. If it came down to their children or you, who do you think they'd pick? Their sons were getting older, and Declan proved he could not be trusted to control himself around you. We had to sacrifice and put you in a school away from them, where you would be safe from interference by Declan or any of the male Mackenzies. You were a defenseless little girl."

My skin grows clammy. I know what my mother is inferring, and she's wrong. None of the Mackenzies would ever hurt me or molest me or whatever disgusting things she is intimating. I was safe there. I was loved there.

"We always tried to do what was best for you, Miranda. And you never appreciated it."

She shakes her head sadly. "We would no sooner get you settled into a school when you would start causing trouble or failing in your courses. We had responsibilities to the horses and our employers, and you were constantly causing distractions and making us have to spend time and a lot of money to find you a new school. I don't know what we did to deserve such a demanding child."

"I'm sorry, Mother," I say instinctively. I learned long ago it was easier to apologize rather than explain or defend.

"Yes, well. We all have our burdens to bear, and you are mine. I can stay for a day or two to help you decide where to go next. You obviously can't stay here with people who pretend to be your friends and play such horrible tricks on you. Maybe you could go back to New Zealand if you haven't burned those bridges. I can reach out to friends in Argentina. There are rugby teams there."

My eyes widen, and a pang in my heart tempts me to rub my chest but I don't want to show that kind of weakness in front of my mother. "I've been here a week. I don't want to leave. They need me." How can I revive a relationship with my parents if we're on separate continents? Why must there always be all this distance, physical and emotional between us?

Mother gives a mirthless laugh as she sits back on the sofa and crosses her legs. She is wearing jeans and a sweater, like I am, but she looks a million times more elegant than I ever can.

"Miranda, they don't need you. You're here because they felt sorry for you. Are you going to stay where you're not wanted because you're too afraid to be independent? Why are you so needy? I'm a strong, independent woman. Why couldn't you take after me? Or be more like Sophie?"

I take the last sip of tea but it's hard to swallow with the tears thickening my throat. "Yes, mother."

I took a nap a few hours ago, but I'm still exhausted. All the sleep I missed last night plus the past couple of weeks from moving and traveling with the team is catching up with me. My eyes are getting heavy and it's a struggle not to nod off.

"You should rest, Miranda. You will see things more clearly once you are refreshed." Mother's tone is kind, with a softness I wasn't expecting, didn't know she was capable of. It's a softness I've always wanted from her. Maybe we're finally turning a corner and on the verge of creating the bond I've been longing for.

I shake my head as I struggle to hold back a yawn. "I don't want to leave you alone. I appreciate you came here to be with me, Mother. I don't want to waste the time we have together."

"Take a nap, and then we will have dinner with the Mackenzies."

"Alright, maybe a nap will help. I'm fuzzy headed. It's hard to think clearly," I say.

Proof of my fuzzy headedness—admitting weakness to my mother. She's like a shark in the water, sensing blood. I brace myself.

"Rest well," is all she says.

I nod and go to my room. My phone is sitting on the comforter, and I check to see if I missed anything. I have messages from Trevor, Brick, and Declan. I save Declan's for last. Trev is checking in and making sure I know he's there for me. Brick was reassuring me she's okay and isn't upset about this morning. I think about Mother telling me I'm gullible. Were they tricking me? Could that be the case?

I don't know Brick very well, but she's been friendly to me. She offered to go shopping with me for a dress. But maybe it was to make sure I chose something unsuitable and looked ridiculous. That's what the girls at school would have done. They told me the wrong jersey to wear for hockey practice, and I had to skate laps until practice ended or I vomited, whichever came first. My "teammates" laughed when I had difficulty walking up the stairs to my room for days afterward. If they thought they could trick me into thinking I was a witch, they would have done it. Then they would have probably tried to recreate the Salem Witch Trials. Maybe Brick is like them, a grown-up mean girl.

Practical jokes are one of the ways teams bond. The rugby team pulled some epic pranks on the new caps. Maybe teasing me is a way to rally team spirit. Being the butt of the joke wasn't in my job description.

Taking a deep breath, I open Declan's messages. The time stamps start when I left the barn.

> Declan: Miranda, leaving to pick up my parents. Please call me.

> Declan: We need to talk. Call me, please.

> Declan: My parents are here, on the way to DD.

> Declan: We're here, are you upstairs?

The next message is from five minutes ago.

> Declan: Miranda, I love you, please talk to me. Can we meet?

Yeah, now he's saying he loves me. But does he mean it? I've been here a week, and he's in love and ready to marry me? Why would he want me? Nobody else has. It has to be all part of the prank.

> Me: I'm tired. Taking a nap.

> Declan: OK. I can get a room, we can nap together. I want to hold you.

Tears rush to my eyes and clog my throat again. I want him to hold me. I need him.

*Why are you so needy?* I hear it as clearly as if Mother was here in the room with me.

I can be strong and independent. I don't need Declan. I don't need anybody. I'm fine alone.

> Me: No. I need space.

> Declan: From me? I don't understand. Please, Daisy, talk to me.

Now he wants to talk to me? How about all those times we talked and he never mentioned he was a unicorn shifter and did I know I was a witch? We always had time to look at real estate ads for farms and auction catalogs for horses because they were things that mattered to *him*. But somehow, we never found time to talk about things that truly matter like I have magical powers and he can turn into a freaking unicorn? Call me crazy but I think those are things we could have managed to work into conversation sometime over the years.

My phone rings. It's Declan. We had snapped a picture together before the Colorado game and I use it as his contact picture. I decline the call.

> Declan: Miranda. Answer your phone. I'm coming to your room.

My stomach plummets. I'm not going to be strong enough to stay away if I can see him, touch him.

> Me: No. Don't. Leave me alone. Why can't you respect me? I will call hotel security.

Three dots seem to go on forever. I don't know what kind of reply he is composing. My tears on the phone screen are magnifying random words. Love. Daisy. Please. No. The last word breaks my heart. I don't want to tell Declan no. I love him. I want him to hold me. I want to go back to this morning before everything went wrong. Back to when someone loved me and the future I dreamed of was possible. Now everything is a nightmare.

> Declan: OK.

All that time and all I get is one word. Two letters. I turn my phone to silent, grab a blanket from the closet, and curl up on the bed to cry myself to sleep. It's over. I'm alone. Again. Always.

I have the strangest dream Mother is in my room, standing over me, speaking softly enough I can't hear her. I know it had to have been a dream because, when I awoke from my nap, I had to unlock the door to leave my room. I don't remember locking it, but I must have out of reflex.

"Oh good, you're awake. Dinner will be here soon," Mother says.

Stretching my arms over my head, my brows lower in confusion. "I thought we were going to have dinner with the Mackenzies?"

Mother sniffs. "They are having dinner together with the casino owner. We aren't invited. We are to get whatever we want from room service. *You* can go downstairs and make a nuisance of yourself showing up where you're not wanted, but *I* have too much pride for that."

"Mother, I'm sure we'd be welcome. I'll ask."

"Miranda, you will do no such thing. We are Quinns and we do not grovel. Well, you don't grovel when you're with me." She looks me up and down and sneers. "What you do on your own is your business. Goodness knows your pride is questionable, but while I'm here, you will behave with dignity and not beg for table scraps."

Shame washes over me. Like it always does.

"Yes, Mother." I hate myself for sounding meek, for not standing up for myself, and even more for not feeling capable of it.

"I ordered us dinner. Chicken almond stir-fry, your favorite." There's a knock on the door. "That must be room service." She waves to the mug on the counter. "I made you tea. I'll answer the door."

She opens the door and gestures for the room service attendant —his name tag says Frederick—to push his cart in.

"Good evening, ladies." A cheerful smile creases Frederick's weathered face. "Shall I set you up at the table?"

Mother sweeps a hand toward the table and Frederick places two silver domed plates on the square table in front of the window overlooking the Boardwalk and Nest. I walk over with my mug of tea.

"Thank you, Frederick." I glance at the cart. There's nothing else on it. No dessert, no other entrees, or side dishes. I am stuck with food I absolutely hate.

Mother signs the receipt and Frederick leaves with a cheery, "Have a nice evening."

As the door clicks closed behind me, Mother and I take our places at the table. Lifting the lids, I'm disappointed to see we both have the chicken almond stir-fry. There are almonds everywhere, like extra almonds were requested.

"I know this is your favorite, Miranda. I was thrilled to see it on the menu." She picks up her fork. "Remember how you'd always ask for this when we'd go out to eat when we visited you at school?"

"What?" I've never asked for this meal, and they rarely visited me at school. The times I would see them wouldn't be categorized as "visits." They were dropping me off at a new school or picking me up to take me to another school. We weren't having cozy family dinners. I wasn't ordering chicken almond stir-fry.

Mother motions with her fork. "Eat your dinner, Miranda. It's going to get cold."

I pick up my fork and scrape the almonds off the best I can and spear a piece of chicken. They're everywhere. Beyond being scattered on top, it's like they put a layer of almond on the plate first, added the chicken stir-fry and then piled even more almonds on top. There is no way to avoid them. I take a small bite of chicken and try to control the shudder when I taste the almond slivers I couldn't scrape off.

"What's wrong?" Mother asks sharply.

"Nothing." I try to surreptitiously free another piece of chicken from its almond prison.

"Don't you like it?" Her voice is harsh, and my shoulders tense.

"I don't like almonds," I admit quietly, looking down at my plate.

"Since when?" she demands.

My hands tremble. "I...I've never liked almonds, Mother." I look up through my lashes to see her face darkening in anger.

She slams her fist against the table, and I jump. "Don't lie to me, Miranda. You've always loved almonds. Why are you being cruel? I came here for you, ordered your favorite dinner, and all you've done is lock yourself in your room and refuse to eat what I order for you. You have always been ungrateful. I don't know why you hate me so much." She snatches both plates from the table, storms into the small kitchen area, and dumps both meals into the garbage, plates and all. "No wonder you don't have any friends. You're a selfish, miserable human being."

She stomps out of the room and slams her bedroom door shut. Her weeping carries through the door. What happened? How am I wrong? I didn't ask her to come here or order dinner. I put down the fork I'm still holding. Should I apologize? I'm uncertain what I'm saying sorry for. Rising from the table, I walk to the window to look out on the view as I finish my tea.

It's evening and I can't see the ocean, but I can see a few brave souls walking along the Boardwalk. I wish I could join them, leave this room and have time to think. But I know I need to stay here. If Mother comes out and finds me gone, there will be more yelling and guilt. I don't know why it's like this. What I keep doing wrong. I need to try harder. I look into my empty mug and the bits of tea leaves left at the bottom of the cup. *This* I remember having during my childhood and when I'd see my parents at school, not chicken with almonds.

Mother's sobs have quieted. I get ready for bed because I'm exhausted again. Hopefully, everything will be better in the morning. Maybe today is a nightmare and I'm going to wake in Declan's arms. Maybe all of this isn't real. I wrap my fingers around the clover pendant he gave me yesterday and wish with all my heart.

# 24
## DECLAN

WE ARE MEETING TEAGAN IN THE PRIVATE DINING ROOM OF THE STEAKHOUSE in Devil's Den. It's me and Sophie at a large table, dark wood decorated with a large floral arrangement at the center and elaborately folded cloth napkins. Are those...wolves? And a unicorn? Bloody hell. I've never noticed this before. Next team dinner I'm taking notes to see if they do antlers for Stone's moose.

I took Carter back home and packed a bag. If Miranda is staying here tonight, I am too, even if we aren't sharing a room.

"Where's Miranda?" I ask.

"She's not coming down for dinner," Sophie says. "I spoke with Doreen and Miranda wanted to stay in their room and get room service. She doesn't want to see you, Declan."

I know that's not true. Miranda loves me. As I love her. I turn to exit the steakhouse.

"I gotta speak with her. I'm going to get her."

My parents have walked up with Teagan in time to hear me. Dad puts a heavy hand on my shoulder and squeezes.

"Declan, calm down. Have dinner and we can talk things over. It may be for the best to leave things be for tonight. You will see her at the rink tomorrow and can talk then."

Shaking my head, I try to shrug off his hand, but he doesn't remove it. Instead, he uses it to guide me to a chair like I'm still a boy and not a grown man almost seven feet tall. I reluctantly sit as everyone else takes their places around the table.

I look at my mother. "Something is wrong. She loves me. Why doesn't she want to see me? This morning we were blissed out and talking about getting married. About our future. Now she won't talk to me at all." I shoot a glare at Sophie. "If she didn't have all of this sprung on her, we would still be okay."

Sophie glares daggers right back at me. "Oh no, this isn't my fault. You're the one who fell into bed with her without talking about important things like the fact you're a fricking unicorn. And how has the fact she's a witch never come up through the years? It's always poor, poor Miranda. You know I love her like a sister and consider her one of my best friends, but it's always a crisis with her."

"Are you on drugs? Seriously? Why are you being such a bitch?" I can't believe she can say she loves her like a sister in one breath and be vicious in the next. This isn't like my sister. She's outspoken and spunky but she's loyal.

She lays a gentle hand on my forearm. "I know you love her, Declan. You're a kind man with a loving heart, but she's going to break it." She looks at our parents. "You know it as well as I do. Tell him. Don't make me look like the bitch here."

"Sophie, Declan, language," Mother chastises. "I love Miranda like she's one of my own. Always have. I believe you are fated for each other, but fate isn't always kind. I understand she's had a shock and I hope tomorrow she is back to the woman you love. But Declan, you have to accept your love may not be returned."

"She loves me." I pound my fist on the table, making the silver-ware rattle. I rarely display fits of temper. Everyone describes me as a quiet and even-tempered man. But this isn't an ordinary situation. My future—my heart—is at risk.

Teagan clears her throat. "Let's have dinner and discuss how we can help Miranda learn what she needs to if she embraces her witch powers. We can also guide her if she chooses to renounce her gift. It is rare, but there have been those who chose to deny their birthright. If it is her choice, we will help her. No matter what, she is part of my family now. Both the Devil Birds and also the Sisterhood of Witches."

We eat dinner. I'm sure it's delicious, but it all tastes like ash to me. As soon as we are done, I race from the dining room and upstairs to Miranda's room. I knock on the door. Okay, maybe I pound on it. I'm showing restraint because I could easily break it down. I'm about to knock again, harder, when Doreen opens it.

She's smiling, but it's all teeth. Like a rabid honey badger. "Good evening, Declan."

"I need to speak with Miranda." It's rude not to return her greeting, but I'm a desperate man.

"I believe she's gone to bed. You can speak with her in the morning."

"Miranda," I call out as my family and Teagan approach.

"For god's sakes, Declan," Sophie says. "What is wrong with you? You're in a hotel—you can't be bellowing like you're calling sheep back to the barn."

"Declan," Teagan says. "Is there a problem here?"

"Yes, there's a problem here. She won't let me see Miranda."

"Doreen?" Mother asks.

"Nora, Miranda has had a very trying day. She's exhausted, and she's gone to bed. Please tell your son"—Doreen looks at me like I'm vermin—"to please leave us alone."

"Declan?" Miranda walks into the room behind her mother. She is in pajamas and looks sleep rumpled and adorable.

"Miranda. Darling. We need to talk. Please." I try to enter the suite. But Doreen blocks my way. I'm ready to push past her, but my father grabs my arm.

"Steady on, son," he says.

Miranda pushes her hair out of her eyes and shakes her head.

"We have nothing to talk about, Declan. Leave me alone." She turns and goes back to her room, closing the door and breaking my heart.

"You heard her. Declan." Doreen gives me a steely eyed gaze. "I'm sure you're disappointed your affections aren't returned. But please respect my daughter's wishes. If you continue to harass her—"

"Harass her?" my mother exclaims in disbelief. "Trying to get an explanation and talk to his girlfriend is not harassment."

"Nora, you've been my best friend since we were girls, and I love you like a sister. I've known Declan his whole life and I know he is a good man. But I must respect Miranda's feelings even if I don't agree with her. I'm sorry." She turns to me. "Declan, I don't want to have to call the authorities on you, but I will if it's what's necessary to protect my daughter. Please don't make this difficult. Good night."

"Protect her? From me? Don't be ridiculous," I shout as she closes the door. The sound of the dead bolt engaging is the last straw. I can't believe she doesn't want to see me. How has everything perfect gone horribly wrong in a day? I spin away from the door and punch the wall in frustration. I hear the bones crack before the pain registers. "Fuck," I moan as I cradle my hand to my chest. I didn't even put a dent in the wall, but I've broken my hand. This is the worst day of my life.

---

The team has a top-notch orthopedic surgeon on staff who x-rays my hand quickly and confirms the break. They call it a "boxer's fracture," but Coach calls it a "fucking dumbass fracture." He's right. I should have controlled my emotions better. I'm not a violent man, but I was seeing red.

I'm on the bench watching practice. With my right hand in a splint for the next two to three weeks, there's no practicing with the team and no playing in the PHL All-Star game in Florida. I *am* a dumbass. It was such an honor to be picked, and I let my temper and frustration get the best of me and ruin it all. If my team won there would be prize money, significant prize money, that would make my ability to get a farm much easier. And I threw it all away because I lost control. I let my feelings for Miranda distract me from hockey. I want her to be my future, but I can't lose sight of everything else because she's here.

Nate Crosby is in my spot and he's doing well but he's a different type of player than I am. He's a wombat shifter and smaller than I am. Everyone is smaller than I am, but he is one of the smaller guys on the team. Still a big guy, he's over six feet tall, but small for a team loaded with wolf, bear, and other large animal shifters. He's a faster, more agile skater than I am which throws the timing of passes off. His stick isn't as long as mine and he can't snag pucks sliding past on the ice to rescue the play like I'd be able to. Carter is getting frustrated Crosby isn't where he expects him to be. Carter has a hard time adapting sometimes when he's stressed. They'll work it out.

Coach blows the whistle for lines to change. Carter and Crosby skate over to get water. I put their bottles on the board to make them easier to grab. At least I can do something useful.

"We gotta work on our timing," Crosby says. He's serious where Carter is more of a goof.

Carter growls. "Ya think?"

"You'll get it," I say, trying to de-escalate the situation.

"I know we'll get it. Sucks we have to." With that scathing remark, Carter skates away. I know I screwed our team by losing my temper. They have every right to be pissed at me.

"Hope you heal quickly, Mac, this isn't how I wanted to move up to the first line," Crosby says as he leans over the board to put his water bottle back on the shelf. He gives the board a stick tap in farewell and goes toward the far goal to practice tip in shots with our second goalie.

"Are you happy now? You broke his heart and hand," Sophie shouts from up in the stands.

What the hell? I turn around to see what she's going on about and see Miranda and Doreen climbing the steps to take them to where my family and Daphne are sitting.

My breath catches when I see Miranda. She's beautiful, but she looks exhausted and fragile. A shell of the lovely, vibrant woman from last week. Hell, from the day before yesterday. Is she ill? Her normally cream and roses complexion in her cheeks looks sallow, her eyes are flat like gravel from the barn's driveway, not serene. It looks like she's lost five pounds she had no business losing in a day. While part of me wants her to be heartbroken like I am, I don't ever want my Daisy to suffer. I want her to be happy and healthy. I love her, even if she doesn't love me.

"What?" Miranda asks, turning to scan the ice. I'm easy to pick out since I'm the tallest. When she doesn't see me, she looks at the bench and sees me sitting there. I wave my splinted hand and curse myself when I see her go pale and sway slightly as if she's going to faint, but she doesn't. She edges around her mother and comes down to the spot behind the bench where there's a small gap in the protective glass.

Her eyes are shiny with tears as she reaches out for my hand.

"Declan." She runs her fingers over my splint with the hand not holding mine. "What happened?"

"You happened, Miranda," Sophie spits. "You always fucking happen."

Miranda's eyes widen, and a flush replaces the sallowness as she releases my hand and turns to face Sophie. "Excuse me?"

She doesn't say it politely. More in a "What the fuck did you say to me?" tone I never expected to hear come from my sweet Miranda.

"You heard me," Sophie takes the last step down, losing the slight height advantage she had to stand toe-to-toe with Miranda.

"The entire team heard you, you banshee, but I don't know what the hell you're talking about."

Miranda's accent is no gentle Irish lilt. It is a full-blown brogue.

"You sleep with Declan, freak out because you're a witch, and dump him. You refuse to speak to him. He punches the wall and breaks his hand. It's all your fault." Sophie jabs Miranda in the breastbone and, with her wolf shifter strength, pushes her back.

I surge to my feet, wanting to catch Miranda in my arms, hold her, shelter her from pain, but a wall of plexiglass separates us. "I'm the idiot who punched the wall. That's not Miranda's fault."

Miranda turns to me. "Why?"

I want to tell her because she broke my heart, and I was frustrated. Sophie isn't wrong in her facts, but she's got it all wrong somehow.

"Because you're a heartless bitch," Sophie screams.

"That's enough," Coach bellows. Carter is in the tunnel next to where the girls are, and he's not separated from them by plexiglass like I am. He reaches out an arm and hooks Miranda around the waist and pulls her over the wall. She yelps in surprise.

Coach comes up behind them. "Miranda, go back to your office, please."

Tears spill down her cheeks, and she looks stricken. With a tight nod, she takes off down the tunnel, Carter following her. I reach, with my broken hand, to open the gate to follow too.

Coach stops me. "Sit your ass down, Mac. Miss Mackenzie, you are a guest at this practice. If you can't control yourself, you will need to leave. We don't allow fighting on the ice *or* in the stands."

He turns toward the ice. "Bedard, run drills with the coaches."

To me, he says, "Stay here while I handle this." He points a finger at Sophie. "Simmer down."

He's lucky Sophie isn't more in touch with her witchy side because he'd have turned into a toad in that moment if she could have managed it. Instead, he walks down the tunnel toward the locker room and his office while typing on his phone.

I look up at the stands where Ma, Doreen, and Daphne are sitting. Daphne is rubbing her belly and looking at her phone. Coach is probably texting her about this shit show. Doreen is looking down at me with a hint of a smirk on her ruby red lips. She's a beautiful woman. My teammates have been checking her out even though she's old enough to be their mother. She does nothing but repulse me. She's like a beautiful red apple full of worms. You don't know it's rotten until you bite into it, but then it's too late. Miranda will always be lovelier than her. It hits me in a flash. She is jealous of Miranda. Her own daughter. She's like the evil queen in an animated film. She has to be the fairest of them all.

When I look at it through that lens, everything makes sense. I'm living a fucked-up version of Snow White and my friends are a bunch of hockey-playing dwarves. I start to rise from the bench, but something compels me to look back at my mother. She gives me an almost imperceptible shake of her head and the words, "Trust me," echo in my brain. I turn back toward the ice and nod. To anyone else, it will look like I'm reacting to something on the ice, but I know Ma knows the nod is for her.

Doreen watches practice for a few minutes but soon leaves. Carter comes back on the ice and comes to the bench to grab water.

"This is a clusterfuck, man," he says. "Something's not right."

"Carter, are you joining us today?" Coach asks.

He rolls his eyes and skates away. He's right. Something is terribly wrong, and it's not limited to timing passes. But the fact he sees it too doesn't make me feel any better. Practice continues, and Ma comes down to talk to me before leaving.

"Declan, I know things look bleak now, but we will figure out what is going on."

I look over Ma's shoulder to where Sophie is talking with Daphne. She seems calmer.

"Sophie is being weird, too," I say. "There's something going on with both of them. They'd have spats now and then as girls, but Sophie has a vicious edge to her I've never seen before."

"We will sort this out, but you need to control yourself. Trust me. Pushing Miranda isn't going to do any good."

I give a tight nod and try to swallow the lump in my throat. I have never felt more helpless in my life. How many times must have Miranda felt like this? Every time she had to switch schools and try to make new friends and adapt. I want her to have security, I want to give her roots. But I can't tie her down. She has to choose. Please let her choose to stay with me.

Ma leaves, and Coach joins me on the bench. We watch the plays unfold on the ice for a few minutes before Coach speaks.

"Mac, we can't have scenes like this happening. We can't have you losing control and doing dumbass stuff like punching walls and trying to push your way into hotel rooms. I know you have feelings for Randi—"

"I love her."

"Okay, you love her. But we can't have this kind of drama. It's disruptive to the team. If you two can't get your shit together, Randi is going to have to go. She's become my friend over the years from hanging around Kennie, but the team has to come first. They're my responsibility."

My heart sinks. I can't be the reason Miranda loses this.

"No, you can't do that," I say. "If we can't work it out then trade me. Or I'll quit and forfeit my salary. She loves working for the team. She loves hockey. Do you know she was a two-time state champion?"

"She was?" he asks. "I didn't know she played."

"She did, right wing. She was wonderful. Her dream is to get a front office job with a major sports franchise, and she hopes it's here with the Devil Birds. I'm not going to be the reason she doesn't get the chance."

"Well, then, make sure you get it straightened out. I don't want to lose either one of you."

"Please make sure Miranda knows her job isn't at risk. Even if we aren't together, she doesn't

have to leave. Don't tell her I volunteered to go, though, tell her you'd choose her to stay. That matters to her."

Coach looks at me, not saying a word. It's uncomfortable. Finally, he nods.

"Okay. But I pray you two work out whatever craziness is happening and are happy. You two are a good match for each other. This past week was the happiest I've ever seen Randi. You bring out a side of her she hasn't shown before."

Hopefully both of our prayers are answered.

# 25

## MIRANDA

I don't know what to think. Declan's hand is broken. Sophie is being vicious. My head is foggy, nothing makes sense. I thought this was going to be a wonderful year. It's by far the worst one of my life and we're not even through the first week. I love him, but there is a wall between us. Trevor is following me down the tunnel. I hate he's missing practice but I'm grateful to have my best friend with me.

"Do you want water?" I ask as we enter my office.

At his nod, I go through to the dining room and grab bottles for each of us. I grab a bottle of orange juice, too. Maybe my blood sugar is low? I take a seat on the sofa and Trevor sits next to me, stretching his arm along the back, inviting me to snuggle against him. I don't even care if he's sweaty from practice—I need the comfort.

"Randi, what's going on with you? You were all in love with Declan and now you can't stand to be near him. I know you're not fickle."

I sigh. "Trevor, I'm so confused. I do love Declan. I've always loved him. But he's kept secrets from me for years. Important secrets. I'm a witch, apparently? And he didn't tell me. How could he do that and claim he loves me?"

"Randi, Mac thought you knew. He thought you were being private about your powers, that's why he never brought it up. Did you guys ever talk about him being a wolf shifter?"

"No. Why would we? I don't know anything about shifting and when we saw each other, we had other things to talk about."

"Exactly. If you didn't talk about him being a shifter, why would you talk about you being a witch?"

I fidget uncomfortably, and he wraps his arm around my shoulder. It's embarrassing to say what I need to say, but Carter is the person I can trust.

"I don't believe I really am a witch. I think Declan and Sophie were teasing me like they did when we were kids. I think Brick played along with it. I never turned anyone else into a shifter before. If I've had powers all these years, why hasn't that happened?"

"How often do you point at people and tell them to shift?"

He has a point. "Well, never. But you'd think other things would have happened. What if I pointed at you and commanded you to shift right now, would it work?"

He shrugs and the mountain of pads he's wearing moves beneath my cheek.

"I don't know. You can try. This is going to sound crazy, but yesterday you had this...energy...about you that you had never had before, and you don't have today. The witches I've known have kind of... I don't know...a frequency humming in the background. I feel it with Teagan. I felt it when I met Bedard's mother. I feel it with Mac's mom. Sophie has it, but more faintly. You had it yesterday, and it was at a super high frequency—the most I felt from anyone. But it's gone now."

I stand and start pacing my office. "So maybe Sophie put a spell on me as a joke and it's worn off. My mother says I'm not a witch. She is, but the powers didn't pass down to me. I'm human." I nod decisively. "What happened yesterday was a joke. Sophie's mad at me for some reason, maybe because I'm with Declan. I don't know. This is her way of getting back at me."

Trevor steeples his fingers and rests his chin on them. It's his thinking pose. "That's possible, I guess. But why would she do that? She's supposed to be one of your best friends. This is hurting her brother, who she loves, not just you. I don't know. Something is weird here. You're not acting like yourself."

I throw my hands up. "Until last week, you hadn't seen me in a year and a half. Who I was in college is not the same as who I am now. You don't know who I am."

Trevor stands and wraps me in a hug. "Randi, you haven't changed that much. You are the same kind, sweet, and shy woman I've known since you were eighteen years old. Some things don't change."

Coach appears in my doorway. "Carter, head back to the ice. I need to speak with Randi."

I step out of Carter's embrace and nod at Coach. Before he walks away, he gives me a kiss on the cheek and assures me everything will be okay. I can hear his skates clomping as he walks out of the locker room.

Coach is carrying a mug of coffee from the dining room as he walks in.

"Okay if I close the doors?"

I nod and he closes the door to the dining room and also the door to the locker room. This can't be good. He grabs one of the chairs in front of my desk and spins it around to face where I'm seated on the sofa again. Taking his seat, he rests his elbows on his thighs and clasps his hands between his knees. His pose should look relaxed, but it doesn't.

"Randi, I don't know everything going on with you and Declan. Frankly, I don't want to know. But we can't have it impacting the team."

Oh no. I knew this was going to happen. It was too good to be true. I'm going to have to leave again. I should be used to this, but for the first time in years, I had hoped maybe I'd found my place. I blink rapidly, trying to keep the tears from falling and take a sip of water to ease the lump in my throat.

Nodding, I murmur, "I understand. You have to do what is best for the team. Are you giving me notice or is my termination effective immediately?"

Coach sits upright like he was hit with a taser, causing the chair to tip back slightly and the legs to bang as they hit the floor.

"What?" he asks with a look of bewilderment on his face. "You're not terminated. You're doing a great job, and we want you here. The issue is Mac. If he can't control himself, then he's going to find himself traded. None of us wants that. We like him and he is a skilled player, but he has to be focused on the game. If he can't because you're here, then he's going to have to go."

"Wait. What? *He'd* have to go?" It's my turn to shake my head. In confusion. Is he saying they would pick me over Declan? I'm not being sent away? I've never been picked.

"You're family. Part of the Devil Birds family, but you're also like another sister to me. You're Kennie's best friend, I've known you since you were roommates your first year of college. Mallory and Daphne love you. You're doing great at your job. As far as I'm concerned, you're here as long as you want to be."

I can't hold back the tears. No one has ever picked me or said they wanted me to stay. But I don't want Declan to have to leave. I tell Liam that.

"No one wants Mac to leave. But if he can't control himself and be around you without being in a relationship or whatever is going on with you guys, then he'll have to move on. He's a grown man and a professional athlete. His job is to play ice hockey. If he can't keep his personal business off the ice, then he doesn't need to be here." He shrugs. "Some teams love to have the drama and be the attention of social media influencers. We don't. We are here to play damn good hockey."

He takes a sip of his coffee and gestures to me with the mug. "I'm not saying you need to date him or have anything to do with him.

Your position here is independent of whatever relationship you have with him. But we can't have scenes like we did today distracting the team. None of it was your fault, I know that. I had no idea the Mackenzie clan was this volatile."

"They aren't. I don't know what's going on with either of them. Sophie, it's like she hates me, and I don't understand it."

Coach rises from his chair and swings it back around to face my desk again. His hand stays resting on its back.

"Well, I hope you two can get along or stay out of each other's way. She's here for the next couple of months as Carter's dance partner. We have expectations of Carter going far on Celebrity Dance Dare. The further he goes, the more publicity for the Devil Birds, which is good for all of us. We need Sophie focused on dancing with him and not fighting with you. If she can't handle it, we will find another partner for Carter. It's part of the contract, hopefully she knows what's good for her."

After Coach walks out, I go and get myself a mug of hot water. My tea is steeping and I'm staring off into space when Bedard pokes his head in from the dining room.

"Are you drinking different tea? It smells...um...nice. Peach, ginger. Do you know what else is in it?"

Well, that's random.

I nod. "Yeah, it's a blend my mother made. I used to drink it as a child, and it was very comforting. I don't know everything in it."

Opening my desk drawer, I hold up my bag.

"I have extra tea bags if you want to have some," I say.

"Yeah, great. Thanks. I don't want tea right now, but I think Kendall would enjoy a mug with me after dinner."

"Sure. Here," I say, holding out the bag. "Take them all. There are more back in our suite. I'll restock."

"Great, thanks."

"Of course. You're welcome. I hope you and Kennie enjoy it."

He smiles and walks away.

I down my tea in a few gulps. My head is pounding. I think I need to get some more sleep. I'll bring my files with me, and I can work from there later today.

I walk through The Nest and out to the Boardwalk. Like always, the icy wind coming off the Atlantic Ocean takes my breath away. I wish I could snuggle against Declan and share his warmth like we did before. I tell myself the tears stinging my eyes are from the salt air, but I know they are from my broken heart. When we're apart, all I want to do is be with him. I love him. But then when I see him, all the doubts creep in and I'm angry all over again.

I'm usually even-tempered, but in the past day my emotions have been all over the place. It's like I'm crazy. I want things to go back to how they were. I want to go back to how I was. But not alone. I don't want to be alone any longer. I want the future we whispered about with children and a home. With these feelings of doubt or mistrust, I don't know if it's possible. Part of me knows what Dec says about not talking about things because he thought I knew makes sense. We never talk about his wolf, I've never spoken with Kennie about her cougar, or Carter about his wolf. No one asks why my hair is black or my eyes are gray. It's how you are—there's no reason to discuss it.

But what mother says makes sense too. She would have seen things from an adult perspective I had no concept of as a child. I don't remember Declan and Sophie picking on me, but I was always a target at my schools. It makes sense I was with them too. I don't know. I'm confused. This headache isn't helping either. Hopefully, a nap will help my head clear. I need to be able to think clearly and figure out what I'm going to do.

The hotel offers a welcoming warmth when I enter. Trevor is waiting at the elevator.

"Hey Randi. Sophie needs to change into dance clothes for our practice. I'm meeting her upstairs."

I nod tiredly. Trevor puts his arm around me, and I lean against him as the elevator whooshes upward. We don't speak, we don't have to. When the doors open, I glimpse Nora entering the suite I'm sharing with Mother. I guess I won't be able to sneak in to take my nap. Oh well. Trevor is coming with me while Sophie changes in her room. We are a few doors from mine when I hear raised voices coming from my suite. Mother and Nora are yelling at each other. Before I can rush ahead to see what's going on, Trevor grabs my arm to stop me and puts a finger up to his lips. We creep silently to the door of the suite and discover it's ajar. Nora dropped her mono-grammed wallet to stop the door from latching. Why?

"You promised you were going to teach her about her powers, Doreen," Nora is saying. "You didn't. Why? She was terrified to discover she was a witch. How did she not know for all these years?"

I peek through the crack in the doorway. Nora is facing the door and mother's back is to me. I know Nora sees me and I hear her voice in my head telling me to listen. A sense of peace and love washes over me as I slip to the side in order to hear without being seen. Trevor makes the okay sign with his fingers and when I nod, he takes off for Sophie's room.

Mother's laugh doesn't hold humor. "It was simple. She didn't have any. I put a suppression spell on her powers. It held all these years until she mated with your son. As for why, they are *my* powers. She got them from me, and I didn't want to share."

The elevator doors slide open, and I glance down the hall. Teagan is striding toward me, but stops for Trevor, who is on his way back. She listens to what he has to say and nods. Looking my way, she mouths some words and waves her hand. I feel like a barrier has slipped between me and the door. I take a step back in surprise.

Trevor and Teagan reach my side and she gives my arm a light squeeze. "I put a barrier spell up. We can hear what is said in the room, but they can't see or hear what is going on out here," she whispers.

"In case Sophie can't keep her big mouth shut," Trevor murmurs.

I nod.

"Her powers are her gift. It is not your place to deny her," Nora says.

Mother tosses her head like a cantankerous mare I used to feed apples when I lived with the Mackenzies. "I'm her mother and I can do whatever I want with her and her powers."

"Why are you doing this to her? You're her mother, you love her, why are you hurting her?"

"I don't love her. I never loved her. I had her because my mother's will contained a trust providing additional funds for the support of a child. If I didn't have a child, I couldn't get the money, it would be donated to an animal charity. It was *my money*. I suffered through a pregnancy and childbirth and earned every penny. You were willing to take her on with your litter, so it worked out. I had my money and didn't have to deal with the brat."

Mother is spewing this venom in such a matter-of-fact way, like what she's saying isn't unnatural and vile.

"I would have left her with you until she turned twenty-one and the money ran out, but she had to come into her powers early and you were eager to teach her. She's *my* daughter and if she was going to learn about the craft it's my place to teach her. Not you. You have your own daughter. Miranda's powers come from me and if I don't want her to have them then she won't. They are mine and I don't want to share."

Sophie calls from down the hall. "What's going on?"

Thank goodness for Teagan's spell.

"Your mothers are having a chat," Trevor says in what is the understatement of the year.

Sophie shoulders her way past me to enter the suite and runs into the barrier Teagan placed. She staggers back in surprise.

"I want to hear what they have to say," Teagan says with a shrug. With a snap of her fingers, a tub of popcorn appears in her hand, and she offers it to us. Trevor takes some. I shake my head when she offers it to me. I can't.

She grimaces. "Sorry, bad read of the room. How about this?"

With a snap of her fingers the popcorn disappears, and a tumbler of whisky pops into existence. From the color and aroma, I know it's from the Mackenzie distillery. It's the good stuff. Teagan doesn't skimp with her magic. I already have a pounding headache, it's not like a hangover is going to make it feel any worse. I take it and sip, closing my eyes as the fire slides down my throat. The fog filling my head clears a tiny bit. Like a weak ray of sunshine made its way through thick clouds. I turn my focus back to the conversation between mother and Nora.

"I took her away from you and suppressed her powers to stop her from causing shifts left and right. I put her in whatever school would take her." Mother stops pacing and faces Nora again. "When they kicked her out because we didn't pay the rest of the tuition, we'd stick her in the next."

*That's* why I moved from school to school? Because they didn't pay their bills? I didn't have to go to boarding school. I could have gone to the public school wherever they lived or did online home-schooling. Oh, yeah, she didn't want me around.

"If you want me to stop disrupting Miranda's life and making your son miserable, it's very simple," Mother says. "Give me five million dollars and I'll leave them be."

"Five million," Nora exclaims. "It was a million dollars before."

A million dollars? What?

Mother laughs like any of this is funny. "That was eight years ago, Nora, inflation. That million dollars is gone. I kept my end of the deal. I let you pay her tuition and remain in one school to finish high school and let her attend college where she wished. I put up with her visits until she turned twenty-one. I didn't interfere. I wouldn't be here now if your brat of a daughter didn't poke her nose into my business. But she did, and here we are. If I'm inconvenienced, then you will be too."

"She's an adult who can make her own choices. Why should I give you anything?" Nora asks.

"Can she really make her own decisions? You know she wants to please me. She always has. Desperate for her mummy to love her. Pathetic." Mother shrugs her shoulders nonchalantly, like none of this matters. "I told her how you didn't want her anymore and insisted we take her away. How she wasn't safe with you. How she didn't see a unicorn and to stop lying. I've told her lots of things, and she believes me."

Tears slip down my cheeks. Trevor hugs me from behind, and I grasp his arms like they are my lifeline. In a way, they are. Sophie is gasping and sputtering over being called a brat. Like that's the worst thing in the world. Teagan snaps her fingers again, and a box of tissues appears. I wish I had witch powers, being able to conjure up French fries or cookies whenever I want would be handy. Especially on days you hear your mother hates you and lies to you like it's her hobby. But...I do have powers. But my mother has been suppressing them and the suppression is slipping since I caused Brick to shift. I look at the glass of whisky—empty. Would Teagan snap me another if I asked? Before I can, she snaps, and it's refilled. I take a grateful sip.

"Give me the money, and Miranda and Declan can get married, give you the grandbabies you want. Live their boring happily ever after. Don't give me the money and I'll introduce Miranda to people I know from the racing circuit. I know lots of men who would like an innocent like Miranda. She wouldn't be innocent for long. Not that she is now since your son tarnished her, but she's still innocent enough they'll enjoy breaking her in."

I retch. The whisky threatening to come back up. I can't believe what my mother is saying. Trevor is growling like Declan does. Like Declan did. Sophie is silent. I think she's finally shocked.

"And it's not only Miranda who will be affected. Declan's hand is broken. It would be a shame if Sophie's dance career was ended by an injury that never healed properly. You know, maybe five million isn't enough. I think ten million is more than fair."

I've heard enough. "Remove the barrier," I tell Teagan in a low voice, handing Carter my tumbler. He gulps down the remainder and bends to place the glass on the carpet.

"Are you sure?" she asks.

I nod. Before she does, she hands Trevor the tissues and takes my hands in hers. She murmurs some kind of incantation, and power ripples from her hands to mine and through my body. I don't know if it's a protection spell or something else, but I have strength and confidence in what I'm about to do.

The air shimmers as Teagan removes the barrier and I enter the suite. Mother spins around and gives me a loving smile.

"Miranda, you're back early. Have you had lunch? Nora and I were discussing where we could take you and Sophie for a treat. Weren't we, Nora?"

How can she lie this smoothly? If I hadn't heard what I did, I would have believed her.

"Actually, Mother," I say coolly, walking toward her, "I've been here for a while. I heard everything you said. I'd ask how you could do that to me, but you've already explained how I was essentially an annuity for you, and you hate me. Is there anything else to say? I didn't want to believe people who told me you were a narcissistic piece of shit, but I guess I should have."

"How dare you speak to me like that," Mother shrieks and raises her hand to strike me. Before she's able to land the blow, Sophie shouts, "No!" and holds her hand up with her palm facing us. Mother's hand stops in mid strike like it hit a wall and she wails in pain.

"That's for Declan," Sophie says with a nod.

I want to give her a high five, but she's been a bitch to me, and the temptation is to make it a high five to her face. I'm not going to risk it.

"You bitch," Mother shrieks and lunges toward Sophie. Trevor steps in front of Sophie to protect her. Like she can't protect herself, but the intention is sweet.

"Mother, you aren't getting a dime from anyone, and you are to pack your things and leave. You are to never contact me again..."

"You're dead to me. I wish you had never been born," Mother shouts.

"Yes, well, whatever. I consider myself an orphan since Father never stepped in to stop you so, pretend you never knew me. Hopefully, with enough therapy, I can pretend I never knew you."

Hotel security enters the suite. Teagan must have summoned them. Sophie, Nora, and Teagan join hands and cast some kind of protective spell. I barely hear it with the blood rushing in my ears. I feel faint, like an adrenaline rush has suddenly run out. Trevor guides me to the sofa and gently pushes me forward to guide my head between my knees. He strokes my back and murmurs soothing words as sobs rack my body. Nora sits on my other side and runs her fingers along my scalp. Cocooned between the two of them, I could easily be lulled to sleep. I hate showing weakness before my—I stop myself from thinking of that...*creature*...as my mother—*her*.

"You're behind a cloaking spell. She can't see us," Nora says as if she can read my mind. Maybe she did. I don't know anything any longer.

Teagan announces, as head of the Atlantic County Coven of the New Jersey Association of Covens, under whose jurisdiction Doreen falls as a resident witch of New Jersey, she is performing the witchy version of a citizen's arrest and suppressing Doreen's powers because of her continued assault against my magic. She will have a trial before the Witches' Council. Who knew witches had a council, too? I guess everyone gets one? I picture Oprah pointing, saying, "You get a council. And you get a council," to an entire room full of paranormal folk and giggle. I think it's more from shock than from humor. Then, I groan because giggling jarred my brain and makes my head hurt more. In a matter of minutes, Doreen is marched out of the suite, hopefully right back to the rock she slithered out from. My head is pounding.

"You've had quite a shock, dear. Come to my suite and lay down," Nora says. I would have nodded in agreement, but my head couldn't take it.

I'm about to rise when suddenly Bedard is in the doorway. "Don't drink the tea," he exclaims, slightly out of breath.

"What?" I ask. What the hell is he talking about?

"The tea from your mother," he says, "It's not good for you. There's an herb in it that makes you susceptible to the power of suggestion."

I laugh. I can't help it. Could this get any weirder?

"Are you saying my mother was poisoning me?" I ask in disbelief. I don't know why I'm shocked, it would be completely on brand for her.

Bedard shakes his head. "No, not poison. Well, not yet. Teagan told us what was going on. Maybe that was next."

Us? I look over to see Declan standing in the doorway, looking unsure of his welcome. Nora tells him to come in. He leans against the wall while Bedard explains.

"I'm a chemist and my mother is a kitchen witch. I know about herbs and chemicals. When I smelled your tea today, it niggled at me. That's why I asked for the tea bags. I wanted to examine them." He's standing tall and lecturing like he must have back in his classroom in Canada.

"I examined the leaves and herbs in the blend and consulted with my mom over FaceTime. She could see them and one of the herbs used is on a restricted list because when brewed and ingested it makes the drinker vulnerable to suggestion. It takes away their ability to exercise their free will. A witch can cast a spell making the victim vulnerable to them, they won't be influenced by anyone else. It's like supernatural branding."

I think about how many cups of cursed tea I've had in the past day, hell, in my life, and my stomach lurches. Leaping to my feet, I rush to the bathroom, slamming the door behind me. I retch and try to purge every drop from my system.

Through the door I hear Sophie. "Wait, I drank the tea too."

"You did?" Nora asks, aghast.

"I have for years," Sophie replies, "whenever I visited Doreen. She sends me care packages with it in it. I got some for Christmas. Was I under its effects too?"

"Probably," Bedard says.

There's more chatter I tune out as I flush the toilet. At the sink, I swish water and spit it out to remove any traces of the tea. I think back to the times Declan lovingly made me tea and what a gift it was and how those beautiful memories are tainted now because she weaponized tea. It's ridiculous, tea as a weapon. It's like an episode of *Midsomer Murders*, but less believable.

I leave the bathroom and take the bottle of water Trevor is holding out for me. "Thanks." I look at Bedard. "How long do the effects last? When will I be free of its influence?"

"About seventy-two hours."

I look at Declan, who hasn't said a word. I know lies about him were planted in my head and while logically there is no reason to doubt him or his love for me, I still do. I need to let this evil brew leave my system before making any decisions about my future. He nods his head once in what I take to be understanding, straightens, and leaves the suite. The longing to chase after him is strong, but I resist. Anything we say or decide needs to be done with a clear head. I don't want there to be any doubt.

"Kendall says you are welcome to stay in her guest room," Bedard says.

I nod. "I think it's for the best."

I throw my things in my bag. I'm a nomad again. Someday I will have a home. I hope it is with Declan.

# 26

## DECLAN

I WANT TO GET DRUNK AND STAY DRUNK FOR AT LEAST THE NEXT THREE WEEKS until my hand heals, and I can be on the ice. Maybe longer if Miranda no longer loves me. I don't know if I can stay here if I'm not with Miranda. I could survive being here when she was across the ocean and I didn't know what it was like to hold her, love her, share whispers in the dark. There is no way I can go back to how we were before. If we aren't together, I need to be traded or go back home and do something else with my life. Alone.

She was being drugged by her mother. It's like something out of one of the murder mystery shows we watch together. I guess I should be relieved it's tea and Doreen didn't go full-on poison apple like the evil witch she truly is.

As I enter my parents' suite next door, Dad hands me a glass of whisky.

"What are you doing here?" he asks. "Why aren't you with Miranda?"

"Miranda has been begging me to give her space. I am. Until that blasted tea is out of her system and she's clearheaded, I don't want to put pressure on her. She knows how I feel. That hasn't changed and it will never change. Our future is in her hands. So is my heart."

"Ach," Dad says. "That's the Irish part of you. Tap into your Scot, throw her over your shoulder, and carry her away."

"I think kidnapping is frowned upon, Dad. It will be hard to get married if I'm in prison."

"It worked out for your ma and I," Dad says with a wink while Ma blushes. It's amazing they stopped at six kids. "The kidnapping. Never been to prison."

"Married?" Ma asks eagerly. "You're talking about marriage?"

"Aye. That's all I've ever wanted. Even when Sophie was doing those fake ceremonies when we were kids, I wanted them to be real. I love Miranda, she is it for me."

"What fake ceremonies?" Ma asks, a funny look crossing her face.

I look at the ceiling, my cheeks heating. Scrubbing a hand through my hair I blow out a heavy breath. "Sophie would plan these fake weddings. Miranda would be the bride. I'd be the groom. One of the boys or sometimes Sophie would be the officiant. Out in the gazebo. We did it dozens of times."

"Did you say vows? Were you pronounced husband and wife?" she asks, urgently.

I'm getting freaked out now. Cocking my head, I slowly say, "Yeah..."

"And you've slept together? Had sex? Not back then, of course. Now."

My face flushes. I'm a grown man, I don't want to discuss this with my mother.

Dad chuckles. "He's beet red, Nora. You know he has. Are you going to tell him, or should I?"

"Tell me what?" I demand.

Ma reaches out and pats my hand. "Declan, darling, you are already married. According to shifter law, you recited vows, were acknowledged as husband and wife before witnesses, and consummated the union. You're married. If you want to have it civilly legal and sanctioned by the Church, you'd need to do what is necessary there, but you are married, and Miranda is under the protection of our pack now."

"Beyond shifter law, you're handfasted," Dad says. "You're both Scottish and Irish plus a shifter. You're married to Miranda six ways to Sunday, lad."

I'm momentarily elated knowing Miranda truly is my wife, but that quickly fades when I realize what has happened.

"Miranda can't know this. I want her to choose to be with me, not just accept the situation. She isn't a shifter, she isn't bound by the law the same way I am. Her future can't be decided by a childhood game. Does Sophie know her ceremonies were binding?"

Ma shakes her head no, and I breathe a sigh of relief.

"Good," I say. "Don't tell her. We were children, how could they be binding? Isn't there an age of consent or something?"

Ma gently squeezes my arm and gives me a sweet smile. "Declan, darling. The binding happened when you consummated your love. You were both of age then. You've been married since New Year's."

Well, this is the suckiest honeymoon ever, then.

"But if Miranda doesn't want to marry you in a traditional ceremony you'd still be married in the eyes of the Pack and the Unicorn Council," Dad says. "You couldn't marry anyone else unless you had your shifter marriage severed. You're a unicorn. It's not done."

"It's Miranda or no one for me. There will be no one else."

"What are you going to do?" Ma asks.

"Short term, I'm going to give her space. She needs to decide what she wants for herself. The PHL All-Star game is in Florida next week. She will be there for that. I can't play because of my hand. My spot has been given to someone else. The time apart hopefully clarifies things for her. Long term, I don't know. I can't picture a future without Miranda in it. I'll have to get traded or quit hockey. Give up having a farm. I can't be here and not be with her. My wolf will go insane. I'll go mad. I can't watch her date someone else, marry someone else. Have the life that should be ours."

"You're married," Ma reminds me.

"Yes, *I'm* married. She's not. Not in her world. I'm not going to trap her or take her choices away. She's had that done to her most of her life. I love her and I'm letting her go, trusting the universe to bring us back together. I did it when she graduated and announced she was going to New Zealand. Then she came here and fell in love with me. I will do it again and hope she still loves me. But this is the last time."

# 27
## MIRANDA

It's like I'm a leaf blowing in the breeze, flitting from here to there at the whim of the wind, not able to choose its own course. I'm tired of living my life like this. I want to choose my path and where I land. I need to decide what I want and what is best for me. If Declan fit into that life, it would be wonderful. Even though I'm still a bit muddled from what my mother—gah, I hate using the word—put me though, I know I love Declan. I want the future we dreamed of.

"Do you want wine, Miranda?" Kendall holds up the bottle.

We're in the living room of her condo and it's almost like when we were roommates in college, relaxing in our jammies on the couch, gossiping.

I shake my head. "No, sticking with soda."

"Pepsi?" Carter asks, popping his head above the door of the fridge.

"Yeah." I grab another slice of pepperoni pizza from the box on the coffee table.

Trev places my glass on the coaster next to the pizza boxes and settles in the spot on the couch next to me. I'm sandwiched between

Carter and Kennie, enjoying being safe with my best friends. We spent many nights like this in college, the three amigos chilling out, eating pizza and watching movies.

"Thanks," I say.

"So, it was like a ceremony?" Carter asks. Referring to a ritual Teagan performed before I left for Kendall's.

"Yeah, a ritual. Teagan, Nora, Sophie, and the Zamboni driver from the rink." I turn to Carter. "Did you know he's Teagan's cousin?"

Carter nods. "Rhys. Yeah, he's a dragon shifter from Wales. I didn't know he was a witch too."

"He's a wizard from her dad's side. They are descended from Merlin. She has powers on both sides."

"Cool." He raises a brow and waves his slice of pizza at me. "Back to the ritual. Were you all naked?"

I punch him in the arm. "No. We were all dressed and in the living room of Teagan's penthouse. She said you would ask if we were sky-clad, and she told me to tell you to go stand naked on the beach first and then she'll consider it."

Kennie laughs. "Go on."

"We're in the living room, the lights are down low and there's a ring of candles I'm standing in the center of. The four of them are at the points of the compass. They say in unison, 'north, south, east, west,'"

"Oh, dear lord." Trev groans, covering his face with his hands. "Please tell me you didn't say 'Wickham U is the best' after that."

That was the start of a sideline cheer we used to perform. Kendall chokes on her wine and then laughs.

I'm laughing too. "I didn't, but it took all the restraint I had. So, they say that part and then Teagan says, 'Our sister's powers were once bound. What was lost is now found. Our sister's powers are now set free, as we will, so mote it be.' It was beautiful. I felt a weight lift off me and power flow through me. Me repeating the words now won't cast any spells or anything. At my request, Teagan placed a kind of training wheel on my magic. Apparently, I have very strong powers, but I need to learn how to use them properly. She's going to train me. Nora too when she can visit. I can do simple things like turn on the lights or move the TV remote." I point and raise it about four inches off the table before it falls back down. "I need to work on that," I say sheepishly. "But I can't cast spells yet or anything."

"I guess I'll have to use my powers then," Kennie says as she leans forward and picks up the remote and points it at the TV. Our favorite movie, *Bring It On*, fills the screen. There have been times one or all of us would be on our feet doing the cheers along with the actors in the movie, but tonight we cuddle together on the couch with pizza and eventually popcorn and candy. Trev is breaking his nutrition plan by pigging out with us, but he said this was more important and he'd do extra work in the gym to make up for it. He's a goof, but he's my goof.

After the first movie, we take a break before starting *Bring It On Again*. It's just the two movies tonight, since Ken has to get up for work in the morning. We all do.

"I need a car," I announce. "I can't keep relying on everyone for rides and I want independence."

"To being independent." Kennie holds up her wineglass and I clink my soda with her. Trev clinks his beer bottle and echoes the sentiment.

"My old Explorer is in the garage at the house," Trev says. "You can borrow it until you find something you want to buy. Or you can lease it from me because I know you're stubborn and hate feeling like you're taking advantage."

"Thank you." I give him a peck on the cheek. He's right about me feeling guilty, but I know it makes him happy to help me out and it won't be for long.

"You're going to call your family's solicitor or whatever they're called in Ireland about the trust from your grandmother?"

I nod. "Yeah, I texted my Uncle Tadgh the Cliff Notes version of what is going on and asked for the name. He was able to give me the family solicitor's info and called to give him the heads up on the situation."

With the time difference, it was in the evening in Ireland when he called, but I guess with the money the maternal side of my family has, people answer at all hours.

"Hopefully," I say, "there's still something left from the trust my grandmother set up. I have savings and am used to being thrifty. I'll be okay, but I want security. I want to know I can take care of myself and not be reliant on you guys."

I should tell the truth, but I'm scared. I know the tea is still in my system and I shouldn't make any decisions, but in my heart, I know this is what I truly want.

Taking a deep breath, I blurt out, "I want a house."

Kennie squeals and bounces next to me. "There are always units for sale here. We could be neighbors. We could go for walks together and hang out. It would be great. This is a great neighborhood."

I smile. "That would be fun, but I want a house. A plain old boring house with a yard I can plant flowers in and watch them grow. Where I could unpack because no one is going to make me leave. I want to get a dog, maybe a cat. I want someplace mine no one else has control over."

What I truly want is peace, but I don't think they'd understand that. They haven't gone through what I have. Their childhoods were secure and even if Trevor's parents are the high-strung type-A sort, they love him. They've always had a home. Even as adults, they can go back to their childhood homes and be welcomed. The closest I've ever had to a home was with the Mackenzies as a child, but it was never *my* home.

"Do you want to be here?" Trevor asks. "Is this where you want to make your home?"

"I do. I've lived a quarter of my life in New Jersey. I don't have to pump my own gas. They have WaWa. Oh, and you two." I blow a raspberry in Trev's direction.

Trev nods. "The three amigos, together again."

That will have to be enough for now.

---

"Would you like tea, Miranda?" Stella asks as I take my seat on the team plane.

I shudder at the thought of tea. It will be a long time before I'm able to enjoy a cuppa again.

"Any chance you have hot cocoa?" I ask, hopefully.

Stella flashes me a warm smile. "I do. Marshmallows or whipped cream?"

"Whipped cream, please. Thank you."

"Of course."

Sophie walks up the aisle of the jet toward me. "Can I sit with you?"

I nod. "Of course."

"Good afternoon, miss," Stella says. "I'm Stella. Would you like something to drink after takeoff?"

"Hi Stella, I'm Sophie." She holds out her hand for Stella to shake.

Stella's smile widens. "Are you Declan's sister?"

"I am," Sophie says, her eyebrows arching. "Is it the accent?"

"No, you have the same color eyes."

Now my eyebrows are arching. I know there was never anything between Declan and Stella, but my gut reaction is jealousy.

"Oh," Sophie says. To me, she asks, "What are you drinking?"

"Hot cocoa with whipped cream, but Stella makes wonderful tea."

"I'll have cocoa too, please, with whipped cream." Sophie settles in the seat next to mine.

We are flying to Florida for the PHL All-Star game. Trevor,

Bedard, Brick, and Crosby are playing in the game. Crosby got Declan's spot.

I hate that Declan is losing this opportunity. In the three days since everything went down with my mother, I've seen Declan in passing. He's been giving me the space I asked for. While I'm grateful for him respecting my wishes, I miss him. Before the romantic stuff happened, he was my friend, and it's like we don't even have that connection right now.

There are family members of some of the players and VIP fans on the plane to help fill the seats. Sophie is traveling with us, so she doesn't lose training time with Carter. We buckle up in our seats and chat about last night's game before takeoff. Once we are at altitude, Stella brings us our hot cocoa and a plate of snickerdoodles to share.

We each take a cookie and I moan. She heated them and the cinnamon sugar treat melts in my mouth. I glance over at Sophie, and she is chewing with her eyes closed, a blissed-out expression on her face. She must sense my eyes on her because she looks over and gives a half grin.

"This reminds me of when we were girls and Siobhan would let us help—"Sophie puts air quotes around that last word,"—her with the baking and then give us a treat."

Siobhan was the Mackenzie family cook when we were kids. She baked like a dream and would slip me apples and carrots to take to the horses.

I sigh. "I loved spending time with you doing that." Turning in my seat to face her, "Soph, what happened? We were such great friends and lately it seems like you're mad at me, and I offended or hurt you and I don't know why or how. I love you and want to make up for whatever I did."

Sophie turns in her seat to face me. Her tear-filled blue eyes are beautiful, but Stella is wrong. They're not the same color as Declan's.

"Oh Miranda, I'm sorry. You didn't do anything wrong. I wish I could blame everything on your narcissistic psychopath of a mother, but part of it was I was jealous of you."

I'm shocked. "Jealous of me? Why? You're beautiful and talented. You have a wonderful family that loves you." I reach out and take her hand. "Sophie, you have everything I've ever wanted."

She squeezes my fingers. "I know I'm blessed and I'm grateful for that. But I'm selfish. Growing up, everyone loved you. You were this perfect little girl everyone adored. I'm pretty sure you are my mother's favorite child."

I giggle at the absurdity of that. Nora Mackenzie's world is her children.

"I'm not kidding. The two of you get each other in a way she and I don't. I don't know if we're too similar or too different or a bit of both, but it can be difficult. I always wanted her attention, and as her daughter, I felt it was my right. But she was focused on you a lot and I was jealous. Knowing what we know now, and with whatever smidgeon of wisdom adulthood has given me, I'm grateful she was there for you. But sometimes I wanted it to be me and her, and it wasn't, because you were included." Tears slide down her cheeks. "I'm sorry, Miranda."

I pat her hand gently. "Sophie, I understand. We were children and, of course, you wanted your mother's attention and to be separate from your brothers. I'm sorry I intruded. Things should have been different for both of us."

"I hate calling her your mother. I'm calling her Doreen from now on." She gives a watery laugh and uses the napkin Stella gave her with the cocoa to wipe her nose. "Doreen recognized how I felt and used that to drive a wedge between me and you. Between me and my family too. I can see now how she manipulated me. How she used that damn tea."

"It's scary." When I think about how easily Doreen could have poisoned me or drugged me with something stronger, my skin crawls. As crazy as it is, I'm grateful she showed some restraint in her machinations.

Now I'm reaching for my napkin to wipe my eyes.

Stella checks in on us to see if we need anything. "I'll get you tissues." I guess our faces tell the tale.

"Oh, Sophie. I'm sorry too." I pull her into a hug and squeeze her tight. It's weird to be the one initiating hugs but it's something I'm trying to do more of as part of my healing. "We were both victims. Can we put this behind us and start again? I love you and you've been like the sister I've always wanted. I don't want what happened to come between us."

Stella returns with the tissues, and we thank her. After we both take a moment to wipe our faces—Sophie declares she's grateful for waterproof mascara—and declare each other beautiful, we each grab a cookie and settle in our seats.

"I want to move forward in our friendship and be close again. I would love to have you as a sister." Sophie gives a slight grin. "Or a sister-in-law."

I blink rapidly to keep the tears from falling and wrecking what I cleaned up. I would love to be her sister-in-law. To be Declan's wife. But with everything that has happened and has come to light, I don't know if he still feels the same way about me.

Maybe she can read the emotions flitting across my face because Sophie leans toward me, an earnest expression on her face.

"Declan loves you. He wasn't under any spells or the influence of potions or anything. His heart has always been true, and it's always been yours. He's going to give you space because you asked him to. The next move is yours. If you want him, you have to tell him. But please, be sure. It would be kinder to break his heart now than to lead him on and break it later."

The last thing I would ever want to do is break Declan's heart. It's precious and I want it for myself. Letting go of Sophie's hand, I pick up my mug of not very hot cocoa and take a sip. With the time we had spent talking, the whipped cream had mostly dissolved, and the cocoa had cooled to a comfortable drinking temperature. Sophie grabs her mug, holds it toward me and we clink them in a toast.

"To moving forward." Sophie says.

"To moving forward," I echo.

We spend the rest of the flight to Florida gossiping and giggling. Maybe, just maybe, another little piece of my heart has been restored.

---

Even though it's January, the Florida temperatures are balmy compared to what we left behind in New Jersey. For the first time in weeks, I'm cold the second I go outdoors. Buses meet our plane to take everyone to the hotel the team has booked. Turns out it's a Clardmore Hotel.

"Did you know about this?" I ask Sophie.

She shakes her head and looks at me like I'm ridiculous. "No, I have nothing to do with the hotels and I'm not consulted on Devil Birds travel plans." With a grin, she adds, "At least we know the beds will be comfy."

"True. And you can probably get me a free dessert or something at dinner."

Sophie giggles. "Way to dream big, Miranda. I don't know if Declan's going to be able to afford you."

"Who's saying I won't be keeping him in the style he's accustomed to? I have a trust from my grandmother that will help make my future more comfortable."

Trevor takes the seat across the aisle from us. "You've already started spending your trust fund. And it will take some work before you're comfortable." He winks.

"What are you doing?" Sophie asks.

"I can't say anything yet because nothing is definite. As soon as I can discuss it, you will be one of the first to know. I promise."

The buses arrive at the hotel, and Daphne and I oversee assigning rooms like we do on team road trips. Other teams are staying at the same hotel, and they are in clusters in the lobby doing the same ritual. Each team in the league was able to send three players—two forwards and one defenseman—selected by a combination of fan vote and coach choice. Two goalies were chosen from each of the three conferences. The Devil Birds were able to have four players this way. Plus, Liam was named the head coach for the Atlantic conference. That's why I'm here, to be his assistant for everything with the game.

The atmosphere at the hotel and in the arena is incredible. There are meet-and-greets with the players where fans get to have items signed and their pictures taken. The different teams have parties for their fans and there are fun skill challenges for the players.

We are about to take our seats to watch the competitions when Trevor skates up to the bench and signals to Sophie. She goes over and he uses his stick to drop a couple of shirts into her waiting hands. He says something to her, causing her to nod and return to her seat.

"Here, have a jersey," she says.

I unfold it, expecting it to have Carter on the back, because that's what Sophie is pulling over her head. Instead, I see it has the name Mackenzie on the back. I gasp. Tears sting my eyes as I trace my fingers over the white letters. The tidy black stitches holding them on and adding contrast. I've always dreamed of being able to claim this name as my own. Goosebumps break out all over having nothing to do with the chill of the arena.

"How did he get this?" I ask once I manage to dislodge the lump in my throat. My heart is breaking Declan isn't here to wear his jersey with pride on the ice. I wish it was him giving this to me as a form of claiming and not Carter giving it to me as a form of consolation.

Sophie shrugs.

"They had already made Declan's jerseys before he was injured. When Trevor heard they were going to bin them, he got them to give them to him to give to me. But we both decided you're the one who should wear it."

Tears prick my eyes as I pull it on over the Devil Birds long sleeve tee I'm already wearing. Since it's sized for Declan to wear with all his pads, it's huge on me. I could probably add a belt and wear it as a dress. Sophie looks the same in her Carter jersey until she pulls a hair tie out of her purse and uses it to bunch up the excess material of the shirt at her hip in a cute, fashionable way. It always amazes me how people can style their outfits like that. If I tried, it would look like I had an apple attached to my hip. Better to let the shirt hang. It's big enough, I could wear it as a nightgown. If I don't have Declan to hold me, this jersey will have to do.

Brick wins the goalie competition by stopping the most goals in a row. I use my thumb and forefinger to whistle, and it makes Sophie jump.

"What the hell was that?" she asks.

I shrug. "Dec taught me when we were kids. The horses would come over when I did it."

Bedard is the champion of the hardest slap shot event and Carter is crowned the fastest skater. I love seeing my friends do well. I'm sharing high fives with Sophie, Mallory, Daphne, and also whatever fans are around us who are friendly. I celebrate when their players do well too. Not as much as when it's a Devil Bird, of course, but we all love hockey here and celebrate everyone. I think the tea has left my system. I'm feeling like the real me again, finally.

Crosby comes in third for the puck handling obstacle course. The skater has to maneuver a puck through cones similar to an agility dog going through weave poles. After that, they launch the puck over an obstacle and then hit a target in the goal. Whoever completed the circuit the fastest won. Honestly, I was surprised Crosby placed as high as he did, but some of the skaters were overconfident and showboating, and fumbled the puck.

I wish Declan were here. He would have aced the target shooting. A teammate passes the puck to the shooter, who fires them at five targets set up in the goal. The fastest to break the targets is the victor. I've seen Dec do drills like this, and he's like a machine gun.

Ollie King of the Spokane Sasquatch won it, but I know it's because Declan wasn't here.

The actual All-Star Game will be tomorrow.

"It's a shame Declan isn't here," Sophie says, "enjoying the festivities and getting the recognition he deserves. It isn't fair."

"I was thinking the same thing," I say. "I hope his hand heals quickly and he can play the second half of the season, at least. And there's always next year's All-Star Game. I know this is the first of many years he's named an All-Star."

I know he's my All-Star.

# 28

## DECLAN

Stone and I are on the couch in the main area of our apartment with a bunch of our teammates waiting for the skills competition to start. Everyone is making predictions about who will win each event. Everyone is saying I would have been a lock to win the target event. That's nice, but I'm sick of hearing about it. It's bad enough my stupidity ruined this opportunity for me, but I'll be in an entirely different state when, finally, the last remnants of the tea are out of Miranda's system. If I'd not slammed my fist into a wall, if I'd controlled my temper, I'd be there right now, right beside her when she's fully free from any of her mother's remaining influence. I could give her a choice then, and pray she makes the one that will make my heart soar. Part of me would like to go lock myself up in my room and ignore the All-Star Game completely. But I resist showing my bitterness and unsportsmanlike conduct. I need to set a better example than that. What pisses me off is it's my own damn fault I'm not there. It's not like I got injured in a game or anything noble like that. No. I had to lose my temper and punch a wall like a jackass.

My phone vibrates in my pocket to signal an incoming text as I'm taking a swig of my beer. They are announcing the players taking part in the fastest skater competition and have announced Carter's name. He waves to the crowd and points to the stands. The camera pans over, following his gesture, and my breath catches. Sophie and Miranda have prime seats right behind the bench where the players are hanging out between events. They're both wearing jerseys for the Atlantic League team, and they have the Devil Birds patches on them.

"That's cool they have them," Stone says. "They're huge. They must be player jerseys. I guess Carter loaned them his spares."

I'm trying, but failing, to not be bitter I don't get to wear my Mackenzie All-Star jersey. They probably threw them out or took off the nameplate when notified I wasn't able to play. Does Crosby have what should have been my jersey?

Shrugging, I mumble something as I reach into my pocket and pull out my phone.

> Daphne: Wish you were here.

Way to rub salt in the wound, I think. There's a photo attachment. I tap to open it. It's a shot from behind of Sophie and Miranda. Sophie is wearing Carter's jersey. But what makes me catch my breath is seeing Mackenzie on the jersey Miranda is wearing. I don't know how she got it, but it does funny things to my insides to see her with my name on her back. It triggers the primitive parts of me that want to claim her before the world as my mate.

My fingers fly over my screen as I quickly make the necessary arrangements. Draining my bottle of beer, I rise from the couch.

"Who wants to fly to Florida with me?" I ask the group in the room. A cheer goes up and Stone, along with another half dozen of my teammates, start getting stuff together for an impromptu trip to the Sunshine State.

I'm not the type to throw money around, but coming from an obnoxiously wealthy family is handy when you want to charter a plane to take you and some friends to Florida on extremely short notice to watch a hockey game. Being an heir to a hotel chain is an advantage too. We snagged a last-minute cancellation of a suite. Some of us who aren't me are sleeping on air mattresses I had delivered. We're shifters; we can rough it for a night in a luxury hotel.

Hell, I'd sleep on the sidewalk if it got me near Miranda. She's here in this hotel and if it wasn't almost midnight, I'd be trying to find her. Tomorrow morning will have to be soon enough. What's one more night when the possibility of forever exists?

My phone vibrates with an incoming text.

Coach: Hotel bar. Now.

Daphne must have told him of my plan.

Me: On my way.

Some of my crew are already down there when I arrive. My gaze sweeps the bar and I see Coach talking with the coaches of the other teams. Is that why he wants me here? To talk to coaches? Oh crap. Is he going to trade me?

Mallory comes up to me and slips her arm through mine. "I don't know what made you suddenly go as white as a sheet, but don't pass out. You'll put a dent in these lovely floors."

I give a weak smile. "Hi Mallory, Coach texted me to come down here."

She flushes slightly. "Um, that was me. My phone is upstairs drying out. Bubble bath mishap." She tugs on my arm as she walks away. "Come on."

She leads the way through the groups of people gathered and I get some slaps on the shoulders and "Sucks about your hand," and "Heal up soon," comments as we make our way to a side room.

My mopey wolf lifts his head, sniffs, and gives a happy yip. I don't need him to tell me Miranda is here. I can see her sitting across the room on stools at a high table with Carter and Sophie. I don't know how he'll play in the game with one working arm, but if Carter doesn't take it from around the back of Miranda's stool, he's going to have to figure out how.

Maybe Miranda senses my presence because she stops mid-comment and turns to look in the doorway where I'm standing. She blinks twice like she doesn't believe what she's seeing and then the most beautiful smile spreads across her face. I have a moment to savor it before it falls, and she bites her lip, like she's worried or unsure. Oh no, my Daisy has nothing to worry about where I'm concerned.

Unwinding my arm from Mallory's, I stride across the room to reach Miranda's side. Wide gray eyes blink up at me when she whispers my name right before my lips claim hers in the kiss I've been denied for a week. Her arms wrap around my neck, and she kisses me back with the same passion I'm straining hard to hold back. My head clears long enough to realize we can't keep kissing like this, at least not in public.

Miranda must realize the same because she murmurs in my ear, "My room, now."

We don't bother saying goodbye to anyone. I grab her hand with my good one and bulldoze my way through the people milling about, ignoring anyone who tries to stop me for a chat. I guess it's a good thing we don't have the elevator to ourselves, because I don't think I could resist kissing her again. As it is, I'm cursing the fact my family has hotels with over three floors. When we finally reach the tenth floor and step into the hallway, it's Miranda taking the lead and guiding me to a door halfway down the hallway.

She uses the key card to let us into the room. It's the standard room, not a suite.

"Do you have a roommate?" I ask, surprised by how raspy my

voice is, but impressed I used my words and didn't grunt and point at the bed.

"You, hopefully."

Hell yes. I want to make love to Miranda all night long, but too much has happened this week. My brain is saying we should talk. Parts further south are insisting we can talk later. We have a lot of time to make up for. The door closes behind me and I turn, engaging every single lock there is. When I turn back around, I discover Miranda has already taken off my jersey and her shirt underneath and is kicking off her black Converse sneakers, leaving her clad in a white bra and jeans.

My mouth goes dry at the sight. Her breasts are jiggling in her plain white cotton bra and when she undoes the button on her jeans and shimmies to slide them down her hips, I almost swallow my tongue. I know she's trying to get naked and is not intentionally doing a striptease, but this is the sexiest dance I've ever seen.

"Whoa, Miranda, do you think we should talk?"

"Nope," she says, popping the p. "You need to undress and get back to kissing me. We can talk later. I need you now."

Okay, I tried. In a flash, we are both undressed and Miranda is pushing me to sit on the bed. She stands between my spread legs with her hands on my shoulders. One bedside lamp is on. The light and shadows play over her skin, highlighting some areas while obscuring others. I wrap my arms around her waist to pull her closer to me. Even though I'm seated, with my height, I'm able to nuzzle her collarbone and the top of her breasts. I press soft kisses and give tiny nips I soothe with gentle lathes of my tongue. Miranda squirms, but I don't release her from my embrace.

"Declan," she moans, my name on her lips the sweetest sound I've ever heard. "I want you. Inside me. Now."

With one hand in the brace, I'm not sure how we are going to manage this.

Miranda pushes on my shoulders.

"Lay back, let me handle everything. Do you have a condom?"

I do as she says and recline on the bed with my uninjured arm under my head. "Aye, in my wallet." But I'm not coordinated enough to put it on one-handed.

"May I?" she asks, holding up my pants.

I nod. She pulls out both condoms and puts my wallet back in my pocket and lets my jeans fall to the floor.

"Two?" she asks.

"I wanted to have a spare." My cheeks flush with something other than desire. I was afraid I'd somehow screw up getting the first one on.

"No, you only brought two? I don't think it's enough."

Oh shit, my shy, sweet Daisy has an insatiable side to her.

"We'll be home tomorrow night. And don't you have a lot of work tomorrow for the game? Two should be enough." I know I can go more than two times, but I'm not sure she can.

She shrugs. "We can do other stuff if necessary."

My eyes almost cross at the thought of what "other stuff" she has in mind.

She puts one foil packet on the nightstand and studies the one she still holds.

"I watched a couple videos on how to do this, but this is the first time I've done it in person, obviously," she murmurs.

With my broken hand, I'm not going to be of any help either.

"We don't have to..." Not sure if I'm saying don't have to use a condom or we don't have to make love.

"No," she says, ripping the foil. "I can do this."

The way the tip of her tongue peeks out between her berry red lips belies her fierce concentration on the task before her. I want her tongue to do other things, but we have the rest of our lives for that.

"Okay, ready?" She holds up the condom in one hand while reaching for my stiff cock with the other.

"Whoa, how about some foreplay? Kissing? Caressing? I'm not a hunk of meat, Miranda."

It's not that I'm not ready to go, I've been ready for so long it's bordering on painful, but I'm worried she isn't ready...physically... even if she's ready and raring to go mentally. I don't want this to hurt or be uncomfortable for her. I always want her to find pleasure and love with me.

She looks up from my cock with wide eyes. "Oh, no, I'm sorry. It's just that...I felt it, Declan. When the last bit of tea left my system, everything became crystal clear. What I want, how to be brave enough to get it. And this is me being brave. This is me taking what I want. You." She shrugs, giving a wicked little grin. "But yeah, kissing is good too. Whatever you need."

"It's not about what *I* need. It's about both of us finding pleasure. Making love to each other."

Scooting up the bed to lean on the pillow, I motion for Miranda to join me. She crawls up the mattress, and I'm ready to reconsider kissing and foreplay and pounce on her. If she knew I could see her delectable ass in the mirror on the dresser behind her as she crawled toward me, she'd die of mortification. It will be a secret I'll keep to myself. She cuddles up next to me, and I wrap my arm around her. I'm careful not to hit her with my splint. I pluck the condom from her fingers.

"Hi," she whispers. Propping her chin on her hand resting on my chest.

"Hello," I murmur, leaning in to kiss her.

I meant for the kiss to be gentle and languid, but it soon sparks like a wildfire. We are caressing and fondling everywhere we can reach. Since I'm limited to one hand, I make ample use of my lips and tongue. With the three good hands we have between us, we get the condom on and I'm slipping into her slick heat with a moan. We are lying on our sides, face-to-face. Miranda's leg is thrown up over my hip and I'm grateful for the flexibility years as a cheerleader have given her.

The sensations are incredible and I'm determined to last longer than I did our first time together. With my good arm, I gather her close and go back to kissing her, the slow sweep of my tongue against hers matching the slow, steady rhythm of my hips. She's tight and wet. My cock revels in the warm embrace it gets each time it enters her. I love this position. I'm able to squeeze her beautiful ass, look into her eyes, kiss her neck. I'm not worried about crushing her. Even when my hand is healed and other options are available, I'm still going with this at least some of the time. It seems gentler and more intimate. If Miranda's moans and trembles are anything to go by, she likes it too.

However good it feels, it's not giving us the ultimate satisfaction we are both craving. Miranda pushes me to my back and straddles my hips, guiding my length into her until I'm fully sheathed and she's gasping. Leaning forward to rest her hands on my shoulders, she rocks, slowly at first, to find her rhythm and motion. I use the fingertips of my splinted hand to gently push the tendrils escaping from her ponytail away from her face.

"I love you, Declan," she whispers, pressing her lips to mine.

My uninjured hand is on her hip, helping her set the pace she needs to find satisfaction.

"I've always loved you, Miranda. I always will," I promise when we break our kiss to enable Miranda to sit up and change the angle of our lovemaking. She must have found the right spot because her eyes lose focus and close halfway while her breathing turns to gasps. I brush my thumb over her clit a few times and that's all it takes. She tightens around me as she cries out my name. That's what I was waiting for. With a few hard upward thrusts of my hips, I'm tumbling over the edge to my own orgasm.

She collapses on my chest, and I wrap my arms around her. We are both trying to catch our breath. My eyes are closed, but I can feel her trembling and worry she's cold. Then I realize she's laughing. Is that a good sign? She presses a kiss to my jaw and rests her cheek against my shoulder with a sigh.

"I told you the next time would be better," she murmurs.

She was right. And the time after was even better than this.

# 29
## MIRANDA

THE TEAM PLANE FLYING BACK TO NEW JERSEY IS NOISY WITH CELEBRATION. The Atlantic Conference won the game and will have the home ice advantage if a team from the conference makes it to the Dickinson Cup Finals. Some people are staying an extra night, but many of us are ready to get back home. Home. I can't remember ever using that word and it feeling so right, deep in my soul. Sure, I say it all the time for convenience, but I never truly mean it. I do now. New Jersey is my home and where I want to put down roots. Hopefully, I won't be alone.

Taking our usual seats in the back of the plane, we tell Stella what we want to drink after takeoff and settle in with blankets covering us. Snuggling against Declan's side with his arm draped across my shoulders, this is the most peace I have ever felt in my life. Everything is going to be okay. The world goes fuzzy around me until it's all darkness and Declan. I float a bit, like I did when I'd drink Doreen's tea. But there's no struggle this time, no screaming at myself something's not right. Everything's right.

"Psst...time to wake up Daisy. We're about to land."

"Hrmph?"

"You fell asleep, Miranda, we're about to land."

I sit up and wipe the drool from my chin. "I didn't fall asleep. You know I don't sleep on planes."

"Randi, you were asleep. You were snoring," Trevor says from the row in front of ours.

Stone shoves his phone back between the seats. I'm horrified to see a video of me, with my head pillowed on Dec's chest. My mouth is wide open, and a low snuffle is emanating from me.

"You're a mean, mean man, Sean Waller," I say.

"But if I make you French toast, you'll forgive me, right?"

Rolling my eyes, I sigh. "Maybe. But with extra cinnamon."

Why did I fall asleep now? Okay, yeah, I didn't get a ton of sleep last night, but I've flown way more exhausted and been wide awake. Is this what it's like to heal childhood trauma? I should ask Daphne for the name of her therapist. I think I'm going to need to talk to someone neutral about everything I've gone through.

Speaking of Daphne, she is waiting for us when we get off the plane while Logan grabs their bags.

"You fell asleep on the plane," she squeals, grabbing my arm in excitement and giving a wiggle.

I flush hotly. "You could hear me snore that far up?"

"What? No. I walked back to use the restroom and saw."

"You know you can trust Declan to keep you safe while you slept, and you love him." She wipes a tear from her eye. "It's beautiful."

I blink. Is it true? My flippant answer would be to ask her what self-help podcast she got that from and say we made love most of the night and I'm functioning on two hours of sleep. But I've gone *days* without sleep before while traveling and never dozed off. Even on the flights we had before, sitting next to Declan, when I was exhausted from moving to New Jersey, I remained wide awake. Of course, I love Declan. That's never been in question. But do I trust him and know I'm safe around him? I realize I do. There's no one in the world I trust more. Not even Trevor, who I know would do almost anything for me.

"Yeah, Daph," I say, taking Dec's hand. "It is beautiful."

Dec leans down to press a kiss on my cheek. "But not as beautiful as you."

# EPILOGUE – MIRANDA

The days after the All-Star Break are a whirlwind with traveling for games, practices, and watching the league standings to see if we're in the running to make the playoffs to win the league championship trophy and be the first team engraved on The Dickinson Cup.

Declan's hand is healed, and he is cleared to play in the next set of home games this weekend. It's been wonderful to make love and cuddle without worrying about getting conked on the head with a splint. For physical therapy, they recommend he do lots of dexterity exercises with his fingers. I'm always happy to help him with that. The sacrifices I'm willing to make multiple times a day to keep his fingers nimble is a true testament to my love for him. We agree we are going to focus on "dating" for now and will save any talk of marriage until after the regular season is over. We know we're going to be together forever. That makes waiting until April before making it formal bearable.

My new-to-me SUV—courtesy of Trevor—is all registered and insured, so I invite Dec to take a ride with me. It's smaller than the Suburban he drives, but with some seat adjustments he fits. It won't be a long drive, he'll be okay.

Where our driveway meets the road, I turn right. We almost always go left to go to the rink and other places. Going right takes us deeper into the woods, where there are no stores or restaurants. In less than a mile, I see a "for sale" sign on the left-hand side of the road with a "sold" banner across it. I use my blinker out of habit even though no one is around because I am not a heathen and turn down the driveway.

"What are you doing?" Declan asks. "This is private property."

Shrugging, I say, "I know. I want to see what's back here. It's okay."

We bounce along the dirt driveway through the pine and oak trees lining either side. It will need to be graded. I wonder if paving would make more sense. The drive curves and an old farmhouse appears. It's weathered gray and can use some sprucing up, but it's solid. The barn behind it needs work too—a fresh coat of paint, the doors rehung, some of the stalls inside need new lumber—but it has potential.

Turning off Clara—yes, I named her already—I open my door to explore the property, hurrying to avoid Declan's grasp.

"Miranda, you can't go wandering around here. What if we get arrested for trespassing? What if it's not safe?" he says as he gets out to follow me.

"It's fine, I know the owner," I assure him.

"You do? Carter told me about this place being for sale, but it sold before I could view it or put in an offer. Who owns it?"

Going up the weathered steps of the wrap-around porch crying out for a porch swing, I pull a set of keys from my pocket. "I do."

Unlocking the door, I enter the old farmhouse. It's clean but needs lots of TLC to make it the home I dream of. There are four bedrooms and a bathroom upstairs, a walk-up attic that could be a cozy place to relax. The main level has a living room, dining room, and kitchen. I'd like to make it a more open space.

Declan is still standing on the porch.

"Are you coming in?" I ask.

"You...you bought a house?"

Shrugging, I say, "Technically I bought a farm. The house is part of it. There's the barn, pastures, a field of Christmas trees." I point in the general direction of the field of pines and firs.

"I don't want to deal with running a tree farm during hockey season. I'm going to speak with Carter's uncle about it. Maybe he'll harvest the trees planted here to sell on their lot across the street and we can discuss whether to plant new ones. Did you know it takes approximately seven years for a Christmas tree to grow?"

"Uh...no. Daisy, why did you buy a farm? Here. In New Jersey."

"Come in and close the door. You're letting in the cold," I say. Taking a seat on the staircase to the second floor, I pat the step next to me in invitation. Even though I have on a sweater and a jacket, I shiver. I wasn't kidding about him letting in the cold. New windows and better insulation are on my list of improvements for this place.

He shrugs out of his coat and drapes it over my shoulders before taking the spot next to me. I snuggle against him, loving the way his strong arm curls over my shoulders.

"I need a home, Declan. Someplace mine no one can take from me or make me leave. I've never had that. I like it here. I have friends, a job, it's peaceful. I don't want to start over somewhere new again. I want to put down roots here."

Peeking up at him through my lashes, I see he's staring straight ahead through the glass of the front door. I wonder what he is thinking, but I'm afraid to ask.

Swallowing when your mouth has gone dry is tricky, but I manage it.

"I know your dream is to breed horses and coach riders when you retire from hockey. There's a barn with stables and there are pastures. There's room to build a riding ring and set up jumps. We can have trail rides through the woods. We don't back up to the river like Carter does, but there are streams and creeks."

He doesn't say anything, and I'm terrified I've screwed everything up. But I'm doing what I need for my own stability. It's something Kendall and I have discussed, making our needs a priority. She gave up everything for her ex and refuses to do it again. In Bedard, she found someone who accepts that and will compromise while also still fulfilling his own needs. I'm praying Declan will too.

I turn and rest my back against the banister to face Dec. His arm slips from my shoulders, and I miss the warmth. Grabbing his hand to reestablish our connection, I look up into his handsome face.

"I bought this farm. My name is on the deed, but I bought it in hopes it would be our home someday. I know you plan to go back to Ireland after hockey, and I don't know what kind of demands the Unicorn Council will put on you, but is there any chance you'd stay here, with me, on Forget-Me-Not Farm?"

His blue eyes, the same shade as the farm's new namesake, have a sheen of tears when they look down at me.

"Miranda, I was going to buy this farm for us if I had the chance. You snatched it out from under me. The Council is based in Philadelphia for the next ninety-eight years. It runs on hundred-year cycles and moved from Rome last year. I don't care if we're in Ireland or Scotland or Timbuktu. As long as we're together, that's all that matters. Make a home, have a family, grow old together, with you. I would have named it something with Daisy in the name, though."

I give a shaky laugh through the tears clogging my throat. "So, you'll stay here? With me?"

Declan rises from the stairs and pulls me up too. His jacket falls from my shoulders, but his embrace keeps me cozy.

"Miranda, wherever you are is where I am. I want this to be our home. But we're staying with Carter until we get some things done here. A lot needs updating to be comfortable."

We walk hand in hand through the house, talking about changes we'll make and dreams we have for the rooms. Even though we are being careful not to talk seriously about marriage and babies yet, I know we are both picturing the corner room with the peeling yellow wallpaper as a future nursery.

The sounds of other vehicles approaching have us looking out the someday nursery window to see our friends arriving. They are carrying folding tables and chairs, bags of food, and who knows what else. I guess I'm hosting my first party?

"Maybe buying a house this close to the Carters wasn't the best plan," Declan murmurs in my ear as we go downstairs. I grin. Having friends who randomly drop by is something I've always dreamed of. Declan goes outside to help carry things in.

I wander over to the mantel above the stone fireplace. We can't light it yet, so the room is cold, and my hands are in my pockets. My fingers run over what I keep in there as a talisman of sorts. Pulling it out, I look at the small plastic figurine of a black unicorn rearing on its hind legs. This was the start of my collection. One of my classmates had it on a birthday cupcake she was sharing with her friends. I didn't get a cupcake but the other girls at our table did. Francine threw it out because she was cross her unicorn was black and not glittery pink. When they left the dining hall, I stayed behind and rescued the unicorn from the rubbish bin. I washed it off in the girls' bathroom and have kept it ever since.

Placing it on the mantel, I run my finger along the back. "We're home," I whisper.

Coach and Bedard set up tables while Mallory and Kendall cover them with tablecloths. Carter and Stone set up chairs, and Logan directs Daphne to sit in the first one. In minutes, we—friends, family, both blood and found, and teammates—are gathered around the table sharing pizza, wine, and, for Daphne, sparkling cider.

Carter stands and holds up his glass in a toast. "To Randi and Mac, may they have a lifetime of happiness in their future and give me at least a month's notice before they move out."

That gets everyone laughing.

Next, Sophie stands and raises her glass. "Miranda, I know we had a rocky path at times, and it was my fault. Thank you for forgiving me. I'm happy you and Declan have found each other. I know you're not talking about marriage yet." Everyone laughs. "But I look forward to the day I can call you my sister. Until then, it is my honor to call you my best friend."

I start crying and wrap Sophie in a hug. Soon, all the girls are hugging and crying. Even Daphne has managed to wedge herself and Birdie in there.

Declan stands and clears his throat, and we break apart. He motions for us to grab our glasses.

"To friends, family, and teammates. But most of all, to finding a home with the people you love. We are blessed. Sláinte!"

"Sláinte!" We echo, clinking glasses and exchanging hugs. I can't believe how much has happened in such a short period of time. I've gone from being without a home and alone to having the house of my dreams and a found family.

Declan clinks his glass with mine and inclines his head toward the mantel. Of course, he noticed my addition. "Welcome home, Daisy. I love you."

Rising on tiptoes I give him a quick kiss and tell him I love him, too. This Daisy is no longer a tumbleweed. She's going to bloom where she is planted.

---

Did you enjoy Declan and Miranda's story? Want a peek into their future? Get a bonus scene by subscribing to my mailing list at this link. https://BookHip.com/BCQXCTJ

# ALSO BY JENNY FENSHAW

# KEEP IN TOUCH!

Follow Jenny now for her romantic stories, stay for her ridiculous personality.

**Warning: Snort laughing possible.**

If you'd like to keep in touch with Jenny Fenshaw (and I hope you do!) check out Jenny's website for all the ways to connect

https://jennyfenshaw.com/
Or just scan the QR code!

# ABOUT THE AUTHOR

Jenny Fenshaw is a funny, goofy, and creative author of contemporary paranormal romantic comedies who loves daydreaming about ordinary events, making them ridiculous, and including them in her stories. A native of southern New Jersey, Jenny loves to set her stories in the area she knows so well. From the Atlantic City Boardwalk to the Pine Barrens, her stories are a love letter to her hometown just as much as they are the love story of her characters.

When she's not writing, Jenny enjoys watching ice hockey (for research!) and reruns of *Murder, She Wrote*. She has been married to her cinnamon roll of a husband for over thirty years and has a grown son who has the best adventures.

f facebook.com/JennyFenshawAuthor

⊙ instagram.com/jennyfenshawauthor

BB bookbub.com/authors/jenny-fenshaw

www.ingramcontent.com/pod-product-compliance
Lightning Source LLC
Chambersburg PA
CBHW031944240626
47153CB00003B/850